KITTEN

Endearments #2

JACK HARBON

Copyright © 2019 by Jack Harbon

All rights reserved.

No part of this book may be reproduced in any form or by any electronic or mechanical means, including information storage and retrieval systems, without written permission from the author, except for the use of brief quotations in a book review.

Edited by A.K Edits / @AdotKEdits

To the coworkers that inspired some of these characters, my best friends that put up with all my mindless chatter about this book, and my parents who've always supported my dreams.

xx Jack

Content Warning

Alcohol and/or drug use, on-page sex, homophobia, mention and portrayal of abusive relationships, parental abuse (neglect, emotional, mental), abusive partner (emotional, mental), mention of suicide and depression, and mention of terminal illness.

KITTEN

1
YELLOW FALL

"All the girls here need to take them shirts off!"

Kit watched the obviously drunk twenty-something teeter as he announced this to the rest of the dimly lit den. He wobbled dangerously, his red cup tipping and spitting out an amber liquid on the carpet. It wasn't a surprise that people were already drunk. Some of the attendants had pre-gamed before turning up to the function and, after an hour, were already sloshed.

Beside Kit, his best friend Chad snickered. Chad wasn't much of a sloppy partier but the two of them loved watching the drunks slur out words and fall over. At parties like these, that was guaranteed.

"Sit your drunk ass down, Andre," one of the girls shouted at the man standing. Kit was all too involved in watching this exchange go down that he nearly missed Chad holding out the small joint. He took two hits and handed it back.

"I'm heading to the bathroom," he announced, standing and exhaling the smoke. He climbed the steps and headed to the main part of the house. He couldn't locate the stereo system, but the sound of Trina was interrupted only by small bits of conversation he caught while moving through the crowd. He finally reached the bathroom and slipped inside, shutting himself off from the rest of the party.

For a moment, Kit stood there against the door, a smile on his face. This was the reason he'd returned home. As great as things had been out in Washington, New York was his home. The place was filled with plenty of bullshit, but underneath it all, he felt better here than anywhere else.

He quickly did his business and washed his hands. Out of curiosity, he opened the medicine cabinets, grabbing a bottle of lotion. He applied a little and flicked the light off on his way out. When he opened the door, he looked up to see an obnoxiously familiar face.

"Of course, you'd be here," Kit mumbled, pushing him out of the way and heading back to the den. The man caught up with him and grabbed him by the forearm, holding him back.

"Wait up, shit," he complained.

"What do you want, Jaylen?" Kit asked, snatching his arm back. Jaylen knew well enough he didn't like to be touched like that and yet here he was, pulling on him like they were dating again.

"I want to talk."

"Not right now. I'm trying to have fun, not deal with you and your shit."

"Kit," he sighed, an insistent look in his eyes. Kit wanted to shove him off and return to the den with some of his friends but he knew he'd be followed. To save himself the trouble of explaining what all of this drama was about, he glared at Jaylen for a moment and walked to the back door. The two of them made sure they were alone before Kit turned to look at him expectantly.

"What do you want?" he asked, crossing his arms across his chest. Jaylen took a deep breath and said,

"You."

"Corny," Kit said.

"I'm serious. I fucked up. I should have been honest with you, I shouldn't have kept you a secret. And that… thing with Omari was… That's my fault."

That *thing*. That was an interesting way of putting all the times he'd cheated with another man.

"It is your fault," Kit exclaimed, adjusting his voice when he realized that he was being loud. "I'm not some secret you keep in your closet. Niggas like you are out here expecting us to keep quiet, but I'm not messing around with that anymore. If you wanna fuck someone on the DL, you need to find someone in the closet too. I told you a month ago, I'm not doing this with you anymore. And if you think I'd take you back after you fucked someone in my bed, you're even dumber than you look."

Jaylen was silent for a moment. He nodded, his hand reaching out to stroke the other's shoulder. "C'mon," he started. Before he could finish, Kit swatted his hand away and shouldered past him.

"Fuck outta here," he mumbled under his breath. He walked back into the house and maneuvered through the crowd until he was in the den.

"Finally!" Chad exclaimed. He handed off his cup and Kit downed the last of his Hennessy. Chad watched with amusement. "Someone's in their feelings," he said lightly.

"I ran into Jaylen."

"It was only a matter of time. What'd he want?" Chad asked.

"What do you think he wanted?"

"You should take it as a compliment," he smirked. "Got that bomb bussy."

Kit shoved Chad's head and took a seat on the sofa. He relaxed into the cushions and surveyed the room, doing a double-take when he spotted a girl looking in their direction. She twirled one of her loose curls around her finger, bedroom eyes on full volume. Kit nudged his friend.

"She's feeling you."

"Who?" Chad looked around the room.

"Niecy over there."

When they both looked in her direction, she turned away coyly and whispered something to her friend. They both giggled and looked back at the boys.

"Get 'em," Kit said with a smile.

Chad rose from his seat and crossed the room. He took a seat next to Niecy and suavely stretched out an arm around the back of her chair, and it took everything Kit had not to laugh at his best friend. He had game for a white boy, Kit had to admit that.

After a few minutes of people-watching, Kit slipped his phone out of his pocket. When he checked the time, he made a face. Almost three in the morning.

He'd text Chad later and tell him why he had to go. At the moment, Chad was busy. After a few goodbye nods and high fives, Kit was outside and walking down the sidewalk, his cellphone in hand. He took a seat on the sidewalk and waited for his Uber to arrive.

Twenty minutes later there was a car pulling up for him. Kit hopped up and climbed inside, double-checking that his driver knew the right way to his sister's apartment. It was a bit of a drive, but he was too tired to be worried about his bank account at the moment.

His phone buzzed, and when he read the message, he smiled wide. Chad and Niecy were on their way back to her place. He wasn't surprised that his friend had gotten lucky. Not a day went by that he didn't get hit on by girls and guys alike. Not that Kit was left out of the fun, either. Unfortunately, most of the guys that hit on him were on the low. They didn't want anyone knowing about their fun between the sheets. Guys like Jaylen.

Just the thought of him turned his stomach. He couldn't be more over the situation if he were standing on the Empire State Building. Jaylen was persistent, something that had caught his attention in the first place. Kit wasn't stuck up, but dating wasn't something he'd been interested in, and Jaylen hadn't taken that for an answer. He'd wormed his way into Kit's heart, and as a result, things had all gone to shit.

He was done stressing over guys who wanted to play that game. One of his favorite self-help books had taught him that he was worth more than the options being presented to him. Thus was born a more confident, newer Kit Bayer.

Kit tipped well when his driver pulled up to the curb outside of his apartment. On his way to the seventh floor, he made sure to rate her five stars. After he unlocked the door, he pushed inside, searching blindly for the light. His hip bumped into the table near the door and one of the tiny angel figurines fell.

Before he could save it, the porcelain shattered against the wood. He sighed and closed the door, shaking his head. To avoid making any more noise, he tip-toed over to the couch and collapsed face down on the cushions, letting out a sigh. There was nothing better than coming home and falling down onto something soft.

And just like that, Kit was unconscious, his clothes and shoes still on.

Light streamed through the window blinds and Kit suddenly hated that he needed the sun to survive. His head hurt, teetering somewhere between a migraine and a hangover. Slowly, he sat up and rubbed his eyes. Kit jumped in surprise when he saw his sister's girlfriend Trish glaring at him from the recliner.

"What'd I do this time?" he asked instinctively.

"Just your typical lightskin behavior," she said, sucking her teeth judgmentally. Kit couldn't recall anything he'd done lately, but he was sure there was something. When he didn't respond, she glanced back at the broken porcelain on the ground.

"Did I do that?"

"Yes, Urkel." She stood and made a noise of disapproval. "Bria said she wanna talk to you, too. You in trouble." Trish left him alone in the living room.

"I'm completely innocent," Kit mumbled, standing up. His head pulsed painfully but he ignored it and grabbed the broom from the closet. Making quick work, he swept up the porcelain and trashed it. When he was done, he tentatively knocked on Bria's bedroom door.

"Come in," she called out. Kit pushed into the room, glancing between the two ladies on the bed. "How'd you sleep last night?"

The tone of her voice wasn't as warm as it usually was, and Kit didn't need to be a detective to figure out that she was less than pleased.

"Uh… I slept alright. Why?" he asked.

"Because that was your last night sleeping in until noon without spending the day job hunting."

"What's that mean?" Kit didn't like the sound of this conversation already.

"It means that starting today, you need to get out there and look for a job. It's been three months since you graduated, Kit. You keep saying you're looking for a job but…" She raised her hands in defeat. "I love you, but if you're going to be living here, you have to help out. So, you've gotta get out there and find some kind of job."

As she talked, her voice became softer. Kit knew she didn't like confrontation like this. It was too close to their childhood. Because of that, he was willing to keep his cool and not pout. As much as he hated admitting it, he knew she was right. He was running out of money by the day, from food to clothes to movies, and he had no way of making more.

"I mean… Fine." Kit knew he could make a big deal out of this, but Trish wouldn't hesitate to check him if he got out of line.

Bria's shoulders relaxed. "Thank you."

"Yeah," Kit said, shrugging.

"Also," she started. "You owe Trish a new figurine. You broke her favorite one last night when you came stumbling in."

He wanted to correct her and say that he wasn't stumbling because he hadn't drunk that much but kept his lips pressed together.

"Gotcha," he replied. "I'll start looking today. Is that good?"

"It's perfect," she said.

"The coffee shop around the block is hiring if you're interested," Trish offered. Kit made note of it and nodded, slipping out of the room. He returned to the couch and kicked off his shoes. Logically, he knew he couldn't be mad, but starting off his morning by being told he needed to do something with his life wasn't exactly as great as a plate of pancakes in his face.

Rather than sulking, Kit sent Chad a text. If he was going to go looking for work, he'd need someone to keep him entertained along the way.

———

That night at dinner, Kit, Trish, and Bria sat around the small table in the kitchen talking about all the exciting things they had planned. Trish swallowed a spoonful of soup and said,

"We're still looking for our Danny Zuko. I hope we can find her by next week. Then we can start planning dates and things like that."

Trish was directing an all-female version of *Grease*, one of her favorite musicals. Kit had been interested in helping out until he found out that there would be no male roles. He'd never been in a musical before, but he liked Kenickie the most and would have loved to play him.

"I'm sure you'll find the perfect Danny," Bria said, smiling at Trish. She stirred crackers into her soup and looked up at her brother. "What are you looking forward to?"

He shrugged and picked at his food, separating all of the peas from the rest of the vegetables. "I don't know. Hopefully some calls from the places I applied to. I filled out like, eleven applications today, so I'm sure I'll get at least one response."

"Hopefully," Trish said, glancing up at him. "That figurine was seventy bucks."

Kit rolled his eyes and smiled. "I'm not going to forget. Don't worry. I'll hit you back with some money."

"You better," she said.

Kit was glad Bria had finally settled down with someone like Trish. Back when they both lived at home, she was always dating girls that she knew would piss off their parents. He remembered the many nights the three of them would scream at each other, his parents mad that she was interested in girls and his sister mad because they couldn't accept her. It was the reason he'd been single until college. When he moved away, he went wild.

Trish had straightened his sister out. Figuratively, of course.

Gone was her rebellious behavior, and instead she could be who she really was. Rather than sneaking out and getting tattoos that would only enrage their conservative, highly religious mother and father, she was spending time inside, working from home. She'd mellowed out way more than he'd expected.

"And you, Bria?" Trish asked. "What's on your busy schedule?"

"I'm going grocery shopping on Saturday and I can't wait."

Kit snorted. "So exciting, Bri."

"Whatever," she grumbled. "You don't ever say shit when I bring home them little Cutie things."

"Okay, that's because those slap," he laughed. "You should get some pizza rolls too. I need more of those."

"Mhm," she said, giving him one of her dismissive glances.

Kit started to speak when his phone buzzed. He stopped himself and pulled it out. He didn't recognize the number. He held up a finger and excused himself from the table.

"Hello?"

"Hey, Kit, sorry for calling you so late and on my personal number, but I got your voicemail and I've got something you definitely don't want to pass up," Ira, the man from the temp agency he was using, said.

Kit had never been happier to hear that nasal voice. "Oh yeah? What is it?"

"It's with Yellow Fall. Have you heard of them?"

"Sounds familiar, but I don't know where I've heard it," Kit said. He took a seat on the couch and opened Bria's laptop. He typed the name into the search bar and navigated to the company's homepage.

"It's this new advertising agency. You might know

them from that ad they ran for Grandeur's new cologne."

How could Kit forget about that? The tagline of Grandeur's cologne had been "Drive women mad," and the ad depicted gorgeous, muzzled women in straitjackets and a padded cell, a shirtless man lounging between them. Kit could see the vision of the advertising team, but the ad had angered plenty of people. Deemed misogynistic and insensitive to both women and those suffering from mental illnesses, Grandeur quickly pulled the entire ad campaign.

When he'd first heard about it, Kit questioned whether it was an oversight or an unsavory marketing scheme. Outrage made people talk, and to many companies, it was worth the hit to their reputation so long as it brought in customers.

"Uh… are you sure this is the place for me?" he asked. He wasn't sure he'd want Yellow Fall on his résumé if it was still putting out ads like that one.

"Well, the CEO reportedly fired everyone on the team for that project, and from what I can see, he's done a total revamp of the company. They've had some pretty successful ones. The Christmas advert for Forever 21. The blowout sale for Hamilton and Hale. If you ask me, he's made up for that—pardon my French—bullshit."

"If you're sure they're not going to ruin my other job opportunities…"

"All I'm saying is, you should think about it," Ira said. "They don't say what the position is for, but I'm thinking it's an assistant or something. I only heard about it through word of mouth. Super selective. You know how it is."

"Yeah," Kit said absently. He skimmed a few more paragraphs on the website before he closed the computer. "Well, thank you so much for letting me know, Ira. I'll let you know what I've decided in a bit, alright?"

"Definitely. Have a nice night!"

"You too." Kit hung up his phone and stood. He was surprised to see two sets of eyes on him when he walked back into the kitchen.

"What was that about?" Trish asked.

"Damn, nosy," he teased. "Ira called me to let me know that Yellow Fall is looking for an assistant. Well, he didn't tell me what exactly the position was, but that I'm probably qualified for it. Entry level."

"Yellow Fall?" Trish huffed. She shook her head vehemently. "Turn it down."

"*Trish*," Bria exclaimed. "I know you don't see it for them at all, but Kit needs a job. Unless you want to start pitching in more money for rent and food?"

Trish glared at both of them before sighing.

"It's not like I'm going to start working for them and suddenly hate women," Kit offered.

She shot his optimistic comment down with an eye

roll. "Doesn't mean you won't be working for a bullshit company."

"All companies are bullshit, Trish. Eat the rich." When she didn't smile at his joke, he added, "Okay, how about this. I wait and see if any of the other places I applied are interested, and if not, I'll check out Yellow Fall?" He knew that when Trish formed an opinion, there was no way she'd change her mind quickly. She was hardheaded and stubborn, but that was just another thing about her that Bria had fallen for.

"Kit, you can do whatever you want, but just know that if you get hired at that place, I'm always going to have something to say. I'll keep it cute though."

"See, everything is working out perfectly," Bria said happily. "Trish is going to find her Danny Zuko, and Kit is going to get a job and help out. We'll have to get you some new clothes, though."

"I have clothes, Bri," he said.

"Seriously, what's wrong with what he has on?" Trish looked him over and shrugged at his khakis and button-up.

"Well, for starters, Kit owns approximately *zero* ties or solid-colored shirts. All of his shoes are Nike and none of them are dressy. And you need a haircut too."

"What's wrong with my Nikes?"

"Don't blame me, blame white corporate America," she shrugged.

"Fine. We'll go shopping Saturday afternoon. Trish, you can come if you want."

Trish crinkled her face. "I don't want."

Kit laughed out loud and said, "I don't either. But Bria's word is law around here."

"You bet your ass it is." Bria winked at him across the table.

2
SELL YOURSELF TO ME

"I LOOK FUCKING STUPID," KIT SAID TO HIMSELF, turning to look in the bathroom mirror. When he'd tried them on in the store, the shirts all looked nice. Now he just looked like a child playing dress up in his father's closet. He knew he'd need to get his pants tailored to fit him properly but that would have to wait until after his first paycheck. He didn't have the money today. On top of that, he was already running late.

"Kit, hurry your ass up. A bitch gotta pee."

"Alright, Trish, jeez," he said. He opened the bathroom door and maneuvered around her, heading to the couch and grabbing his phone from the cushion. Bria stood by the front door, watching him. When he looked up at her, she gave him a reassuring smile. Despite his jittery nerves and the constant negative 'what ifs' running back and forth in his mind, he smiled as well. She had that ability.

"Don't take no for an answer. You'll do fine, okay?"

"Doubt it," he muttered, adjusting his tie. "But thank you. I'll let you know how it went once I get done, alright?"

"Sounds good," she said. Bria stepped out of the way and let him open the door. She made sure his messenger bag was properly laid across his chest then pecked him on the cheek. "Go get 'em."

The city was as busy as it always was. That might have been good if he wasn't already running late. As it was, the constant traffic on and off the sidewalks was a mess, and he had to bob and weave through the crowds to make it to the subway on time. He collapsed into his seat and pulled his phone from his pocket. Almost mechanically, he put in his headphones and turned on his music. The last thing he wanted to deal with this morning was subway performers and people chest-boxing over the last seat.

He opened Chrome and typed in the company's name. Yellow Fall.

From Wikipedia and a few other sources, he learned that the company had been created in 2014, and up until recently, they were quite unknown. It wasn't until their campaign with Grandeur that anyone knew who they were, and not for any good reason. He was impressed by how well Yellow Fall had turned itself around. Had this been a handful of other companies, their doors would've been closed and this would have been a stain on Ari Naser's career as the CEO.

At his stop, Kit stepped out of the subway car and took in a deep breath. When he glanced down at his watch and saw that he had fifteen minutes to get there, he took off, careful not to bump into anyone.

Fighting someone before his job interview was a guaranteed way to end up on WorldStar. On top of that, Ira had pulled a lot of strings to get him this interview—a lot more than anyone else at the temp agency might have done—and he wasn't going to waste that.

He made it to the Yellow Fall building with five minutes to spare. Rather than heading to the receptionist's desk immediately, he dipped into the bathroom and looked over himself. He brushed his hair again, styling it perfectly, and sniffed under his arms to check if he needed more deodorant. Bless Bria and her constant DIY projects. The deodorant she'd made him still held up even though he'd been jogging for nearly ten minutes.

Kit popped a mint into his mouth and left the bathroom, confidently marching up to the front desk. The brunette woman looked up at him and smiled expectantly.

"I'm here for the interview with Ari Naser. Kenneth Bayer," he said.

While she searched for his name, he looked around the room. It was simplistic, a few modern chairs stuffed in the corner that surrounded a table full of magazines, framed images of ads they'd done hanging on the walls, and a beautiful Persian rug spread out underneath him.

"Well, I have you scheduled for an interview, but not with… Not with Ari."

"No?" he said, leaning in closer to her notebook. He saw his name but couldn't read who he was scheduled to meet with.

"No, it says you're to meet with Roman Li." The name sounded familiar but he couldn't place his finger on where he'd heard it. The receptionist looked up at him with an embarrassed smile. "Is—is that okay? He's just about done with his other—"

Before the woman could finish her sentence, the elevator doors opened, and a woman came running out with mascara tears streaming down her cheeks. She headed right for the bathroom without a word. Kit blinked and looked back at the receptionist.

"What was that about?" he asked, laughing nervously.

"That… was the woman from Mr. Li's eleven o'clock interview."

"Oh. Cool. Coolcoolcool." Kit's nerves were back

on one hundred. He'd been at sixty for a good minute but now he couldn't even pretend to not be nervous.

"Right," the woman said, looking back at her book. "You can just head up to the sixth floor. You'll know his office when you see it."

Kit nodded sluggishly and slowly made his way to the elevator. Before he could get too far, the woman called his name and tossed him a small toy.

"What's this?"

"Stress ball," she winked. "Trust me."

Kit said his thanks and stepped into the elevator. His hand shook as he reached forward to press the floor number. When the door closed, he held his face in his hands and took deep breaths.

"Fuck, fuck, fuck, fuck," he whispered. He thought about slapping himself to get out his nerves but refrained. He could do this. He didn't cry easily, and at the end of the day, whatever this Roman guy said didn't matter to him. The worst he could say was no and that was that. The sliver of confidence that Kit built up evaporated the moment the elevator doors parted again. He took an uneasy breath and stepped out.

The receptionist hadn't been wrong. He could clearly tell where Roman Li's office was. It was the only part of the floor outside of bathrooms and a kitchen that had interior walls that *weren't* made entirely of glass. In fact, Roman's office walls were floor-to-ceiling mirrors. He could see his own reflection, and he suddenly felt very small.

"Fuck," he said to himself once again. Kit puffed his chest up and walked straight ahead, right down the aisle that led to the room made of mirrors. He raised his hand to knock but the door opened instead.

"Come in," the man behind the door said, stepping aside so that he could enter. Kit nodded and stepped inside the office. He was immediately hit with the smell of sandalwood and spotted a tan candle burning on one of the shelves behind his desk. The flame was dangerously close to the books.

Kit took a seat and turned to look at Roman but caught his breath. The mirrored walls of Roman's office were two-way. He could see all of the same people talking and working and they couldn't see him.

"Surprise," Roman said casually, taking a seat across from Kit. He folded his hands together and placed them on the desk, taking a long look at Kit. His thick brows were unmoved, a blank expression on his face. With his sharp cheek bones and strong, prominent nose, he looked as intimidating as he did beautiful.

"You've got… Uh, you've got a nice office here. I've never seen one like it before," Kit offered.

"Let's not do that," Roman said.

"Sorry."

"Tell me, why are you here, Mister…" Roman

leaned down to look at a sticky note on his desk. "Mr. Bayer?"

"Honestly? I'm here because I need a job and Yellow Fall is something that really interests me."

"Interests you how?"

"Well, for starters, you guys... You didn't exactly have the ideal rise to fame. But the company's turned itself around and I can really appreciate a group that recognizes their mistakes and fixes it to the best of their ability."

Roman nodded slowly and smirked. "Had it not been for their PR nightmare, I wouldn't be here today."

"Small victories," Kit said, clearing his throat.

Roman's dark eyes sparkled the same way he'd seen Chad's when they were at the club. Whether Chad was looking for a guy or a girl, he was always excited by the thrill. The thrill of the hunt. Kit broke the intense gaze and looked to the table behind Roman. It was a mess, but at least it was distracting, something he could focus on rather than the fact that he was pretty sure he was sweating far too much.

"Since you know quite a bit about the company, which of my campaigns are you a fan of?"

Suddenly Kit remembered where he'd seen Roman's name before. He was listed as the Chief Creative Director on the company's website.

"I—I'm a fan of them all. You've really managed

to… to turn the company around and point it in the right direction, and I think—"

"Kenneth, don't kiss my ass. I already pay people to do that."

"Sorry," Kit said. "I liked your Hamilton and Hale one. It was smart. It didn't talk down to people looking to shop there. A lot of these commercials act like the customers can't tie their shoes and need to be talked to very slowly. But not Hamilton and Hale."

"Mission accomplished, then," Roman said. Though he still seemed determined to embarrass and rush Kit, his tone softened the next time he spoke. "I have your résumé right here in front of me but I don't really care about that. It's all just fluff. Especially since I'm only looking for a personal assistant. Instead, I want you to tell me about yourself. Better yet, sell yourself to me. Convince me that you're worth my time, my money, and my respect."

Kit felt on the spot again. He kicked himself for not looking up the interview process when he was researching on the subway. He wanted to say something, anything, but froze up, his confidence shot. Roman waited for him, obviously entertained by his fear.

"You don't have anything to say?"

"I… I…"

"Kenneth, Kenneth. You came to an advertising agency and you didn't expect a question like this?"

Kit said nothing. His face reddened, hot with humiliation. "It's for a personal assistant position. I didn't think—"

"Right. You didn't think," Roman said, standing up.

As he passed the corner, his hip bumped the desk and the cup of pens and pencils nearly spilled to the floor. "I'm going to make a pot of coffee and enjoy my lunch. You can show yourself out. It was… interesting to meet you, Mr. Bayer. Hopefully one day you'll be properly prepared for your next interview."

Roman left the room, shutting the door behind himself.

Kit was left in silence.

He felt sick to his stomach, a mixture of anger and sadness churning deep in his gut. He wanted to flip the desk and fall to the floor in tears. He'd been humiliated with one single question. One task, and he couldn't even do that. And being talked down to like a child? It made him see red. He stood and reached for his messenger bag. As he started for the door, Bria's words came back to him.

Don't take no for an answer.

He dropped his bag and turned around to face the office again. He wasn't going to take no for an answer.

The first thing he did was move the cup of pens away from the edge to avoid it nearly spilling again. He set the small tin of paperclips and the rolodex in the same area as well. After that, Kit gathered up the small stack of files and alphabetized them by the words on the side tab. He turned around and did the same to the papers on the table behind the desk. Last but not least, Kit rearranged the bookshelf so that the candle wasn't in danger of setting the whole place ablaze.

When he was done, the office looked brand new. He checked his watch. Only fifteen minutes had passed. He didn't feel like crying anymore, but he was still upset by Roman's dismissal of him. He was a human being and he didn't deserve to be talked to like that. Kit snagged a sticky note and a pen, scribbling down two short words.

'Sold yet?'

He stuck the note to his résumé, slapped that down in the center of the desk, and stormed out of the office. The gazes from the other glass rooms fell heavy on him, but Kit ignored them as he marched to the elevator. Kit met eyes with the receptionist on his way out and caught her smiling at him.

3
RUN ME MY MONEY

Kit was still in a funk by the time he got home. He'd tried stopping by the ice cream shop a few blocks from his house but that only made him more upset. Not only was he out of a job opportunity, but they didn't have his favorite bubblegum ice cream either. He unhappily flicked his tongue over the plain chocolate cone as he searched for his keys in his pocket. He closed the door softly and turned to see Trish and Bria cuddled up on the sofa.

"You're home pretty late," Bria said. She reached for the remote and paused the movie playing. "How'd it go?"

Kit simply laughed. Bria's shoulders sank.

"That bad, huh?" she asked.

"That bad. He was a total prick to me. Acted like

I was an idiot because I was stumped by some question, and it wasn't even a good question."

"What was it?" Trish asked.

"He told me to sell myself to him. I had to make him want me, show him what I could do. Like, Trish, you said your old manager had you sell an item of clothing to her. He wanted me to do that, but I'm looking to be an assistant, not some sales associate."

Kit placed his bag down and kicked off his shoes, plopping down on the other couch. He could only half-heartedly eat the cone of ice cream, but Bria smiled and happily took it when he offered. "I don't know," he said. "I spent all day applying to more jobs, so I want to focus on those. This job would have paid great, but no use crying over spilled milk. Or spilled pens." Neither Bria or Trish got it, but it at least made Kit smile.

"I'm sorry," Bria said, placing her hand on his shoulder. "But don't give up. Eventually someone will want to hire you in an instant. Just keep trying."

"I will," he assured her. This may have been a rough start, but Kit was pretty confident with himself. If he had to, he could get a job working fast food. *They* probably didn't gleefully embarrass the people they were looking to hire.

That thought still stung Kit.

He'd been treated like he was less of a person in Roman Li's office, and he had half a mind to write him a letter. Being in New York, he'd become accustomed to assholes in suits glaring at homeless people on the sidewalks, but even still, the arrogance of some people surprised him. Kit wondered if he'd approached the situation differently, maybe the outcome could have been different. Maybe if he'd strode in the room like he owned the place, Roman might respect him more.

He kicked the idea clean from his mind. No, he wasn't that kind of person. He'd nearly become that guy in college, and he refused to go back there. He could only be himself, and if people didn't want that, they could move on and leave him alone.

Lost in his thoughts, Trish's gaze brought him back to reality. He couldn't exactly decipher what she was trying to communicate with her eyes. Finally, she said, "You'll be fine."

He nodded and looked back at the movie. He hadn't even realized it was playing again. Trish's comment drew a small smile from him. She was right. He'd be fine.

"Dude, you'll be fine," Chad promised. He stood outside the club with Kit, nonchalantly tapping away on his phone. He seemed far too relaxed considering the two of them hadn't been to a gay club since their sophomore year in college, and that one hadn't even been in New York. He'd heard horror stories about the clubs here, and the last thing he wanted to do was look like a fish out of water.

"You better not ditch me, you hear me? I don't care if Michael Ealy himself walks in and wants to eat your ass like vanilla cake. If you leave me, I'm fucking your shit up, got it?"

"Damn, insecurities," Chad laughed, stuffing his phone in his pocket. "I'm not gonna leave you all by yourself. You've got too much of a baby face for me to leave you with the sharks. Besides, if we stay by the bar, we get more drinks from these older queens."

"I'm not gonna complain about that," he smiled.

"You need to get yourself a sugar daddy. One with a nice penthouse and hella money."

"Gross, those guys are usually perverts. Probably even serial killers."

"Oh please," Chad said, rolling his eyes. "All I'm saying is, if a daddy wants me to sit on his face *and* pay me for it, I'm not turning him down." Kit heard two boys behind them make noises of agreement. He cracked a smile and looked back up front at the bouncer.

The two of them stepped closer, waiting with bated breath to see if they would be let in. Thankfully, after a quick look up and down, the bouncer opened the rope and let them inside.

The club was exactly how Kit imagined it. Alcohol-fueled bodies writhed and grinded on the dance floor, businessmen laughed and toasted at the tables in the corner, and the older men perused the room like it was hunting season. The two of them took seats at the bar and ordered drinks, turning to face one another.

"I'm still not over your interview, dude. He really said he hopes one day you're more prepared for interviews?" Chad asked. He stirred his Cuba libre with the straw. Kit swallowed down his shot of vodka and nodded.

"Is that not a bitch thing to say to someone before you sashay out of the room?"

"He sounds like a complete asshole," Chad said. "Was he at least hot? Because you can probably get away with being hot, suave, and a douchebag, but you can't be an ugly bitch."

"Yet here you are," Kit smirked.

"Blow me from the back," Chad retorted.

"To answer your question, yes. He was hot. But that doesn't excuse his actions." It didn't matter to Kit that Roman had beautiful eyes or a smirk that, under the right situation, was probably sexy as hell. He treated people poorly and that turned Kit off. Kit turned to the bartender to order another shot and did a double-take at the man across the room.

"What's he look like?" Chad asked.

"Turn around. He's right there."

Slowly, Chad twisted in his seat to look for him. Kit described his angular face, sharp nose, and perfectly-styled facial hair, and Chad eventually found him seated at the other end of the long bar, lazily chatting with a much younger man. The kid giggled and playfully shoved his shoulder. Roman stiffened and turned around, clearly disinterested in talking to the boy. The younger man made a nasty face and spun Roman around, said something insulting, then dumped his red drink on Roman's lap.

Roman jumped up and shoved the boy away.

"Holy shit," Chad laughed. "So much for suave. Serves his ass right."

Kit threw back the other shot and slammed the glass on the bar. "Not quite," he said, hopping up from the bar. Before Chad could stop him, Kit chased after Roman, following him into the bathroom. He could hear him cursing under his breath, viciously scrubbing at the red stain on his tan slacks.

"Motherfucker," he growled.

"Karma's a bitch, ain't she?" Kit asked, leaning against the wall. Roman spun around and glared at him.

"Did you know him?"

"What?" he asked.

"Did you know that guy? Ask him to pour that on me as some kind of petty revenge for your shitty interview?" Roman moved to the sinks to wet a paper towel.

"You really think I thought about you enough to stalk you to a club and enlist some twink to dump his Cosmo on you? You must think you're the center of the universe and not just an asshole worthy of dumping drinks on."

"So, what, you just came here to gloat?"

"Exactly. You got exactly what you deserved. You don't get to treat people like objects that you toss away when you're done with them."

"I have a few hundred dollars in my wallet. If I give them to you, will you disappear?"

"I hope your pants are ruined and you're embarrassed when you leave," Kit said, turning and heading for the door.

"Wait!" Kit stopped and turned around. "I'm sorry I was a dick. I need your help, though."

"I already helped you. Your office looked like shit."

"I need your help *again*," Roman said through gritted teeth. "I can give you five hundred dollars if you just go down the block and pick me up some pants. The store doesn't close until ten, so you've got about twenty-five minutes."

Kit stared at him skeptically. There was no way in hell his pride was so high that he couldn't walk out to his car with a stain on his pants. But Roman didn't smile or laugh. His brows remained knitted together, hopeful that he would take the offer.

"More."

"Huh?"

"Give me some more money," Kit said.

"Five hundred is plenty," Roman retorted.

"Then you can save it and walk out there looking like an idiot." Kit started for the door again before Roman called out to stop. He held his smirk back and turned around. "Like I said. More."

"One thousand. Just get me some fucking pants already." Roman yanked a Benjamin from his wallet and handed it to Kit. "Thirty for the waist, thirty-six for the leg. Hurry, please."

Kit rolled his eyes and took the money. He found Chad and pulled him up from the chair, tugging him out the back door.

"Whoa, what's going on?" he asked, regaining his balance as they walked.

"He's paying me one grand to buy him some new pants."

"Jesus, I thought you just said you didn't want a sugar daddy."

Kit rolled his eyes and quickened his pace. As obnoxious and entitled as Roman seemed, Kit wasn't above doing him a favor as long as it brought in money. He'd need some extra cash, especially if these other jobs never called him back for an interview.

They found the store and he glanced down at his phone. They'd made it with just over fifteen minutes left. The two of them split up and went looking for a proper pair of pants for Roman. Chad jokingly held up a pair of corduroy pants that made Kit's skin crawl. Kit was just about to give up when Chad called him over.

"These look like the ones he was wearing, right?" Chad asked. Kit looked them over and smiled.

"Yep."

They brought the slacks to the cashier who'd been glaring at them since they walked in. He could imagine how irritated the woman was. She'd just started closing up when they arrived. She hastily bagged their purchase and handed him his change.

"Have a good night," she said with a forced smile.

Chad and Kit returned to the club with the bag and Kit hurried to the bathroom to make his delivery. Roman didn't even say a word before he tore the bag from Kit's hands and unbuttoned his slacks. Kit diverted his eyes and let him change. He looked back up when he heard the sound of a zipper. Roman stared at himself in the mirror and smiled. He was just about to leave when Kit held up a hand to stop him from passing.

"I think you're forgetting something," he said.

"What?" Roman looked at him like he'd lost his mind. "Oh. The money."

"Yeah. The money. Hand it over."

"I changed my mind," Roman said, adjusting the Rolex on his wrist.

"What do you mean you changed your mind?"

"I'm not giving you a grand just for picking me up a pair of pants. That's hardly worth it."

Kit took a deep breath to keep himself from swinging on Roman. When he opened his eyes and exhaled, Roman was looking at him blankly. "If you don't give me my money, I'm going to go out there, order another Cosmo, and ruin your pants all over again. Run me my money, Roman."

"No." Roman stepped around him and opened the bathroom door. Kit's backwards counting was interrupted when Roman said, "I'm not giving you any money until you do some real work. Seven o'clock on Monday. Don't be late."

Kit made a face and turned around to say something when he realized Roman was gone. A moment later, Chad pushed through the door.

"So, did you get your money?" he asked, looking for the wad of cash.

Kit shook his head. "No, but... I think I just got the job?"

4
HGTV BITCHES

"Like, I wouldn't have a problem with all the protests and stuff if they weren't out there blocking the streets and stuff, y'know?"

"*Exactly*. We get it, you guys matter too, but it's such an inconvenience for me. Sit-down strikes aren't a thing anymore."

"Totally."

Mornings like these reminded Kit that he should never, *ever* leave the house without a pair of headphones. Most of the time he could block out asinine conversations with the sounds of Rihanna and Drake, but that only worked when he brought the earbuds with him. Without those, he was forced to listen to people chatter about things they knew nothing about.

And that wasn't even the worst of it. The stop before, he'd had to put up with a couple violently making out across the aisle from him. Anyone with that much sexual energy at 6:30 in the morning couldn't be trusted.

When he reached his destination, Kit practically leapt from his seat. As quickly as possible, he pushed through the crowd and hurried up the steps, unable to inhale any more white privilege from the two women sitting nearby. The walk from the subway to Yellow Fall was twenty minutes if he strolled and ten if he walked briskly. In order to make a good first impression, Kit hurried through the streets, always on his toes. His dress shoes didn't make his movements any easier, but he managed to get to the door with fifteen minutes to spare regardless.

The receptionist's eyes lit up happily and she gave him a wave. It was a small gesture, but Kit grinned proudly and marched up to the elevator. As he climbed inside, he opened his notepad app on his phone and added a new task: learn the front desk lady's name.

The doors opened on the sixth floor and it was a completely different scene than the last time he'd been in the building. Instead of the thirty or so people he'd been greeted by before, there were only seven people in the room. Some still looked a bit sleepy, as if they'd just woken up from their desk-nap.

One woman looked over her shoulder as he stepped out of the elevator and smiled. Unlike the others, she seemed alert and focused. She wore an impressively tall pair of black heels, a royal blue high-waisted pencil skirt, and a yellow blouse opened just far enough to reveal her white camisole underneath. The bright colors popped against her deep brown skin.

"Hello there. Did you bring the coffee?" she asked, tilting her head. Kit blinked, unsure if she was talking to him or someone behind him.

"What coffee?"

"The coffee every assistant brings," she explained, a hint of condescension in her voice. "It's something Roman always has his assistants pick up. Off to a rough start, hm?"

Kit wasn't sure whether this was real life or not. He'd been there literally one minute and there was already somebody coming for his work ethic.

"I'm sorry, did *you* hire me?" he asked, tilting his head the same way she did. "If my memory's correct, Roman hired me, and Roman forgot to tell me to pick up coffee today. If you have a problem with that, you can go talk to our boss about it."

The smile on the woman's face turned vicious, but before she could say anything else, Roman's office door opened and he stepped out.

The sleeves of his white button-up were rolled past his elbows and his hands were stuffed in the pockets of his tailored slacks. They looked suspiciously like the ones Kit had picked up that weekend. Roman looked fresh off the set of *Suits*, and Kit's breath caught in his lungs as he approached.

"That's enough," Roman said. The woman looked between the two of them and softened her smile.

"I apologize, Roman." She turned to Kit. "You too. I get mean when I don't have my coffee in the morning."

"Hm," Kit said simply, looking at Roman instead of the woman. She backed out of the conversation and returned to the table where the others sat. After waiting a beat, Roman said,

"Yolanda Carmichael, Yellow Fall's best illustrator. Gorgeous, deadly, and one of the reasons the company hasn't fallen flat on its ass yet. Also known to get a little bitchy in the mornings." Roman smirked and looked over his shoulder at her. She was now speaking to the table in an authoritative manner.

Kit shrugged half-heartedly. On one hand, he wasn't here for being talked down to. On the other, he loved seeing a Black woman in charge of herself and her work. After all, he *was* just an assistant. He could be gone the next week. What did she owe him?

"Tell her to bring her own damn coffee, then," Kit muttered under his breath. Roman chuckled and placed a hand on Kit's back, turning him around.

The gesture would've felt patronizing if it weren't for the fact that Kit secretly liked it.

On the door beside the elevator hung a small whiteboard with eight names. Beside each of those names were various types of coffee.

"Most of the time, these orders never change, but some change their orders when seasonal drinks come out, so you'd do well to look over the chart every now and then. Forgetting the drinks will lead to seven very angry employees glaring at you. And if you think Yolanda was bad, wait until you forget to bring mine."

Kit took a step closer to the board and read over everything. Most people liked their coffee black, but three of the employees had very specific combinations. He took a quick picture so that he wouldn't forget. When he slipped his phone back into his pocket, he noticed Roman staring at him.

"What?" Kit asked.

"Those are the orders for today."

Kit was silent for a second before he realized what he was saying. "*Oh*. Right, I'll get right on that."

THE LITTLE COFFEE SHOP AROUND THE CORNER FROM Yellow Fall was packed with various forms of hipsters. Some wore beanies and tapped on their iPhones while others reeked of last night's blunt and Febreze air freshener. He slipped around a girl with bangs and a sundress and pulled his phone out to list off his order. The cashier's eyes widened for a moment before relaying the order back to one of the employees.

"Sorry about this. My boss and the rest of his team are picky," Kit explained.

"You're from Yellow Fall, aren't you?" the woman asked. Kit glanced at her nametag. Michelle.

"I am, actually," he said cautiously. "How'd you know that?"

"My manager was telling me about these customers who come in and order a ton of drinks. They all end up working at Yellow Fall. I just figured..."

"Ah, yeah, seems like coffee runs are part of the job here. It's my first day, so I'm a little out of my element."

"It's my first day too!" Michelle exclaimed. When she laughed, her brown ponytail swished from side to side and her dimples became more pronounced.

"Is work as crazy for you as it is for me?"

Michelle leaned over the counter and lowered her voice. "Let's just say," she began, "I still don't know what these different sizes mean. I barely know how to make plain coffee, let alone all these fancy drinks. I just really need the job."

"Girl, you don't have to tell me," Kit chuckled.

Michelle told him she'd call his name when his

order was ready and he took a seat, scrolling through his phone to avoid looking at other people. He thought about calling Bria to let her know that his first day was going alright and his first task was pretty easy, but she was more than likely still asleep. Bria and Trish had been up all night working on costumes for the musical.

Instead of waking her, Kit opened his favorite word game app and half-heartedly tried solving the puzzle. The distraction worked, because soon enough Michelle called him up. He stood from the scratchy seat and pulled a few bills from his wallet to pay.

"Good luck on your first day!" Michelle called after him.

"Thanks! You too!"

Kit used his back to push the door open, then hurried down the street, careful not to move so fast that he might spill the drinks. He stepped out of the way of a woman screaming into her phone and gunned it for the door before it could close behind the last person who'd entered. Kit narrowly made it inside but managed to do so without spilling.

When he returned to the sixth floor, he could practically hear the relieved sighs of his coworkers. Were they his coworkers? He'd have to ask Roman later.

Kit placed the coffee down in the center of the table and began disbursing the cups. Yolanda's smile seemed genuine for a moment when he handed over her drink. Once the others had all received theirs, Kit took a seat and relaxed. He glanced at the woman in front of him as he poured sugar into his cup.

She stood out from the rest of the crowd, not only because of her clothing choices—which were, to put it kindly, a bit outdated—but because she didn't seem as talkative as the rest. Her chestnut hair fell down to her shoulders, her makeup was gorgeous, and her cheeks went rosy when she caught Kit staring. He realized he was watching her intently and apologized, smiling in embarrassment.

"You're fine," she assured him. Her voice was like honey, and he instantly felt welcome being around her. If Kit had to guess, she was in her mid-to-late forties. "Can I just say that not all of us are like Yolanda? She can be rude sometimes, especially to Roman's assistants, but the rest of the team doesn't get that way. Barbara Lovejoy, by the way. Everyone here calls me Barbie."

"Don't worry, you guys seem fine. Today's just weird for everyone. And it's good to meet you, Barbie. I love that name." Kit laughed and looked towards Roman's office. He wasn't sure whether or not he was being watched. Maybe that was exactly what Roman wanted his employees to feel. After all, the head of the Creative Team couldn't let his employees start slacking.

"Well, you did a great job with the coffee. Mine's—"

As Barbie tipped her coffee back to take a drink, the lid came off, spilling down the front of her wool sweater. She let out a startled cry and put the drink down. Kit jumped up and rushed to the small kitchen across the room, grabbing a handful of napkins next to the microwave. He returned and helped clean the woman up.

"Damn these cheap cups," she said under her breath. When she took her sweater off, she found that her dress underneath was completely dry. "Thank god," she said, laughing at herself. "I'll just wring my sweater out and drink what I can get from that."

"Here," Kit said, securing the lid on his cup and handing it to the woman. "I really shouldn't be drinking coffee anyways." The surprise on Barbie's face made him glad that he'd offered her the drink. She seemed touched.

"I couldn't—"

"Somebody's gotta drink it," Kit shrugged. Behind her, he could see Roman wave him over. "I just got plain coffee, but I did add a little sugar."

"Thank you so much," Barbie said, her eyes crinkling with a smile. Kit grinned as well and slipped away. He closed the office door behind him and took a seat. Roman glanced at Barbie and shook his head.

"She's lucky she's the best at copywriting or she'd be fired," he said stuffily.

"You of all people should understand a spill," Kit retorted, instantly defensive of Barbie.

Roman rolled his eyes and reached under his desk. He returned with a stack of papers, a small box, and a credit card.

"What's all of this for?"

"The papers are everything you need to sign before you become an official employee. Bank account forms so you can get paid, confidentiality agreements, all of that. The card is for company purchases. Expenses around the office mostly, like catered lunches and coffee runs. Remind me to pay you back for what you spent this morning. And in that box is a tablet. It's to be used only for work purposes. You'll plan my schedules, organize my calendars, and occasionally respond to emails if I'm unable to. Think you can handle all of that?"

Kit nodded and looked everything over. It was a lot to take in. "Yeah, I can manage."

"Good. Once you get finished with those papers, I'll need you to start working on your first assignment. You'll be redecorating this floor."

"Um…"

"'Um, what? You said you could handle it, did you not?" Roman asked impatiently.

"Okay, well, it's just that I'm not one of those interior designing, HGTV bitches. This wasn't in the job description," Kit replied. Roman glared at him from across the desk.

"Then *hire* one to do the work for you if you don't think you're up for the task." Roman said this as if it were as simple as one plus one. "And I don't want to hear you say anything more about 'bitches.' We don't use that type of language at work."

"Right," Kit said, stuffing the company card into his wallet. "You only use it when describing employees like Yolanda." He sent a pointed look at Roman and saw the stern look on his face soften for a moment. His frown twitched like he was about to smile, but he kept it together and continued to look at Kit without amusement.

"I don't want this place to look ugly, understand?"

"Because it's so gorgeous now," Kit muttered. Roman narrowed his eyes.

"Do you want this job or not, Kenneth?"

"*Yes*, I want this job, jeez." Kit hated hearing his name spoken with the same level of frustration his parents used. It brought him back to dark places, where respect was something only for adults. "Please stop calling me that, by the way. If you all can call Barbara Barbie, you can call me Kit."

"Okay," Roman said, shrugging impassively. "Start making some calls. I want this to be done by next month."

"You want me to redesign the entire floor in a month?" Kit exclaimed. This really was an HGTV show.

"I believe in you," Roman said without any real support in his voice.

Kit sighed through his nose and stood up. He pulled his phone from his pocket and tried his hardest to keep from storming away. Roman was right. If he wanted to keep this job, he needed to start acting professional. He couldn't get angry and throw temper tantrums anymore. This was the adult world, and it was a mean, mean place.

As Kit opened the door, he heard Roman call out to him.

"Thank you for getting the coffee orders correct. You did well."

So maybe it wasn't so mean after all.

5
NO DAYS OFF

Roman didn't look up from his desk as he said, "You're late."

"You're the reason for that," Kit replied, reaching over the desk and placing the cup of coffee in front of the man. Beside that, he put down a bag of fresh donuts. To top it all off, he moved to the shelf behind Roman and set up the bouquet of flowers. "You do know that most people order flowers ahead of time, right?"

"I didn't know I wanted them until this morning. They look nice." Roman's eyes remained on the paper in front of him. He circled a paragraph with his pen and leaned back in his chair. After another moment of reading, he finally looked up at Kit. "What?" he asked.

"This is where normal people say 'thank you.'"

Kit cocked an eyebrow up at him. Roman gave him a humorless smile and shook his head.

"Be thankful I haven't fired you yet. What's your schedule look like today?"

Kit flipped open the cover on his tablet and tapped open his calendar. Before this job, he'd only ever used that to type in when the biggest parties were scheduled and when his favorite shows were coming back from their hiatuses. "Well, I'm meeting with Alma Middleton in like, ten minutes. After that, I'm free. Do you need me to do something?"

"Alma Middleton?"

"She's the interior designer I found. Have you never seen her show, *Middleton Makeovers*?"

"Do I look like I watch that channel?" Roman asked.

"Fair enough," Kit shrugged. He reached into the bag and pulled one of the donuts out. Roman's eyes grew in surprise. "What?" Kit asked, his mouth full. "It's a middleman fee."

"You're the one who should be thanking me, then, correct?"

"*Anyways*," Kit exclaimed, "Alma is hella talented. I watched her shows back in school."

"I keep forgetting that you're a child," Roman sighed, adjusting the silver tie that hung from his neck. It was messy in a way that still looked attractive. GQ who?

"Old age will do that to you," Kit mumbled, finishing off his donut. He licked his fingers clean. When he looked back, Roman was staring at him intently, dragging his thumb across his chin as if in deep thought.

"What?" Kit asked. He turned around and swiped his face for any crumbs. He didn't want to meet with Alma looking raggedy. Roman continued to look at him with an indecipherable expression on his face.

"I have to get going," Kit said finally.

"Do I need to sign your permission slip?"

"You attract more bees with honey than with vinegar."

"Go, Kit," Roman said, shaking his head. He grabbed his pen and flipped to the next sheet of paper. Kit watched him for a moment longer before he cracked a smile and spun around, marching out of his office.

Just as Kit exited Roman's office, the elevator doors opened and a Chinese woman in a pinstripe skirt suit stepped out. Her black curls fell over her shoulders in waves. She looked TV-ready—and for good reason. When she met eyes with Kit, her expression warmed.

"You don't know how excited I am to meet you," he said when they were close enough. Alma smiled bashfully and adjusted the black portfolio binder up against her hip.

"Please, I should be the one who's excited. I've done work for plenty of homes and home offices, but this... This is something else entirely. Are you absolutely sure we can't film an episode here?" she asked, persuasion in her voice.

As much as Kit wanted to jump at the opportunity, he doubted he would even get the OK from his coworkers, let alone Roman himself. The man didn't seem the type to want his face all over television.

"Unfortunately, I don't think that's possible. You can still take pictures and do a shoot here if you want?" Kit had been to the woman's website and seen that after every makeover, her team took pictures of the work to add to her résumé. She was slowly becoming one of the top designers in all of New York, even without her show.

Alma brushed a strand of hair from her face and said, "Hey, that's a pretty amazing consolation prize. Now, show me what you want to do with this office? Hopefully we're getting rid of this all-glass theme?" Her tone was hushed, as if she didn't want anyone but Kit hearing.

"We should be so lucky," he chuckled. "My boss wants to keep the mirrors around his room, but I'm sure I can convince him to cover them or something. Maybe we can get half the wall to be mirrors and put some chairs underneath it?"

"That shouldn't be a problem," Alma said, pulling

her pen out and quickly scribbling that detail down. "It should take a bit longer since we'll need to remove the whole mirror and place a half wall there, but it's doable."

"Fantastic," he grinned. Kit guided her to the center of the office, aware that nearly everyone in the office was looking at them. With all of the walls being glass, everyone in the office could see him talking to Alma. No pressure.

"Right here, I want to get rid of all the glass walls?" Kit pointed to the room where Yolanda and three others were talking.

"Okay…" Alma said slowly, adding that to her notes. "What do you want there instead?"

"I'm thinking a sitting area. This place feels super cramped with all these glass walls. It would be nice to have something that's more open," he said a bit more confidently. He'd thought about this all night and decided that what this office lacked was a sense of familiarity.

"In the sitting area, there should be a sectional. People can relax, read a magazine if they want. Throw in a bookshelf or a TV or something. Fluffy pillows, too." He'd seen some online and knew he wanted those. Fluffy pillows made everything look better.

"Noted," Alma smiled. When she was done jotting that down, Kit continued the tour, pointing out what he wanted changed and what he wanted kept the same. He loved the small kitchen but didn't like the linoleum on the floor. Instead, he wanted it replaced with hardwood. Something that would complement the new dark brown carpet he wanted put in.

By the end of their conversation, Alma had filled up a page and a half of renovations that needed to be done. "It seems like you've put a lot of thought into this," she said, smiling at him as she closed her portfolio. "Should I be worried that you're going to step in and steal my job from me?"

"That's honestly such a compliment coming from you," Kit said, one hand pressed over his heart. The most experience he'd ever had with designing a room was when he tried getting artsy on *The Sims*. It never turned out all that well, but he still loved the planning portion of it. This was much different. Not only did he have to worry about the act of putting this all together, but he wanted to make sure that the final result was something that Roman would enjoy seeing.

A small voice in the back of his head wondered whether he was more interested in making him happy because he wanted to succeed at his job, or because he wanted to please Roman. He forced himself to ditch that train of thought.

"Yeah, yeah," she teased, giving him a wink. "I've got my eyes on you, Kit."

After the two of them went over the details again,

Kit walked Alma outside and hailed a taxi for her. Just as the woman began climbing inside, she looked up at him and said,

"I'm going to send you an email of all the stores I usually pick out furniture from. If you're not too busy, you should really stop by and look around. They have a lot of beautiful pieces."

"That would be awesome, thank you!"

And just like that, Alma Middleton was gone.

Kit put his hands on his hips and shook his head, smiling to himself. He'd been here for less than a week and he was already meeting the woman he'd drunkenly watched on TV at three in the morning, some passed out frat boy's head in his lap. And to think that was only four months ago…

He turned on his heels and made his way back up to the sixth floor. He collapsed in one of the seats and sighed, staring at himself in the mirrors of Roman's office. Though there was no way to know for sure, he had a strong feeling that the man on the other side of the glass was staring back at him.

Kit stood in the candy aisle of the bodega, flipping through his third catalogue today. Beside him, Chad grabbed another bag of Skittles and a box of Milk Duds. He turned to hand them to Kit, but his face was too buried in the catalogue to notice.

"Ahem," Chad said, glaring at him. Kit looked up in surprise, and in realization, apologized and grabbed the candy. "Are you sure you want to hang out today, man? We can totally reschedule if you're busy with work stuff."

"Naw, man, it's just this one big assignment that has me stressing out. I'm not gonna be out here looking like a moron who can't do his job right."

"But that's what you are, though," Chad said, confused. Kit cracked a smile.

"*I know*, but I can't reveal that until my first paycheck. Then I'll be all, 'Damn, I don't know how to use a copying machine, oops,' or something."

"Well, do you need some help or anything? I mean, I'm not the gay one here, so interior design isn't necessarily my best skill." Kit laughed and pushed Chad into the shelf of chips. "Hey! I offer my services and *this* is how you repay me? The gall."

"Cry about it," Kit teased. They placed their items on the counter and Chad whipped out a few dollars to pay for it. "Help would be nice, though, yes. I'm trying to redesign an entire floor of an office building. I'm kind of like a fish out of water."

"And he gave this to you as your first job? Thank you, have a nice day," Chad said to the cashier. The two of them stepped outside and he dug around in his bag for the Skittles.

"Yeah, he's kind of a dick about a lot of things. I'm surprised he hasn't gotten his ass beat by now."

"No, we saw him at that club. I'm sure that ass gets beaten on the fucking regular."

"Consider me officially jealous," Kit chuckled. He closed the book in his hand and sighed.

He knew if he put too much pressure on himself to do this job right, he'd end up making a mess. He needed to calm down, take it slow, and tackle it in chunks. He and Alma had already done quite a bit of work in terms of the base of the room, now all he needed to do was hammer out the finer details.

"You know, you could be getting the same kind of play if you actually put yourself out there," Chad said lightly, glancing at Kit out of the corner of his eye. Kit rolled his eyes and began walking towards the crosswalk. "Don't give me that look," Chad said.

"Don't suggest stupid stuff, then."

"It's not stupid, it's true. If you just got back in the game, you could be smashing all kinds of dudes. I know this one Puerto Rican dude that deadass told me he wanted to get in your guts, bro," Chad said, giving his friend a pointed look.

Kit almost wished he wasn't such close friends with Chad because there was no way Chad would let him forget that they used to be the biggest hoes in school. They had plenty of wild stories to tell, especially when it came to guys who so bluntly explained what they wanted to do. "All I'm saying is, you have options, Kit. Jaylen's not the end-all be-all. You're cute, you're single, and you can do a split on the dick. Stop sleeping on yourself and start sleeping on top of other guys."

"Yeah," he said quietly.

If only it were that simple.

Every thought of intimacy ended up bringing him back to Jaylen. Every time he thought about himself sleeping with someone, he was dragged back to the times he'd spent with his ex. He couldn't shake the memories. They were stuck to him like magnets, each of them decorated with a different lovely event they'd experienced together. He ached to tear them all off, free himself of the oppressive thoughts, but as hard as he tried, he couldn't. Hating the other man was all he could do now.

Before the silence between them could get too uncomfortable, Kit's phone went off. He glanced at the caller ID and sighed. Just what he needed. "Yes, Roman?"

"Drop what you're doing and get to the office."

"What? I'm in the middle of something right now."

"Get to the office, *now*, Ken—" Roman caught himself. "Kit."

Kit could see that Chad had a vague idea of what the call was about. He felt bad for inviting his friend out only to ditch, but he couldn't just ignore Roman's demands. Eating Skittles wouldn't pay the bills, unfortunately.

"Alright, chill, I'll be there in a bit."

"Hurry," Roman said, hanging up a moment later. Kit bit back a smart comment and let it go. When he looked to Chad, he could see his friend was slightly upset.

"I'm sorry," Kit said immediately. "He told me I was supposed to have the day off. I mean, I met with Alma three days ago and all I've done since then is work my ass off for him. Today was our day, and I'm a dick for having to go."

"Kit, chill," Chad said, waving his hand. "We'll hang out after you get done doing whatever it is he needs you to do. I'm not mad, I promise."

Kit finally took a breath and eased up. One of his biggest pet peeves was when people cancelled or plans changed during the last minute. Naturally he was opposed to being the person to cancel. While Chad wasn't fuming or anything, Kit still felt bad about leaving.

"I promise, I'll make it up to you."

"Just go." Chad smiled. Kit gave him a quick one-armed hug before he waved down a taxi and climbed inside.

Kit made it to Roman's office in a decent amount of time, and though he looked relaxed, his mind raced. What was the emergency? Why was his free day cut short? Roman stood with his back to the door. He spun around when he heard it open, the deep lines etched in his forehead easing away.

"What took you so long?" he asked, irritated.

"I thought it was my day off, my mistake." Roman rolled his eyes at Kit's sarcasm and handed a receipt over. "What's this for?" Kit asked.

"I need you to get my dry cleaning. Now."

Kit stared in disbelief. "You mean to tell me that I rushed over here to get your laundry? Roman, I'm not sure you know what an emergency is, but—"

"Kit, stop talking and *go*. I have a meeting in thirty minutes and I don't have my fucking shirt. I'd get it myself, but I still have paperwork I need to finish before the meeting. I'm not going to say it again," he said loudly, his voice just under a shout. Kit looked at him and clenched his fists. All of this over a fucking *shirt*. He snatched the paper from Roman's hand and yanked the door open. Before leaving, he paused. In a low voice, he said,

"I'm beginning to wonder how many assistants you've had to hire in the past six months alone.

Wouldn't surprise me if they all quit." He closed the door and stormed back to the elevator.

Unbelievable. Screaming at him over a goddamn shirt that wouldn't make a bit of difference. What was wrong with the shirt he had on now? What was so special about this shirt that Roman couldn't go without wearing it?

He stepped outside and read the receipt. The cleaner wasn't far, thankfully. Kit crossed the street and narrowly dodged a taxi, flipping the driver the bird once his heart began beating again. His phone vibrated in his pocket but he ignored it. Roman could go fuck himself for all Kit cared.

Oleander Cleaners was relatively empty when he entered. A woman stood at the front twirling her hair around her fingers as the man behind the counter went looking for her items. Kit stepped up behind her and finally checked his phone. Surprisingly, it wasn't Roman who'd been texting him. He opened Chad's message and made a face.

"Again?" he sighed. Following Chad's instructions, he logged into Twitter to see if Jaylen really was tweeting about him. Just as Chad said, there the guy was, subtweeting him once more.

"Thinking about the trip to Florida again. Fuck."

"I mess everything up. I mess it all up, always."

"If you love something, take care of it."

Kit could feel his anger rising once more. He was

so tired of this back and forth game. One minute, Jaylen wanted to brag about all the ass he was getting now that he was single again. The very next minute he was in his feelings all over again, bitching and moaning about not having someone to hold at night. Though he didn't follow Jaylen anymore, Jaylen followed him. Kit began writing a tweet himself when he heard the man in front of him speak.

"You're next."

He dropped his phone back into his pocket and stepped up to the counter, handing the receipt over. "My boss needs his shirt," he said, shrugging. The employee nodded and walked to the back. In his irritation towards Jaylen, he'd nearly forgotten that he was supposed to be irritated with Roman as well. The grown man who threw fits when he didn't have his shirts.

Was this what being an assistant meant? Getting treated like a mule 24/7? Kit had seen *The Devil Wears Prada* before but had assumed it was just a movie. Bosses couldn't be that bad, could they?

The cleaner returned with his item a minute later and thanked him for stopping by. On his way out, Kit grabbed a mint and popped it into his mouth.

Roman took the shirt gratefully and unbuttoned it quickly. "He got the stains out, that's good," he said to himself. He looked up, surprised to see that Kit was still standing there. "Can I help you with something?"

"Actually, you can. You can tell me why you'd bother letting me have the day off, then freak out when your dry cleaning isn't here. It was my day off, and you got an attitude whenever I was rightfully upset about having to rush down here. I could have been doing something important, like a doctor's appointment or something," Kit ranted. He glared at Roman, who seemed amused by his anger.

"Are you done?"

"I'm glad this is so funny to you. I'm seriously considering quitting and just working at McDonald's. At least working there, I'll get to deal with many different types of douchebags, not just one." Kit caught himself before he could say anything more. This was the kind of attitude that had gotten him in trouble back home. He tried his hardest to think before he spoke, but every now and then…

"This is your job, Kit. This isn't some hobby you do whenever you want some cash. I'm not paying you to show up whenever you feel like it. I'm paying you to be here when I need you to be here. I'm paying you to watch your tongue while you're at work. I'm paying you to do the things I ask without any lip. If that's not something you can handle, maybe you should quit. Maybe you *should* go work at McDonald's. Like you said, plenty more unsavory people there. Your work ethic will fit right in."

Roman pulled his shirt over his head and tossed it to the chair next to where Kit stood. Kit was too stunned by the man's body to even come up with a comeback. He never would have guessed that beneath all those suits and undershirts, Roman had the body of an underwear model. Kit had to force himself to look up when he realized he was staring down at Roman's Adonis belt.

"Look, I can be a handful," Roman continued, sliding his arm through the sleeve of the button-up shirt. "I can be a huge prick. Hell, I can be a lot like Yolanda." This earned a reluctant smile from Kit.

"But?" he asked.

"But nothing. That's just how it is here. You think people here work for me because they like my personality? Do you think I took over as Chief Creative Director because I'm nice and I always make people feel good? No, that's not how things work. People work for me because I'm good at my job. We have customers because my team is good at what we do."

"Being nice doesn't hurt anyone, either," Kit suggested.

"Business is not nice. Your feelings will get hurt, Kit. There are people who would kill for the success you have. Money makes people into the worst versions of themselves. You start seeing the side of people most of us manage to keep hidden. So, either you man up and you do what needs to be done, or you go home. Do you want to go home?"

Kit fought the urge to roll his eyes. He wasn't going to give Roman the satisfaction of being right, but he knew that he was. He knew that Roman wasn't his friend. He was the boss of everyone on this floor, and if Kit couldn't work with that, he'd just have to go home.

"No, Roman, I don't want to go home. I just wish you'd stop treating me like I'm nothing but an assistant."

"But you are just an assistant," Roman said. "Look, I get it. I'm not nice when I'm upset, but again… Either you deal with it, or you quit. I'm not going to make the decision for you, because believe it or not, you do good work. That's why I can handle your piss-poor attitude towards me. Judging from the way you left my office after our interview, I know that you won't hold back when someone tells you that you can't do something. You like proving people wrong and making them look stupid. Am I wrong?"

"No," Kit said. He thought back to his and Bria's move to New York. Their parents had beaten them over the head with the fact that moving away was going to be their biggest mistake. And look where they were now.

"That's why I keep you around. Had you been

anyone else, I wouldn't have hesitated to kick you to the curb. But then I'd be proving *my* boss right. I had to fight to get another one after the mess that was my last assistant. The truth is, you're smart, and you work hard."

Kit glanced up at Roman. "I'm also your last option. Aren't I?"

Roman's lack of an answer was answer enough. Roman continued. "I spoke with Alma Middleton about how things are going with the renovations. She told me she was impressed with how knowledgeable you were about design. You had a clear, cohesive idea."

"She said that?" Kit didn't mean to smile, but he couldn't help it. Alma had complimented him, yes, but he'd worried she was only being nice. That she said the same thing to Roman proved she truly felt that way.

"She said that. She's impressed with your work, and so am I. I'm not going to apologize for not being nice, but I will say that I'm pleased with what you've done in such a short time. I appreciate how much you value your job and want to do something well the first time around."

"I shouldn't have called you a douchebag. It was unprofessional, and I'm not trying to lose my job over something this small. I'm sorry," Kit said.

"Don't make a big deal out of it," Roman said

dismissively. He began buttoning his shirt up, and Kit almost sighed with disappointment.

"What's the deal with that shirt anyways? The one you had on before was just as nice."

"This is the one Ari told me he thought looked nice. I have a boss to impress as well," Roman said with a smirk.

"Yet you act like a god."

"I'm still a god, don't let this one instance make you think otherwise. Anyway, you're free to go. Thank you for getting this for me. Thank you for coming by on such short notice."

"It's my job," Kit shrugged. He pulled his phone out and looked at the message he'd begun to type back at the dry cleaners. "It was a distraction from real life stuff anyways."

"What's going on?"

"Do you really want to know or do you just want me to leave?"

"Kit."

"Alright, fine. My ex is on Twitter whining about me again. It's annoying as hell. And the best part is, he isn't even out of the closet, so most people think he's talking about some chick. Half the time, I just want to tag myself in the tweets for him. Either that, or beat his ass."

Roman chuckled and pulled a hand mirror down from his shelf. He looked over himself, checking his pearly white teeth and reworking his already-perfect hair. "Violence isn't the solution. Why don't you just talk to him?"

"Would you want to talk to someone who A, didn't acknowledge your presence when you both were in public, and B, cheated on you? He's lucky I haven't put him on blast about everything he did to me. He knows I see this stuff that he posts. He knows."

"Sounds to me like you're not over him."

"That's disgusting," Kit said, shaking his head. No, he was *absolutely* over everything he and Jaylen had. Most of the time.

"I don't mean romantically, I mean in general. If you didn't care, if you were really over him, his social media wouldn't bother you. No amount of tweets, statuses, or snaps would really make a difference. Indifference is the true sign that you've moved on. And it doesn't sound like you're indifferent."

"I'm not indifferent. I'm still mad about what he did," Kit said without thinking. "I'm mad because he's a total jackass and I liked him in the first place. Sorry about cursing."

Roman waved his hand. "It's fine. I won't bludgeon you with any more advice because frankly I have very little interest in your love life, but I will say that sometimes people need to see things are over before they understand. If you show him that you're no longer interested, maybe he'll get the hint. Don't be nice about it. Be mean. Being mean sometimes gets things done, you know."

Kit sighed. He'd tried that. All it did was make Jaylen want him back more. "I shouldn't be bothering you with this stuff anyways. I'll be in early tomorrow." Kit stood and walked to the door.

"I'll see you tomorrow. Thank you, again," Roman said.

"Thank you, too."

"For?"

Kit smiled softly. He wanted to thank Roman for the compliments. For explaining how things worked at Yellow Fall. For trying to help him out with Jaylen. Instead, he said, "Just thank you. Later." He closed the door and walked to the elevator, still longing for one more glimpse of Roman's bare chest.

6
FUCKING KEVIN

"*Party at Katrina's house on Saturday. Wanna go?*" Kit read over Chad's text message twice before he answered.

"*Not sure. Wanna get food on Monday for sure, tho?*"

"*Hell yeah!*"

In front of Kit, three men painted the wall with large rollers, slathering on a warm beige color. Alma hadn't been kidding when she told him these guys worked fast. In just two hours, they'd already painted almost the entire floor. He'd have to tip them extra for their hard work.

Kit felt someone step beside him and he looked to his right to see Yolanda. She stared at the painters as well, the look in her eye much more critical.

"You went with this color?" She sniffed once, obviously unimpressed.

"Not a fan?"

"I personally wouldn't have gone with that shade, but…" She smiled at him but Kit knew she wasn't being any bit of kind.

Kit shrugged, "Well, when you're faced with a task this important, I hope you do a better job than me."

Yolanda surprised him by laughing. "A job like this is beneath my paygrade, sweetie. You have fun, though."

She sauntered off towards her desk. Kit stared her down, silently stewing over her insults. He reminded himself that he needed this job. He needed it for Bria. And in a way, he felt like he needed to keep his job for Roman. His compliments were two weeks old by now, but he still found himself thinking back. Roman said he did good work and that he was determined to succeed. Kit didn't want to let him down.

After a minute of brewing, he let the anger pass and focused on how nice the office was starting to look. The old furniture looked completely out of place with the new style, but that was a slow process as well. He'd already ordered a really nice sectional for the sitting area, and a meeting table was being delivered in two days. He still had plenty of work to do, but the office was coming together quite amazingly. If everything went well, the office would be done before the deadline he'd been given.

"Oh my gosh," an excited voice behind him exclaimed. Kit turned around to see Barbie stepping out of the elevator with wonder in her eyes. "Kit, did you design all of this?"

He laughed with embarrassment. "I did, yeah."

"It looks so good!"

Kit realized that Barbie hadn't been at work to see how bad things had looked before the workers had cleaned it all up, so she was now seeing the near-final product. He smiled again, "Thank you. I'm honestly kind of shocked that it came together like this. I expected it to look like a hot mess."

"Come sit down with me, honey. We'll talk," she said, ushering him over to the kitchen. He took a seat at the table and watched her open the fridge and pull out a cup of yogurt. "I always knew you'd do a good job of the office," she informed him.

"Why do you say that?"

"We all saw how you stormed out of Roman's office after your interview. When he came back, he asked us who'd reorganized everything. He didn't sound angry, either—which is an amazement in itself," she laughed. "Everybody knew it'd been you. It doesn't surprise me that you'd also be good organizing this whole project."

Kit blushed and looked away. This was almost too much praise for one day. It was a welcome change compared to Yolanda's criticism, though.

When he glanced over at Yolanda, her brows were knitted together, and she was mumbling to herself, flipping through papers. He was reminded of what Roman had said about himself. He didn't work here because he was nice. He didn't make the money he made because he had a great personality. He succeeded because he was talented.

"Yolanda doesn't like the office," Kit whispered, playfully rolling his eyes. Barbie's smile faded for a moment.

"Yoyo doesn't really like anything. She reminds me a lot of my husband."

"Oh?" Kit leaned forward and placed his chin in his hands. "Tell me all about your husband."

For the next thirty minutes, Barbie brought him up to date on all the drama she was having with her husband. Not only was he skipping out on taking the kids to their recitals and practices, but he rarely did household chores, leaving her to pick up his slack. And just the other night, he'd called her a bitch—something he'd never done before.

Kit listened and nodded at all the appropriate times. He couldn't believe someone as gorgeous as Barbie was putting up with BS from fucking *Kevin*. Kevin didn't deserve her.

She was just about to tell him about Kevin's *mother* when Roman stepped out of his office. Barbie sat up straighter and jerked her head towards him. Kit turned to see Roman staring at him and smiled. "Do you need me, sir?"

Roman gave him a pointed look then returned to his office.

"Guess that's a yes," Kit said to Barbie.

"Good luck," she winked.

Kit walked into Roman's office and leaned against the door frame. "What's up, boss?"

"I need you to set up a few appointments."

"I can do that," he said. He crossed the room and took a seat in the chair opposite of Roman. Roman took a moment to scribble down a few lines on his pad of paper then handed it off.

"Here's a list, but I'll go over everything. August 27th, I need you to schedule a meeting with Arthur Danby, head of Alainment Enterprise. He's got this new company that he wants us to do some advertising for. On the 29th, reserve a Cadillac for me. I have to go out of town for the day. And on the first of next month, reserve a table for nine at Eleven Madison Park. Clear your schedule for that night, too."

"You're taking me to dinner?" Kit asked, looking up. Roman stared at him without amusement which only made Kit smile wider. "I'm teasing."

"Did you get all of that?" Roman continued.

Kit scanned over the short list and nodded, "Yep, not that complicated. I'll have it all done before lunch."

"Good, thank you. That's all."

Kit stood and stuffed the list in his pocket. "How do you like the office so far?"

The man glanced at the office in front of him and shrugged with one shoulder. "It's not too bad. What really matters is the furniture inside, so don't mess that up."

"Your confidence in me is inspiring," Kit sighed melodramatically. He looked out through the glass. It was better than *not too bad*. It looked great, and not even Yolanda's opinion could make him think differently. "I'll let you get back to work. If you need me, come get me. I'm here to assist you with anything you need."

"I'm aware, Kit. Go," he said. He failed to keep from smiling. Kit returned the expression then closed the door to his office.

―――――

"God, Bria, are we almost done?" Kit whined. Bria gave him a pointed look, a pomegranate in her hand. Kit sighed and stuck out the basket.

Bria grabbed another pomegranate. "You don't complain this much whenever *I'm* the one getting food, do you?" When Kit looked in the other direction and ignored her question, she said, "Exactly. So, stop complaining, help me get this grocery shopping done, and we'll get you a suit for dinner next Wednesday night."

"I'm starting to think you just like dressing me up in fancy ass clothes," Kit laughed. He followed Bria around to the next display and looked down at all of the various vegetables. He didn't have the slightest clue what to do with them but he trusted Bria. She was a master chef.

"Do I think you look so much cuter in fancy suits and ties? Of course. But you also have to remember that jobs like these have a weird obsession with appearance—especially advertising. Like, presenting something in a pleasing way is literally your job."

"Alright, *What Not to Wear*, what do you propose I look like?"

"I'm thinking… fitted suit with a tie that adds a splash of color. A fun pattern that shows people you're not stuffy but you also realize you're eating at an expensive restaurant."

"Which reminds me," Kit said, interrupting her, "I looked online and I almost had a fucking heart attack. It's three hundred dollars per person."

Bria nearly choked on her gum. "*What?*"

"Yeah, three hundred. Nine people makes that almost three grand for one meal." Saying it out loud didn't make it any less insane for Kit.

"That's rent money in some places… Kit, you

better eat all that damn food, I'm not playing. Eat it or you don't get to come home."

"I'm going to! I just hope that Roman's paying, otherwise I might have to cut the reservation by one. I can't afford that."

"How much do you have left?"

"After rent, I've got like, a rack. But I need to portion that off so that I can start saving up for my own place," he said. Bria looked up from the potatoes.

"You're moving out?"

He could see the surprise on her face. There was also something else. It was almost… disappointment.

"Not right now, but I figured you and Trish would want your own space some time soon. I've been there for a while now and I think I should let you guys get back to what you had before I came home." He shrugged and tossed a potato in the basket.

"I mean, you don't have to rush out anytime soon, Kit. I love having you around. I missed you while you were at school. I'm not looking to kick you out by the end of the year."

Kit shook his head and said, "No, I know, I just thought… I don't know." He met her eyes and shrugged with one shoulder. He thought she might look away but she stared up at him for a moment.

"Don't go just yet. Okay?"

"Yeah, okay."

This seemed all too familiar. Kit was reminded of

the last day at their parents' place before he went off to school and she moved out of town. She'd made him promise that he wasn't going to leave her for good. They were all each other had now. They were stuck with each other for life.

"You ready to go?" he asked, looking down at the basket in her hand. They had plenty of fruits and vegetables inside. He doubted they'd need to come back for a while. Bria seemed grateful for the change in topic because she exhaled and said,

"Yeah, let's go."

He followed her to the self-checkout aisle at the front of the store and helped her punch in the numbers for the food. They bagged the items and Bria carried them on her arms. She patted her pockets for her wallet and her eyes grew wide. "Shit."

"What's wrong?" Kit asked, scanning the last item.

"I don't have my wallet on me."

"Oh, I got it. No big deal."

"I'll pay you back," she promised him. She looked at the total and nodded. "Remind me to give you a hundred and twenty when we get home."

"Sure thing," Kit said. He reached into his pocket and pulled out his little leather wallet. As he searched for his card, Bria called his attention. He glanced over at the tabloid magazine she was pointing at and rolled his eyes. Those magazines put out the strangest rumors.

The machine beeped to accept the card. "Alright, let's get outta here," he said, slipping his wallet back in his pocket. He took the receipt and headed towards the door.

"You ready to get all snazzy, Mr. Bayer?"

"I'm ready to look like a million bucks," he chuckled.

7
SOMETHING YOU WANT

Bria had once again impressed Kit with her styling skills. He'd been skeptical of the suit she'd picked out for him at the store, but now that he looked at himself with a fresh shave and styled hair, he looked pretty damn dapper. No one at the restaurant could possibly tell that he'd lived off ramen for two years.

On his way to the door, Kit stopped by Bria's room to say goodbye.

"Be careful, and have fun!"

"I will!" Kit replied. He waved to Trish, then was out the door and down onto the street. Right on time, his Uber pulled up to the curb. He hopped into the back and pulled his phone out to check his teeth.

"Damn, Eleven Madison Park," the driver said, whistling. "Got a fancy date tonight?"

Kit smiled at his comment. "You could say that."

Roman wasn't Kit's date by any means. Knowing Roman, he would be on edge all night. Even if Kit *could* pretend that this was a date, Roman's tense nature would ruin the fantasy in a heartbeat. He was regal and controlled and always kept his chin up and his back straight. This environment was his element. Kit wished he could say the same.

For three hundred dollars, he could buy enough chicken nuggets to send himself to the hospital. He couldn't imagine what they'd be eating tonight. Whatever it was, it had better be good. Kit didn't plan on wasting his night eating a bunch of bullshit.

The driver pulled up to the curb just outside of the restaurant, and Kit's stomach did a flip. It was even more beautiful in person than it was on Google. Kit was frozen in his seat for a moment, unsure whether he was ready to go through with this or not. Sure, he could act semi-formal at the office, but this was going to be three hours of being on his best behavior.

"Good luck in there," the driver said reassuringly. Kit nodded at him and stepped out onto the street. He rated his driver well and looked up at the building once more.

"Well, there's no time like show time." That saying didn't sound right to him, but he didn't give himself time to rephrase it. Kit pushed through the doors and was greeted by a hostess. She looked through her book until she found the reservation under Roman's name.

"Right this way," she said, guiding him towards the table. Kit smiled at Barbie when she waved excitedly.

"We were just starting to wonder where you were!" she said once he was seated at the table.

"I'm not late, am I?" he asked. Kit looked down at the time on his phone and let out a sigh of relief. He'd made it there with a few minutes to spare.

"Cutting it close, hm?" Yolanda said. She looked stunning in her gold cocktail dress. Her hair had been styled up into a neat updo, and her makeup looked painstakingly perfect. She took a sip from her glass of water and smiled.

"You look nice tonight, Yolanda," Kit said. Her smile faltered for a moment, and Kit could tell that she was a bit confused by his compliment. She'd subtly insulted him just a moment ago. Without giving her time to respond, Kit turned to Roman. "Sorry I kept you waiting. I lost track of time while I was getting ready, and the drive here was—"

"You weren't late, Kit. You're fine. I'm glad you made it here alright. We do these things every now and then to help build team morale. It gets stuffy spending all day in that office, so we come out, treat ourselves, and enjoy each other's company away from all the desks and paperwork." Roman adjusted his ruby tie and shrugged with one shoulder. Like it was nothing to drop a few thousand dollars in one night.

"That's really cool of you to do that for everyone." Kit could smell the man's rich cologne on his clothing, and he tried not to make it obvious that he was utterly intoxicated by it. There was something about seeing Roman outside of the office that truly did it for him. Sure, he was the same old uppity hardass, but it was a bit like seeing a professor outside of the classroom. It made Kit just a little happier.

He cleared his throat and looked around for a waiter. "So, when does the food get here?"

The moment the words left his mouth, four servers appeared around the table, each with a tray of mugs and some strange nugget of food on the side. The servers placed the mugs down before each guest. Kit leaned in to look at his, slightly skeptical whether or not he wanted to eat it.

"This is the thyme-infused mushroom tea, and on the side is the white truffle brioche," Roman explained.

"A bunch of words I don't know the meaning of," Kit said under his breath. Barbie giggled at his comment.

"The brioche is my favorite, I just wish they'd make it bigger," she said. Kit nodded, unimpressed with the tiny morsel that he'd been given. He knew truffles were expensive, but still. He could probably fit seven of these things in his mouth and not even struggle.

They didn't taste half bad, though, and that was what mattered. Kit chewed tentatively, looking around as everyone else ate and made conversation. Yolanda sipped from her tea and talked with Barbie about her husband Kevin, and for the first time, Kit could almost see a glimpse of kindness in the woman. Her advice was pretty sound, and Kit couldn't argue that Barbie deserved better than whatever Kevin was offering her.

Kit took a sip of his tea and made a face. "This is different than the shroom tea I had in college," he murmured. His coworker next to him, Logan, chuckled and nodded in agreement. Kit was glad at least one person was enjoying his snide remarks. Roman seemed to be completely ignoring him and only talking to the others at the table.

The servers returned again with the strangest looking lollipops Kit had ever seen. A woman placed the plate in front of him, and he narrowed his eyes, trying to figure out whether it was safe to eat.

"Yogurt with cocoa butter and fried lentils," Roman said, as if answering Kit's question. Kit made a face. By the color of the yogurt, he assumed it was plain. Once more, his face contorted, and he struggled to look like he enjoyed it.

When he glanced up, Roman sat glaring at him. Kit shrugged bashfully. What was he supposed to do, eat something he didn't like? He pushed his plate forward a bit and tried to choke down the tea once more. This process went on for another hour. The servers placed something in front of him, Kit took one bite, and usually found the food prettier than it tasted.

There were a few things that he did enjoy, like the carrot tartar, but the portions were much too small for him to really get into it. When two hours rolled in, Kit put down his napkin and excused himself to go to the bathroom. There was only so much Roman-glare that he could take before he needed to leave.

He stepped into the men's room and sighed. Even the inside of the bathroom was beautiful with its deep sinks and marbled countertops. He nodded at the attendant standing in the corner and checked himself out in the mirror. He still looked nice, like a million bucks, but his heart wasn't in it. Each time something else had been placed in front of him, Kit felt his spirits sink a little lower.

This wasn't his scene. If he was going to eat a three-hundred-dollar meal, he wanted it to actually feel that way. Here, it felt as if he were only eating appetizers at a formal party.

The bathroom door opened again and Roman stepped inside. He jerked his head and the restroom attendant nodded, stepping out so that they were alone.

Kit sighed. He knew he was in for it now.

"What's wrong, Roman?" Kit asked, not bothering to look at the other man. He knew there would be a scowl on his face like there'd been all night.

"I could ask you the same question, Kit."

"I'm fine. I don't know what you're talking about."

"You've had a look on your face since you got here," Roman said. Kit turned to look at him, his brows crinkled.

"So have *you*." He crossed his arms. "You've been staring at me like I'm some idiot who's never been to a nice restaurant."

"I'm staring at you because you're being *rude*. This meal is supposed to be special and you're treating it like it's no big deal."

Kit bit his tongue. He was this close to saying that it wasn't, that this dinner didn't matter as much to him as it did to Roman, but he didn't want to seem ungrateful for Roman spending so much money on him.

"Look, I know you don't know me all that well, but this whole thing isn't really my scene." He gestured around the room to emphasize just exactly where they were. "I understand that you were trying to do something nice for everyone at work, but this whole dressing up, pinkies out while drinking champagne thing? That's not who I am."

"This restaurant was rated three stars by Michelin," Roman said.

"Roman, I don't know what that means. I'm happy that the Michelin Man loves to eat here, but I'm not like you guys."

"That's not who…" Roman started. He shook his head. "Look, whether you like this restaurant or not, you need to act like you have some sense about you. I heard all of your snarky comments. You're lucky the chef wasn't around."

"I obviously wouldn't insult the chef to his face, Roman."

"How is that obvious? You've been acting like an ungrateful brat since you got here."

"And *you've* been acting like a stuck-up dick since I got here, too. Nobody else but you has a problem with me making jokes, and that's because nobody else is so preoccupied with appearances like you."

"Kit—"

"Don't even deny it, either, Roman. You freaked out when I said I wouldn't buy your pants for you. You got all pissy because you didn't have the shirt that Ari liked. And now, when I'm making jokes and everyone else is laughing, you don't like it. You don't like it because you're so used to everyone acting all stuffy around you, but that's not me."

"It's not stuffy."

Kit snorted. "It's stuffy, and uptight, and bougie as fuck. And I'm none of those. I don't worry about shit like that because at the end of the day, I don't need to convince anyone that I'm something I'm not. Maybe you get off on being perfect for everyone, and that's your prerogative. You're allowed to do that. But if you ask me, what makes you insufferable sometimes is the fact that you don't let yourself have fun. You're too worried about looking good to everyone that you never have a good time with anything. My suggestion is to loosen the fuck up, do what you want, and pull that stick out of your—"

Kit's words were silenced by Roman reaching forward to grab his shirt. His grand speech caught in his throat, too thick to swallow down. And when Roman yanked him forward, chest to chest, a flash of worry crossed his mind. Not that he'd said something wrong, but that he might actually be dreaming.

Roman's long fingers laced through the back of Kit's hair, and he stared into the younger man's eyes. His lips pressed together tight, thoughtful, and before Kit could question whether he'd actually cross this line, Roman leaned forward to kiss him.

For just a second in time, Kit's environment disappeared. He wasn't in the bathroom of some high-end restaurant. He was in Roman's arms, his heart thudding against his chest so hard that he worried Roman could feel it as well. Kit was overcome with the tickling sensations of Roman's beard against his cheek and the way his shuddered breaths washed over him, warm and inviting.

Kit was greedy, as he was in most aspects of his life, and he turned his head and deepened the kiss. A shiver ran up his spine as his tongue brushed against Roman's. The whimper he let out surprised even him, but from the pleasured grumble racketing around in Roman's throat, he couldn't muster an ounce of shame. It felt good. Fuck, it felt so good.

He pushed him back against the counter, and surprisingly, Roman didn't complain. He complied.

They worked their mouths together hungrily, like there was no tomorrow or yesterday, only this frozen, present moment, and only retreated when they needed air. Roman's breath was hot on Kit's lips, and it came out ragged, in uneven tremors. Kit remained still, eyes closed, waiting for the sound of his alarm or Trish's voice to wake him from the fantasy. This had to be some kind of elaborate wet dream Kit was having. When he finally peeled his eyes open and looked up at Roman, he saw that it was real. This was really happening.

"Was that 'doing something you want?'" Kit asked, his voice barely loud enough to hear it himself.

Roman nodded, the corner of his mouth pulling up into a lazy, satisfied grin. He looked completely content with his decision. Roman lowered his head and kissed Kit once more.

It was almost cruel when Roman retreated from the kiss. He left Kit with an emptiness in his chest, a deflated balloon where his heart was. When he turned to his reflection, Roman straightened out his clothes and wiped at the corner of his mouth. He sniffed, then glanced at Kit's reflection.

"This didn't happen," he warned. He held that eye contact until Kit nodded in agreement. Then he left the bathroom in only a few smooth, languid strides.

Kit brought his fingertips to his lips, brushing them over both. There was a tingle, a current of electricity that Roman had left in his wake, and when Kit's breathing finally returned to normal, he comprehended the weight of this situation. All of his suspicions—and hopes—had just been confirmed.

A little uneasy and off-kilter, Kit returned to the table, careful not to stare too long at Roman. He was afraid that if he did, his face would grow as hot as his entire body had felt only moments before.

8
PERSONAL USE

Kit couldn't stop thinking about what happened at Eleven Madison Park with Roman two days ago. He'd gone to bed after dinner with the man on his mind, and when he woke up, there Roman still was. The kiss was the last thing he would've expected from him. He was all about how something made him look, but last night, this didn't seem to be the case.

Just as Kit had encouraged him to do, he had done what he wanted without thinking things through. While that was great and Kit was glad he finally let his walls down—even just for a moment—he couldn't help but wonder what this meant.

Would they go right back to just working together, or was this the beginning of something else entirely? The thought scared Kit as much as it excited him.

This was uncharted territory, and for Kit, the opportunity for something new always brought up a mixture of feelings.

The worst thing about this whole situation was that he had nobody to turn to. He'd considered talking to Bria about it, but he knew, without a doubt, that she would talk his ear off about how irresponsible he was being. He finally had a job that he could make a good living from and he'd gone and kissed the boss. He'd crossed a line that he never should have crossed because of what—horniness?

Chad was also off the table. Kit loved his best friend to death, but he knew the second he told Chad about what happened, the guy would continue to push him towards that direction. Sure, it wasn't the *worst* reaction he could get from somebody, but he wanted to take things slow. He wanted to think this over and not get ahead of himself by going towards Roman based on pure emotion. Chad was usually nothing *but* pure emotion.

And then Trish. Fat fucking chance she'd talk to him about this. She'd only just begun to come around to the idea that he worked at Yellow Fall in the first place. If she knew his boss had kissed him, Kit knew exactly how that looked. But this wasn't Roman taking advantage of him. Kit was more than familiar with that kind of relationship—and he'd never let something like that happen. He had a mouth on him, one that could cut deep just as well as it could kiss softly.

These thoughts clouded his mind all morning on the subway. He tried distracting himself by looking through news articles, but all he could think about was Roman and the way his lips felt and the way Kit had wanted him to do more than just kiss him. The doors opened and Kit hurried out of the car, heading towards the coffee shop.

Since starting his job, this had become a second nature to Kit. He rattled off the orders to Michelle and watched as she got to work on preparing his drinks. While she worked, they made their usual small talk. She'd just gotten a little tabby cat over the weekend and she was nervous about leaving him alone for so many hours.

Before he could go, Michelle stopped him. "Hey, Kit, I have a question for you. How do you feel about parties?"

The question caught him off guard, mostly because all they normally talked about was weather and stupid reality TV shows they'd watched the night before. Kit shrugged and said, "I like them. Why?"

"Well, I was kind of tasked to invite a bunch of people to this party my friends are throwing and I figured I'd invite you. You'd probably like my friends, they're interested in all the same stuff I am, but they're a lot funnier." She turned and called out for a Daniel to come pick up his latte. "So, what do you say?"

He had to admit a party sounded nice. All the stress from work had slowly been building, and he needed to decompress and clear his head. On top of that, Chad had been bugging him constantly that they needed to go out again, whether it be a house party or a club. He would have jumped at the opportunity.

"I'll have to see what my schedule looks like, but I'll try to make it," Kit said. He put the cupholders down on a table and pulled a pen from his pocket. He scribbled his number on a napkin and handed it over. "That's my number if you wanna text me more of the details, okay?"

Michelle smiled and folded the paper up, slipping it in her pocket. "I'll text you later today. Have a good day!"

"You too!" Kit gave a wave and headed out. In the past few weeks, Kit had grown guilty over constantly bailing on Chad when it came to party invites. This would be perfect for the both of them.

He carried the coffee to the table in the lounge area and turned to wave everyone over. Barbie hopped up from her seat and crossed the room to greet him.

"Hey, cutie! You seem happy. What's going on this morning?" she asked.

He smiled coyly. "Nothing, really. Just had a good morning and I'm optimistic that my afternoon will be just as good." Kit nodded at each of the people thanking him for picking up their drinks.

"Thanks, Kit," Yolanda said. Kit didn't detect a hint of sarcasm or condescension in her voice. Both he and Barbie watched with shock as she walked back to her desk.

"Did she just…" Kit started.

Barbie nodded. "Yup. Today really must be a good day for you."

Barbie excused herself and Kit flopped down on the large leather sectional that had been delivered earlier this morning. The couch marked the last piece of furniture that needed to be shipped before the redesign was complete. Though all of the pieces hadn't technically arrived in under a month, Roman hadn't punished him. Not that he would've minded that too much…

Kit played around on his phone for a bit until he noticed that Roman's cup of coffee sat unattended on the table still. He made a face then stood to grab it. It was still warm, so he decided to give to Roman. Maybe he hadn't heard him come in or didn't look up through the two-way mirror. The fact that Roman had fought him on keeping at least part of that feature made Kit roll his eyes.

He knocked on the door lightly before entering Roman's office. When he entered, Roman didn't bother looking up from his papers. He continued examining the files while Kit stood in the doorway. Eventually the younger man cleared his throat, drawing his attention away.

"What do you need, Kit?"

There it was. Despite everything that had gone down at the restaurant, the tone of Roman's voice hadn't changed in the slightest. He still acted like he *hadn't* had his tongue halfway down Kit's throat against the counter in the bathroom.

"You didn't come get your coffee. I thought I'd give it to you." Kit stepped forward and handed the drink off. "So, are we going to talk about…?"

"Finish your sentence, Kit, I'm not a mind-reader," Roman sighed. Kit rolled his eyes and considered snatching that drink right back from his hand.

"Are we going to talk about what happened at Eleven Madison Park? Y'know, the whole, 'my boss grabbing me and kissing me' thing? You were there, you probably remember."

Roman placed the paper in his hand down and took a slow sip of his coffee. While he drank, his eyes remained trained on Kit. Kit crossed his arms, an expectant look on his face. Roman swiped a drop of coffee from his lips before he finally said, "No."

"No?"

"No, we're not going to talk about it. Not here. This isn't the time or the place for that kind of conversation," Roman said.

"But a 'Michelin three-star restaurant' was?" Kit asked, still snarking at the rating Roman had reminded him about.

"We weren't at work, Kit. We weren't in a business setting. So yes, that *was* the time and place. But we're not there, are we? We're at work, being *professionals*. I don't ask any of my employees or team members about their personal life when I'm here because I don't care. Not when I'm at work, I don't." Roman turned the page in his file and went back to reading.

"Well, I just came in here to say that you probably shouldn't ever do that again because your breath is actually really gross," Kit said. Being a mature adult was boring, and his petty side wanted some much needed time in the sun.

"No, it isn't," Roman replied. It took all Kit had not to stomp his foot and demand Roman's attention.

"Whatever, Roman." Kit turned to leave when Roman called out to stop and come back. Reluctantly, Kit dragged himself back to his office and closed the door. "What?"

"You shouldn't be worrying about what happened

at dinner, anyways. You've got bigger problems than that," he said. He handed over one of the papers he'd been looking at. Kit took it and tried to make sense of what he was seeing.

"What is this?" he asked.

"That's a list of everything you've purchased on the company card this past month. I've highlighted one very specific charge that I can't make sense of. You went to a marketplace and spent over one hundred dollars on groceries?"

"Huh? I don't buy groceries…" Kit made a face and looked back at the paper to find the highlighted portion. That didn't make sense to him, but looking at the date, suddenly it clicked. Last month when he'd gone to the store with Bria.

"Oh shit."

"Oh shit, indeed. I'm sure you know that the card is only to be used for the company. Coffee charges, supplies if we're having a party, buying new furniture, paper, things like that. Not grocery shopping."

Kit shook his head and pulled his wallet from his pocket. "This was a total accident. My sister didn't have her card and I used mine. I must have swiped the wrong card. Here, I have the money, and I can pay you back with right now." He pulled a few bills from his pocket and placed them down on Roman's desk.

"I totally didn't mean to do that, and I can guarantee that it won't happen again."

Roman looked at him intently for a moment, probably deciding whether or not he believed Kit. Finally, he said, "You're fine. I'm sure you wouldn't have been dumb enough to actually use the card for personal use. Still, I want you to go through these statements and make sure you don't see any kind of suspicious activity."

Kit looked down at the stack of papers and tilted his head. "That's just the stuff that *I've* used the card for?"

A smirk pulled on Roman's lips. "No, this is for all of the cards in this department. But consider this your warning. Go through all of these, look for any weird amounts, over one hundred, and make a note of them."

Kit glanced at the papers again. That sounded awful, but if he didn't want to lose his job, it was what he had to do. He sighed and grabbed the papers from the file.

"I have a feeling this is supposed to be your job but you're passing this off on me."

"While you're going through those files, look for any place where I asked about your feelings."

Kit's mouth fell open. Roman had never sassed him with such a quick, cutting response. That shock turned into a smile. "Wow."

Roman shrugged with one shoulder, watching as Kit made his way to the door. He cleared his throat before he said, "The office looks nice, Kit. I didn't think you could pull it off, but I'm pleasantly surprised."

Kit looked over his shoulder. "You should trust me more often, Roman. You might be surprised at what I can do."

9
YOU NEED TO BEHAVE

THE SMELL OF COFFEE AND FRESH SCONES FLOATED around the coffee shop, and it was nearly enough to distract Kit from his work. That wasn't saying much, however, given the fact that he could have easily been distracted by watching the paint on the interior walls dry.

If there was ever a small chance that accounting was the path his life would lead to, going over these credit card statements squashed that entirely. This wasn't for him. This was so obviously not for him.

Kit shook his head and tried regaining his focus on the papers before him. He'd just made it to the middle of August's statement, and he placed his finger on the paper so he wouldn't lose track again. Three hundred dollars on the two coffee tables. *Damn,* he thought to himself. He couldn't remember them being that expensive. Still, it was nothing out of the ordinary. The next few purchases were for the small kitchen in the corner of the office. A gunmetal refrigerator for two grand. Three new couches at seven hundred each.

"I overdid it," he chuckled to himself.

"Overdid what?"

Kit looked up to see Michelle watching him expectantly. The morning bustle of uppity Suits had died down and now the store was quite peaceful. She leaned against the counter, a bright smile on her lips and strands of hair that had escaped her bun framing her round face.

"Oh, I'm just going over my expenses for work. I kind of got ahead of myself with the interior design." He sighed and closed the folder. He didn't have to be at work until noon—Roman had thankfully given him a few hours to himself today—and he figured he could read the rest of the file when he was feeling more up to it. If that ever happened, that was.

"Ew, who works these days?" Michelle teased.

"I wish I could relate to that mindset," he chuckled.

"Work is boring! Let's talk about my party. Did you ever decide if you could make it or not? I was told to tell everyone I invited to invite other people. They want a *huge* group of people to show up," she said. She wiped down drips of coffee from the counter and blew the hair from her face with one big puff of air.

"I actually did," Kit said. He took a slow sip of his coffee before continuing. "I don't have any work that Friday night, so I'll definitely be there. Thank you for reminding me, though, I completely forgot to invite my friend. He loves all kinds of parties. That's where he thrives best."

"Invite him! He sounds like fun," she giggled. A customer entered the store and stepped up to the counter, cutting off their conversation momentarily. With this lull in the conversation, Kit pulled out his phone and dialed Chad's number. He picked up on the third ring.

"Heyo, Kit! What's good, bruh?"

"Hey, you doing anything this Friday?" Kit spun his pen around his fingers, fidgeting as he waited for an answer. He really wanted the two of them to have some more time together considering he'd had to bail on a lot more kickbacks since he'd started working.

"Hell yeah I'm free this Friday! Why, what's going on?"

"Well, I got invited to go to this party, and I want you to come with me. Consider it me making up for being hella flaky on you the past few weeks."

Chad made a *psh* sound. "Please, dude, I know

you gotta work, it's cool. We're not in college anymore, we can't just spend every day together eating Doritos and watching dumb shit on YouTube."

Kit smiled fondly. Those nights had always been his favorite during school. No matter what problems they were having with their grades or their friends, Chad and Kit managed to always find time to hang out and take a load off from all the stress of the real world. Having this separation made Kit uncomfortable. It did help that Chad wasn't holding it against him, though.

"We're gonna make up for all this time we've lost, I promise," Kit said.

"Good! Hit me up with the details and I'll be there."

"Perfect. Talk to you later."

"Later!"

Kit hung up the phone and let out a breath of relief. Michelle stared at him, her chin in her hands. When he glanced at her, he blushed. She must have overheard his entire conversation. "He said he'd be there," Kit grinned.

"Yay! I can't wait!"

For the next hour, Kit made himself buckle down and finish reviewing all of his expenses. Outside of an occasional swipe at the vending machine in the lobby,

Kit had no other personal expenses. He was relieved to know that he hadn't accidentally used the card more than once. One time being scolded by Roman was enough.

At noon, Kit gathered his belongings and said goodbye to Michelle on his way out the door. He hurried to the building around the corner and made his way up to the sixth floor. The elevator doors opened to reveal Roman standing in front of them, his eyes trained on where Kit would be.

"Oh," Kit said in surprise. "Hey?"

"Let's go." Roman stepped into the elevator and pressed the button to take them to the ninth floor.

"What's the rush?" he asked, nervously shifting his messenger bag higher up on his shoulder. Roman slipped his phone from his pocket and glanced at the time before he said,

"I have a meeting at twelve-fifteen. New client."

"Ooh, exciting stuff. That is exciting, right?"

"Yes, it's very exciting. We get to deal with another helicopter parent telling me how to do my job." Roman's deadpan tone amused Kit. In the beginning, it had gotten on his nerves, but since he'd been around Roman more, he'd started playing a game. Whenever Roman got like this, he'd try his hardest to lighten the mood by being upbeat and cheery. He knew it wouldn't work and that it would only irritate Roman, but that was the point.

"On the bright side, you get to make a lot more money and buy some more exquisite suits!" Kit's voice was saccharine sweet.

Roman's eyes slid towards him, skeptical. "Stop being so happy."

"Stop being so mopey."

Roman started to say something when the elevator stopped on the ninth floor. Instead of replying, he stepped out and strode to the large room directly across from the elevator. Inside, four men sat around the table. They nodded at Roman and Kit as they took their seats.

Without having to be told, Kit pulled out his tablet. He had no idea what was going to be discussed, but he didn't want to get chewed out by Roman for not being prepared. He knew his boss was just waiting for that kind of opportunity.

During the meeting, Kit tried to pay attention, but he couldn't keep his mind from wandering. Words like 'fiscal' and 'monthly report' jumped out to him, but outside of that, he had no idea what these men were talking about. It wasn't until they began talking about aesthetics that he had some kind of understanding of the conversation.

Roman leaned close to Kit's ear and whispered, "Write down December thirteenth," in his ear. Kit's body tensed for a moment. The smell of spearmint gum washed over him, and Roman's hot breath on his neck sent goosebumps racing down his back. He cleared his throat and wrote down the date as instructed.

This continued throughout the meeting. Whenever Roman needed an important name, date, or noun written down, he brushed his nose along Kit's ear, whispering what to transcribe. It took all Kit had not to let the tiniest of moans slip out. There was no doubt in his mind that Roman knew exactly what he was doing, and by the end of the meeting, Kit's pants fit snugger and his breathing was more laborious.

He forced himself up from the table and covered himself with the messenger bag, smiling and nodding at the men in the room on their way out. He waited until they were alone to let his shoulders sag. Roman looked him over carefully.

"What's wrong?" he asked, adjusting the cuffs of his dress shirt.

"Nothing," Kit lied. He took a steady breath and headed to the elevator. When it finally made its way back up to them, Kit stepped inside. Roman followed him, brushing shoulders with the younger man. Kit kept his gaze on the wall before them.

"Did you take all the notes I gave you?"

Kit nodded. "I did. Something about a big, fancy party next week?"

"It's a party for everyone else. We'll be going for business."

"*We?*" Kit stepped out into the lobby and followed Roman to the front door. He walked briskly, with a mission, and Kit had to increase his speed just to keep up with him. Roman held the door open for him on their way out.

"Yes, we. I'm going to need you to come with me. I'm sure your obligations to your Xbox can wait."

Kit scoffed and maneuvered around a couple fighting on the sidewalk. "That's rude, first off. I have a date with my Fleshlight." Roman's eyes went wide. "I'm kidding!"

"Kit, what did I tell you about making gross jokes and comments while we're working?"

"Oh please, you were just in my ear on some phone sex operator shit. Where are we going, anyways?" Roman shook his head and carried on towards the corner of the street. Kit adjusted his bag again and hurried to keep up with him. "Roman!"

"We're going to pick out a suit for you. I assume you went over the charges to the card and found no other mistakes, correct?" That hardened look Roman had mastered landed on Kit.

"Yeah, there was just the one spending error. Everything else was great." He wasn't being entirely truthful, but he was sure he could finish up the rest of the charges soon enough that it wouldn't matter that he hadn't finished yet.

"Good. I figured you don't have any tuxedos, so

we're going to find you a nice one for the event next week." Roman pushed through the doors of Wexler Formal Wear. Though slightly annoyed that Roman had him running all over town today, Kit was happy to try on something fancy. It wasn't every day that he got to shop around like this.

Roman waved over a saleswoman and instructed her to collect a few suits for Kit. He looked him over and gave an estimate on his measurements. The blonde woman nodded and hurried to grab four suits that might fit him. While they waited, Kit quickly snapped a few pictures inside the store. When Roman wasn't looking at him, he even got a picture of him with a dog-ear filter on. Kit's finger hovered over the button to save it to his phone. He tapped it and put his phone away quickly.

The saleswoman returned with the suits and gestured for Kit to follow her to the changing room. He thanked her and headed inside. As he closed the door, he took notice of Roman's eyes resting on him. Kit began undressing, putting aside his slacks to step into the dress pants. He looked himself over in the mirror and smiled. He looked good. The fit was a bit strange, but he liked how structured the entire look was.

When he stepped out to get Roman's reaction, Roman shook his head. He brushed past Kit and grabbed the tie from the dressing room. "You can't wear a suit without a tie," he said simply.

"Well, I can't tie a tie, so…"

Roman made a face, then stepped closer to him. He slipped the tie around the back of his neck and began twisting and flipping the fabric this way and that. Kit's nerves were on fire as he stared at the man. Roman's brows knitted together, focused on tying the fabric properly. When he was done, he stepped back and looked at Kit in the mirror.

"You look like you give a damn about appearances, now," he said.

"Shucks." Kit cracked a smile at Roman's annoyed sigh.

After trying on the rest of the suits, Kit settled on the first one. It had been the one to fit the best, and he was sure after a little tailoring, it would look perfect. Roman paid for the suit despite Kit's best protests. With a swift dismissal, Roman swiped his card and motioned for the door.

On the way out, Kit peeked into the bag once more. "So, I'm glad you think I look cute in this suit."

"If only I said that," Roman murmured.

"You don't think I look that good in the suit?" He paused for a moment, tapping his chin. "You're right, I look better out of it."

"Kit," Roman warned him. "You need to behave."

"But Roman… We're not at work. The rules don't apply outside." With that, Kit took off ahead of him, practically skipping down the sidewalk, and though he could have been mistaken, it sounded as if Roman chuckled to himself.

10
MAKE HIM SEE

Kit sat impatiently on his sofa, growing more and more anxious as time went on. Their Uber driver was still late, and he'd told Michelle that he and Chad were going to be there at eight. It was already well past that time.

"You need to calm down," Chad said, biting into his cheeseburger. "It's a party, dude, it's not going to kill you to be a few minutes late."

Kit took a deep breath and tried to chill out. Chad was right. He was being his typical dramatic self. "I know. I guess I've just been getting better about punctuality at work, and it's rubbing off here. You're right, though, I should calm down." Saying it out loud felt like Kit was ridding himself of the stress. Michelle wasn't going to kick him out for being there at nine.

Kit eased himself back onto the couch and

watched as Chad devoured the rest of his food. Chad was a strong believer in pre-gaming food before he went out to a party. He had a low tolerance to alcohol, and filling himself with greasy fries and burgers always helped balance him out and kept him from getting too drunk too quickly.

"You want some?" he offered. Kit shook his head.

"I'm good, but thanks." Kit opened his phone and went over his schedule one more time. For the most part, it was clear. Monday through Thursday he had his typical hours to work, and on Friday he had the day off. Saturday night was the event Roman was taking him to.

Kit tilted his head and considered whether that was the proper way to think about it. Roman wasn't *taking* him to the event, so much as he had to be there for work, but either way he sliced it, he was technically Roman's plus one.

Ugh, get it together, bitch, he chastised himself.

Ever since their kiss at the restaurant, he'd been feeling much more... fluttery around him. There was a newfound energy there that he couldn't quite pin down or put into words. It was a natural response, but one he wasn't used to feeling. Despite his best intentions, neither of them had talked about that night, and through all of the butterflies he felt in his stomach, Kit could also recognize the irritation. He wasn't the kind of person that could let something like this settle in him. He needed to get it out and talk to Roman.

"Earth to Kit," Chad said, waving his hand in front of his face. Kit blinked.

"Huh?"

"Your phone just made a noise. I'm pretty sure that's our car waiting for us."

Kit looked down at his phone to see that it was indeed a notification letting them know that the driver had arrived. He hopped up and grabbed his jacket before looking around the living room. He wanted to make sure he had everything before he went out on the town.

On their way down, Chad briefly mentioned the fact that he'd been talking to this girl but she was a little too kinky for him.

"Kinky how?" Kit asked.

"Kinky like, she wanted to suck on my toes!" Chad's answer garnered a nasty look from an older man walking his dog.

"The question is, did you let her?"

Chad sniffed once then pointed to a white car parked a few feet away. "I think that's the ride." He hurried off towards it, Kit laughing and trailing behind him. They climbed inside and Kit reiterated the instructions the driver would need to take to get to the party.

Once the driver was confident that he knew the

way, Kit sat back in his seat and opened up his camera. He and Chad took the first of many selfies that night, both posing with their middle fingers up and tongues out.

The car finally pulled up to the right location, and the two of them hopped out. Kit straightened himself up and made sure his clothes weren't too wrinkled. Jesus Christ, was Roman rubbing off on him, and not in the way Kit wanted.

Michelle greeted the two of them at the door, squealing when she looked over their outfits. "You two look so *cute*! Hi, I'm Michelle," she said, sticking her hand out for Chad.

"Chad," he said, speaking over the music.

"C'mon, I'll get you guys some drinks and we can talk some more!" Michelle led them into the kitchen, worming her way through the large crowd of partiers. She stopped at the punch bowl and grabbed hold of the ladle. "Jungle juice," she explained. "My friend Dante made it. He's literally the best bartender in town, just wait until you taste that."

Kit took a sip of it and nodded enthusiastically. "This shit is fire!"

"Hell yeah it is," Michelle grinned. She looked completely different out of her coffee shop uniform. Her brown hair, normally tied back into a ponytail, was now in loose curls framing her face. Her makeup was also bolder, deep and smoky, and her outfit teetered on the edge of free-spirited and escort chic. Kit was feeling all of it.

Kit and Chad floated through the party for a good while, making small talk with people here and there. After an hour of playing the room, Chad ended up getting into a very in-depth discussion with a girl who claimed that she could never date a bisexual guy.

For a moment, Kit leaned against the wall and watched as Chad explained to her why that logic was entirely flawed.

"The thing is, being a cheater doesn't rely on your sexual orientation. Just because I happen to like guys and girls, that doesn't mean I'm twice as likely to cheat on you. It doesn't mean that for any other bisexual dude either. All it means is that you're insecure in your relationship with this person, and that's *your* problem, not theirs."

Chad was trying to keep his cool, Kit could see. He often went off on these rants, but Kit never had a problem with it. Chad was right to feel passionate about this.

"Can I steal you for a second?" Michelle whispered in Kit's ear. He nodded, following her out to the balcony of the apartment. With his cup in his hand, he leaned against the railing and looked out at the city lights.

"This party is great. I don't think I told you that yet," Kit said.

"My friends know how to throw a good one, that's for sure. It's nights like this that I'm glad that I saved up enough money to move out here in the first place." She sighed deeply and stared up at the sky.

"How long have you been in New York City?"

She shrugged. "A year and a half? Maybe two? I lose track of time these days. In a way, it feels like I've been here my whole life?"

"I can relate," Kit smiled. "During my summer before college, I moved here with my sister, and I've loved it ever since. I couldn't wait to get away from our old town. New York was where we belonged."

"It sounds like you're reading my life story back to me," she chuckled. "I mean, I left when I was twenty-three, but it's pretty much the same thing. New York was where I was meant to be. I needed to get away from Nebraska and my shitty job at Geek Gang and just… experience shit, y'know? I was way too smart for that dumb ass job, anyway. Here, I've experienced so much. Fell in love with a guy right off the bat. Lost a job. Lost that guy. Got a new job. One time I even got mugged. Bastard stole my Starbucks gift card that I got for Christmas."

"What a dick," Kit exclaimed. He took a long drink from his cup. The booze inside had loosened him up substantially. Now he didn't care if he got a little dribble of the drink on the front of his shirt. "I just graduated college, so I'm back here. Lost a boyfriend. I got a new job, too. And I'm kinda... Never mind."

"Kinda what?" she said. She turned to face him, curious.

"I was gonna say that I'm in love with this guy, but that's the alcohol talking. I don't really know him. I just know I like him a lot. But we never talk about anything between us."

Michelle nodded. "Have you guys done anything, or is it, like, one-sided?"

"Oh, no, it's definitely not one-sided. We went to this dinner a while ago, and he kissed me in the bathroom. It was a wild kiss too. It felt... I don't wanna sound basic, but it felt electric. It felt like how kisses are supposed to feel. You know what I mean?"

"Did the hair on your arms stand up? Did you feel a silly laugh deep in your stomach, but also kinda like you wanted to throw up?"

"Exactly," Kit said, blushing. "But it's been two weeks and we've said nothing about it. I'm getting bored of just sitting there, waiting for him to bring it up."

"Why don't you talk to him about it?"

"I've tried," Kit sighed. He'd tried many, many times to bring it up, but Roman was some kind of master of diversion. Every instance that Kit mentioned the kiss, Roman steered the conversation in a different direction. It made Kit want to shake the man and tell him to knock it off.

"If you want my lame ass advice, I say make him see that you're still interested in him. Do something that will grab his attention and won't let him go. Guys are stupid like that. Sometimes you have to prove to them that what they did actually meant something to you." Michelle shrugged. "It's up to you, though."

Kit looked down into his cup, watching the drink slosh inside.

Michelle was probably right. Though he was intelligent, professional, and confident, Roman probably wasn't the most aware when it came to feelings. Sometimes Kit wondered if he had any feelings at all. Outside of contempt, that is.

"We should probably get back to the party," Michelle said after a moment of silence.

"Definitely," Kit said. He followed her back inside, only to find that Chad was now making out with the girl he'd spent a long amount of time schooling. Kit pulled him away from her and dragged him to the middle of the room to dance.

"Why are you cockblocking, bro?" Chad whined.

"I wanna know what happened to you and her fighting over dating bi dudes?"

"She told me she'd never looked at it like that, and that it was hot that I felt so passionate about it." Chad smiled confidently, and Kit couldn't help but do the same. Before Chad could say anything else, the music changed to a song he and Kit had obsessed over last summer.

"Aw shit, here we go," Kit exclaimed. The corny dance routine came back to them at the same time, and they moved to the music like it was second nature. The girl Chad had been kissing cheered for them, soon followed by a few others in the living room.

"Michelle!" Kit called. She looked over her shoulder, and he waved her over. "Get in on this action," he said once she was close enough.

"Don't have to tell me twice."

She moved between the two of them with ease, and though she didn't know any of the dance moves that Kit and Chad had come up with, she managed to keep up with them—and even throw in a few moves herself.

"Thank you for inviting me to your party," Kit said over the music. "And thank you for talking to me earlier!"

"Don't even mention it!" she said back.

Kit nodded, but he really was grateful for her advice. He hadn't been able to talk to anyone about what was going on with Roman, and finally getting that off his chest was liberating. On top of that, she'd been right.

Kit had to make Roman see him, and he knew exactly how he was going to do that.

11
WE'RE A TEAM

Something was wrong. Kit didn't know what it was, but he felt it the moment he stepped off the elevator that following Wednesday afternoon. It was on the faces of his coworkers. Damien and Logan, the two jokesters in the office, were noticeably silent, and even Yolanda seemed particularly tame. He made a face and crossed the floor to the mini kitchen. He found Barbie sitting with her hands wrapped tightly around a mug of tea.

"Hey, Barbie. Everything okay?" he asked, pouring himself a cup of tea.

"I don't know, honey," she said somberly. He took a tentative sip and looked around the room. Every person that met eyes with him diverted their attention elsewhere a moment later.

He took a seat beside Barbie and said, "Okay,

what the hell is going on? Why is everyone being weird?"

"It's Roman."

The moment the words left her lips, the elevator doors dinged open again. Rather than his boss walking out, Kit watched a stranger step out into the office. His wavy, shoulder-length black hair was brushed back neatly, and his suit looked as if it were tailored by five women with eighty years of experience. He adjusted his tie and looked at everyone in the office.

"Roman's in his office," Yolanda said, forcing a smile. The stranger nodded and headed to the room in the back, not even bothering to knock. An oppressive silence hung over the office.

"Barbie," Kit insisted. "Who was that? Why is everyone acting so strange?"

"That was Ari Naser."

The name was familiar, but it took him a moment to realize that Ari was the owner of the company. He'd been the one who'd fired all of those people involved in the Grandeur scandal. He'd been the one to put all of these people in the positions they currently occupied.

"Oh," he said meekly. It made much more sense why everyone had suddenly clammed up and gone quiet enough to hear a pin drop. "Why is he here?"

"I don't know, but he hasn't been down here

before unless something was seriously wrong," Barbie said. She nervously bit at the nail on her thumb, her eyes wide with fear. Kit glanced back at the office and narrowed his eyes.

What could be the problem? He was sure everyone here had been doing their job the right way. Nothing bad had happened since he'd started working. Whatever it was, he hoped Roman was doing alright. He looked back at Barbie when she stood from the table and grabbed her purse.

"Where are you going?" he asked.

"Lunch. Yolanda's paying. You're invited too, if you want."

Kit shook his head. He wasn't all that hungry, plus owing Yolanda money wasn't very high on his to-do list. Barbie patted him on the shoulder and followed the rest of the employees out of the office. Soon Kit was left by himself. He took a breath and sat back in his seat. His mind began wandering.

Was Roman in trouble for something an employee on his team had done? Or was this something Roman himself had done? What if their conversation was about him? Kit swallowed hard. If Ari had fired an entire team of highly qualified designers and illustrators, he probably wouldn't hesitate to fire some assistant fresh out of college. Did he even have the power to fire Kit?

"Of course he does," Kit said to himself. "Shit."

The door to Roman's office opened and Ari came striding out. He closed the door carefully, his eyes falling on Kit. He tilted his head curiously. "You must be Kenneth," Ari said in a thick Australian accent.

"Y-yes, sir," Kit said, standing and offering his hand. Ari took it and gave him a firm shake. Kit tried to mask the wince.

"I don't believe we've met, which is unfortunate." Ari moved around him and walked to the coffee pot. He poured the drink into a Yellow Fall branded mug and took a long drink. Kit stood still as a statue, unsure how he should react. He wasn't sure whether it was best to keep it casual or be super formal.

"How has your day been?" Kit asked, hoping his voice didn't waver too much.

"Stressful. I'm glad I finally had the chance to talk to Roman. And now, you." Ari turned to face him, his gaze hard. "I wanted to tell you personally. I heard all about your little incident with the company card."

Kit swallowed hard. "Yeah. That was…"

"Unprofessional. Irresponsible. You'd best be thankful Roman's so forgiving. I can't say many other people would be."

Kit nodded and dropped his eyes to the ground. "I promise it won't happen again, sir."

"I'm sure it won't. Crossing me twice isn't something I'd recommend. Get back to work." Ari tossed his cup into the trash and walked to the elevators again. Kit watched him leave before he took a deep breath.

"Don't think so highly of yourself, asshole," Kit muttered. Roman cleared his throat behind him. Kit spun around to face him. "Hey."

"Hey indeed," Roman said, his arms crossed and his eyes stern. "Do you remember when I told you that I was keeping you around because you did your job well? Do you remember that I said I didn't care how you behaved because I knew that at the end of the day, I could depend on you?"

"Yeah?"

"I'm really starting to wonder if I made a mistake in that assumption," Roman said.

Kit blinked. "What are you talking about?"

"I'm talking about you telling me that you finished going over all those credit card statements and that you didn't see any other issues besides the one you made. So, I find it very interesting that when I turned over the statements to Ari, they were filled with little irregularities. Did you even go through anything else besides your own spending history?"

Kit wanted to kick himself. He'd looked over everything once or twice, but he had to admit that he hadn't done the best job he could when he reviewed the other card statements. He'd been distracted with his time with Chad and Michelle, and at home, he,

Bria, and Trish had been preparing for Trish's musical.

"I did a shitty job, Roman. I'm sorry." He figured it was better to own up to his mistake than to try and justify why he hadn't done it right the first time. "Was he here because of me? Did I spend more than just that hundred?"

Roman shook his head. "No."

"What was it?"

"It's nothing," he said, turning to head back into his office. Kit caught his arm and stopped him from leaving. He could feel the muscle in his arm flex, suddenly tense. Roman remained still for a moment before he turned back to face Kit.

"It's not nothing. Tell me."

"Someone's stealing from the company," he sighed.

Kit's brows knitted together. "Stealing how?"

"Through our credit cards. It's not just on this floor, it's every department. They're depositing a hundred dollars into different offshore accounts, withdrawing the money, and closing the accounts."

"Can't you find out who's opening these accounts?"

"Ari's lawyers contacted some of the people in charge of the accounts, but they have no idea what's going on. Someone's using their identities to open them."

Kit's eyes were the size of dinner plates. He'd seen records of a hundred dollars being sent to random accounts, but he'd assumed they were business-related. They didn't seem out of the ordinary at all. Plus, nothing had shown up on his account.

"Wait, this didn't happen on my account. I'm the only one in this department not being robbed," Kit said suddenly. "Does Ari think that it's me doing this?" The idea of losing his job—and potentially spending time in jail—scared the shit out of him.

"No, Kit, you just got here. Plus, this is far too advanced for you."

"If I wasn't so relieved, I'd call you a dick," Kit murmured. "What are we gonna do about this?"

"We?" Roman looked down at him, skepticism on his face.

"Yes, *we*. We're a team, Roman. Whatever happens to you, happens to me." Kit meant every part of that, too. Not only was it in his job description to help out Roman to the best of his ability, but maybe if he'd done a better job of looking over the credit card bills, he'd have been able to save Roman the trouble of getting yelled at by Ari.

Roman stared at him for a long while, examining all of his features. Kit looked back at him, reassured in his promise to help. He gave a small nod before returning to his office. He closed the door, but a minute later, he called Kit inside.

"Yeah?" Kit said.

"Thank you." Roman said it with a kind of sincerity that Kit hadn't seen before. He smiled slightly, then left the man to resume his work.

Saturday night came, and by that time, Kit was certain that everything was going to go according to plan. He wasn't sure how they were going to catch the Yellow Fall thief, but he was positive about this new scheme. He'd thought over what Michelle had told him, how he had to make Roman see that he wasn't going to let that kiss go, and he'd formulated the perfect idea. He was going to show Roman just how much that night at Eleven Madison Park affected him.

He laid out his outfit and then hopped in the shower. Bria and Trish were out doing some preparation for her musical which meant he got to blast his music as loud as he wanted. Migos pounded through the bathroom, and it took Kit just a bit longer to get himself washed up on account of all the dancing he did.

Once he was cleaned up, he changed into his tuxedo. Roman had it tailored for him, and now rather than looking boxy and ill-fitted, the material draped over him better than anything else ever had. He stared at himself in the mirror then pulled his phone out to stunt on Snapchat.

"Okay, but do you see ya boy?" he asked the camera, flipping it around so he could see himself in the full-length mirror. He gave himself a full once-over then posted it to his story. "The next time you'll see me, I'm gonna be at the Mandarin Oriental. You know a bitch like me gets invited to all the best parties."

He laughed at himself and then flopped onto the sofa in the living room. As much as he'd complained about having to work, since he'd become a part of Yellow Fall, he'd experienced so much more than he ever thought he would. Sure, they ate stupid, bougie food that made him roll his eyes and left him hungry, but the things he'd seen and done in the past two and half months more than made up for that. He was living the life every kid fresh out of college wanted.

His phone buzzed in his pocket. He quickly checked it to see what it was, and when he saw that Jaylen had taken a screenshot of his Snapchat story, he rolled his eyes. Jaylen had a way of coming back into his life whenever it was the least convenient, but Kit wasn't going to let him do this again. He was finally in a good place now. He had a job, he had new friends, and he was wearing a suit that cost almost as much as his contribution to rent did. Jaylen could drink bleach for all he cared.

"Team block that hoe," he said, tapping his screen and blocking Jaylen from his Snapchat account.

Not letting that get his mood down, he put on another song and danced around the house until Roman called him. Kit gave himself one last look in the mirror, inspecting all his angles, then took a deep breath and headed down.

It was time.

12
LOOSE LIPS

Kit felt like *that* guy as he stepped down from the staircase outside of Bria's apartment. It was only fitting that he had an equally attractive ride to the event. Pulled up to the curb was a black BMW. The back window came down slowly and Roman's face appeared. Kit expected him to look up at him apathetically, but he didn't. Instead, Roman's eyes wandered up and down his body once before his mouth quirked up into a smirk.

"I'm not opening the door for you, Kit," he said.

Kit rolled his eyes playfully and opened the door, climbing inside next to Roman. "You went all out tonight, didn't you?"

"It's a party. Of course I did."

"You couldn't spring for some chivalry with the

door?" Roman glanced at him out of the corner of his eye and snorted. "Woooow," Kit laughed.

Once he clicked his seatbelt on, Kit told the driver he was situated and they could head out. The man up front nodded and pulled away from the curb. Kit sat back in his seat and looked over himself once more. He wasn't normally all that concerned and nitpicky with his clothes, but as Roman had so eloquently put it, this was a party. He had to look his best for all of these uptight, smarmy businesspeople.

Though Roman didn't say much on the way to the ride, Kit never felt like there was an uncomfortable silence. It was peaceful, quiet—save for the classical music the driver had on the radio. Kit's eyes slid over to Roman, and for the first time, he thought he saw a crack in Roman's façade. He fixed his tie for the fifth time in ten minutes, and after that, he made sure his jacket was smooth.

"Don't be nervous," Kit said softly.

Roman glared at him for a moment. When Kit's face remained sincere, Roman's glare softened. "I'm not nervous," he said.

"Of course not." Kit smiled like he had a secret. "But just in case you do get a little jittery, don't be worried. You do this all the time. You got this. Plus, you have me, and you can't lose when you have me."

Kit waited for Roman to respond. Instead, Roman

seemed to be intentionally looking at everything but him. Kit grinned and went back to his phone.

After twenty minutes, the driver pulled up outside of the massive hotel. Kit tilted his head to look up at it through the window, awestruck. This was the most ridiculously impressive place he'd ever been, and he'd once been to a concert with trained farm animals dancing on stage.

Roman climbed out first, pausing to straighten out his clothes once more. Kit quickly replied to a text from Chad, and when he started to open the door, he noticed Roman outside. He pulled it open for Kit, a bored look on his face.

"Now was that so hard?" Kit asked once he was out of the car. Roman shot him one of his famous icy scowls.

Together, the two of them headed up to the front. A woman in a simple black dress stood at the door, a clipboard in her hand. Roman approached her and told her that they were there for the party with Chelsia Vivienne. Kit nearly choked on his gum.

Chelsia was one of the most popular upcoming fashion designers in all of New York City. She'd worked with Gigi Hadid, both Jenner sisters, and Chrissy Teigen, and that was only in the last two months. It suddenly made all the sense in the world why Roman was fidgeting with his clothing and why he'd shrugged off the price tag on Kit's suit. They *had* to look their best for the host.

The woman in the stylish dress instructed Roman on how to get to the ballroom. After thanking her, the two of them started towards the hotel. Kit reached back for his pocket when someone snagged him by the arm. He nearly fell backwards as he spun around to see who had a hold of his forearm.

"What are you doing here, Kit? You don't belong here," Jaylen said.

Kit felt his heart stop. This couldn't be happening. He couldn't be dealing with Jaylen around his boss. Around so many people who had pull in the business world.

"Let go of me," Kit said, trying to pull his arm away. He didn't want to make a scene outside of the hotel, but the grip on his arm was starting to hurt.

"I saw your video, Kit. You're a completely different person. This shit isn't you. You don't act like that. You don't dress like—this!" He gestured to the clothes Kit had on.

"You don't know anything about what I do anymore, Jaylen. You don't get to know what I'm doing. Now get *off* of me."

"Is there a problem here?" Roman asked, appearing at Kit's side. He looked between the two of them, then his eyes fell on the hand clamped around Kit's arm. His eyes darkened. "What's going on, Kit?"

"Nothing," Kit grumbled, his eyes still on Jaylen.

"Yo, why don't you mind your own fucking business and let me talk to my man," Jaylen asked, puffing out his chest.

"Nigga, I am not your man," Kit said through gritted teeth. He could feel his nerves rattling even more. He was out of control here. Jaylen had him and wouldn't let go. Jaylen was going to ruin all of this for him. The fear and the anger nearly took Kit over. Roman waited for a moment before he reached for Jaylen's hand. He took hold of his middle finger and pulled back swiftly, a loud pop following the motion. Jaylen recoiled instantly, cradling his hand into his chest.

"What the *fuck*!" Jaylen exclaimed. Now free, Kit stalked towards him, pushing his shoulder as he made the other man retreat.

"Stop fucking bothering me, Jaylen. You hear me? Leave me alone. I'm not your man, so stop crying about me on Twitter, and stalking my Snapchat, and trying to get back in my life. Otherwise, I'm gonna have him do so much worse to you."

Jaylen glared at him. He turned and stormed off, never once looking back. Kit took a deep, shaky breath before he tentatively touched the small bruises that he knew were already forming on his arm. They were going to sting for a few days.

Once he recollected himself, he turned around.

Roman stood by the door, watching him carefully. Kit straightened up and approached him. He could feel the lingering gazes of the other attendants outside, but he didn't spent too much time focused on them.

"Thank you," he said. "I'm sorry he showed up."

"Are you okay? He's never done that before, has he?"

"No," Kit said, shaking his head. "It's mostly online. It's my fault that he knew where I'd be, anyway. I was bragging on Snap about it. By the way, what happened to violence never being the solution?"

Roman's concerned expression changed into a conspiratorial one. "We're a team, remember? What happens to you happens to me. I also wasn't a fan of him touching you like that."

Kit bit his tongue to keep from asking why that was. He wasn't sure whether the answer would be as salacious as he hoped. Instead, he simply nodded, took a deep breath, and gestured for Roman to lead the way inside the hotel.

The ballroom was been decorated extravagantly, adorned with gold décor and dinner plates, a live band up at the front, and a golden statue in the center of the room. Kit, trying to loosen up his tension, took a glass of champagne from one of the servers and threw it back in one long gulp. Roman looked at him curiously but said nothing. Instead, he led them over to their table and pulled out Kit's chair for him.

"Chivalry isn't dead," Kit teased.

"I need to talk to someone for a moment, but I don't want you to sit here all night. I invited you for work, but I also want you to have some fun. Okay?" Roman's gaze was pointed and, in the strangest twist of the night, seemed to be filled with genuine concern.

"Yeah," Kit nodded. "I'll try to have some fun."

"Good. I'll be back in a moment." He disappeared into the crowd of socialites and internet celebrities. Kit wanted to call out for Roman to come back so he wouldn't be here alone, but he knew this was important. This was business. Whatever he wanted to do with Chelsia was important for Roman, and for the company.

To keep himself busy, Kit occupied his time raiding the table of food, tasting a little of everything he could get his hands on. Out of all the work-related events, this place had the best food. Eleven Madison Park wanted what this party had, Kit decided. Between sipping on glasses of champagne and dancing with a few recognizable faces from YouTube, Kit found himself letting go of his nerves entirely. Jaylen slipped from his mind, washed away in a sea of tart booze and electric music.

When he needed a break, Kit took a seat at his table and caught his breath, a lazy smile permanently etched into his face. Not only was he having fun, but he was also making connections. Before the wooziness of alcohol hit him, he'd spoken to three different influencers that were looking for advertising agencies for future projects they had, and with how successful Yellow Fall had been, they were curious to hear more. In between Lil Yachty songs, Kit took down their information. Roman was going to be impressed, he could already tell.

"Are you with Yellow Fall?" he heard a man ask. He glanced around until he found a guy not much older than him sitting at the table beside his.

"Yeah! Yeah, I'm Roman Li's assistant."

"That sounds like an incredible opportunity. I hear Roman is a tough guy to work for. You must drink a lot of those having to deal with him every day." The man gestured to the nearly empty glass of champagne in his hand. Kit cracked a smile.

"He's not the easiest boss, but he could be worse."

"You must deal with a lot of stress in that environment. Especially with the money problems Yellow Fall has been having lately. Oh, you're empty." He snapped for a waiter and handed Kit another glass.

"Thanks," Kit said, placing the empty one on the table. Whatever kind of champagne this was, Kit needed to find out the brand because he wanted to drink it every night. He took a long sip of the new glass. "What were we talking about?"

"You were telling me what was going on with the

financial problems at Yellow Fall," the man said with a smile.

Kit blinked and tilted his head. He couldn't remember telling this guy about it. Still, he said, "Yeah, Roman was saying earlier. Someone's—"

Before Kit could finish, Roman was at his side and pulling him away from the table. "That's enough, Kit."

The man he'd been talking to smirked and stood. "Roman, do *you* want to tell me about that problem?"

Roman ignored him and dragged Kit away. Once they were out in the hall, Kit stopped walking and looked back at Roman. "What was that for?" he demanded.

"How much have you had to drink?"

"Not a lot! Just like, three glasses. Maybe four?"

"In forty-five minutes? Jesus, Kit. You *never* talk to journalists about business. You should know this."

The tone of his voice set something off in Kit. It was a light switch shift in emotions, up one moment and down the very next. His stomach churned and his eyes watered. He could tell that Roman was disappointed in him. He could hear it in his voice, the same way his father talked to him years before. The same way his mother shook her head in shame. Like he wasn't good enough. Like he was worthless, just another stupid child that was more of a burden than anything else.

His breaths became shallow, and his eyes were wild, darting from photographer to photographer. Everything was too much. The laughter. The pounding music. The glittering and glimmering and shining of the party. He stuffed his hand in his pocket searching for the card before he took off for the elevator.

"Kit," Roman exclaimed. He barely made it inside before the doors closed and they were heading up to the seventh floor. "What's going on right now?" he asked.

Kit couldn't speak. He knew that if he said anything, he'd fall apart in the elevator. He had to keep it together, just for a little bit longer. When the doors finally opened, he hurried to the fifth room. He swiped the card and bounded inside, finally allowing the tears to fall.

Everything was ruined. Everything was *ruined*. He took a seat on the bed and put his face in his hands. It was all his fault. Tonight was supposed to be about letting loose and having fun, and look how that had gone.

Roman closed the hotel door and took a seat beside Kit. "Talk to me."

Kit didn't know where to start. And then he did. "I'm sorry, Roman. I'm sorry for ruining tonight. I don't know why I said yes to this. I always fuck things up. I always make things into a big mess." He could hear his father say the last sentence with him. That was his favorite thing to say. "I know how much you care about appearances, and Jaylen showed up and embarrassed the both of us. I almost talked to that reporter guy. This wasn't how tonight was supposed to go."

"Tell me how it was supposed to go."

"Not like this! I bought this room because—" Kit caught himself before he said too much.

It was too late, however. "Why *did* you get this room?"

"I wanted you to notice me! That's what Michelle told me to do. You never want to talk about what happened at the restaurant. You always change the subject and make it seem like it didn't mean anything to you. I was gonna 'accidentally' spill something on you and then you'd have to spend the night here with me." As he admitted to his plan, he couldn't help but laugh at himself. It was stupid. It probably would have made Roman more upset with him. "I don't know what I was thinking."

"I'm thinking you don't drink champagne very often. Am I right?"

Kit nodded reluctantly. "It's so good though, Roman," he whined.

"Come here," he said quietly. Kit sniffed hard, unsure if he'd heard him right. "Come *here*," he repeated.

Kit scooted closer and let Roman hug him close. "You didn't ruin tonight for me. You're drunk, and you're reading too far into this. Whoever that guy was isn't a problem. I've dealt with someone who didn't know how to let go either. And I understand your enthusiasm to drink so much. It is good. I'm going to get someone to have that journalist removed for harassing you, and then I'm getting you something to eat to get rid of all the alcohol in your system. Can you stay here until I get back?"

Kit nodded. Roman stood and grabbed the key card from the nightstand. Kit watched him close the door before he brought his knees to his chest and pressed his forehead against them.

He had to be better. He had to do better than tonight, he knew. From what he could see, things were starting to go his way. This job, his new dynamic with his friends, and even how Roman treated him. He couldn't afford to fuck things up now, not when they were going so well.

Still, he couldn't shake the feeling that he was severely out of his league. He could only hope that Roman didn't see him that way.

13
INFERIOR

Kit's eyes slowly parted the next morning, his mouth dry and his head throbbing. It had been a long time since he'd woken up with a hangover, but he was quite familiar with the feeling. Back in college, it was almost a weekly thing, waking up and running to the bathroom before he threw up all over the place.

This was different though. He didn't feel nauseous. He felt dry, and thirsty for a large glass of water. Kit blinked twice, prepared to head into the kitchen to grab water and greet Bria, but instead, he found Roman staring back at him.

He jumped in response, startled by the man lying beside him. Suddenly last night came rushing back to him. The fight with Jaylen. The amount of alcohol he'd downed in under an hour. The reporter. God, the fucking *reporter*. That was where his memory ended. Had something else happened between him and Roman? Kit's heartbeat quickened.

"Did we—"

"No," Roman said simply, as if he knew the question Kit hadn't even asked yet. Kit let out a breath of relief. Had anything close to that happened, he wanted to remember it. He wanted to burn it into his head and remember it forever.

"How come you're in my bed then?" he croaked. He *seriously* needed some water.

"You're in my bed."

Kit rolled over onto his side and looked across the room at the other bed. It had clearly been slept in, but he wasn't sure why he wasn't still over there. "What happened?"

"We had dinner. You were acting loopy, so I put you to bed over there. Around three in the morning, you came stumbling over to my bed, saying you didn't want to be alone. I was too tired to fight with you, so I let you sleep over here."

Though Roman had probably woken up only moments before Kit, he spoke with a clear head. It might have had something to do with the sobriety he'd exhibited last night. Kit chewed his bottom lip, unsure what to say. He didn't doubt Roman's story.

He was the kind of drunk that got lovey-dovey with people, throwing himself on top of them and demanding cuddles before he passed out. The fact that Roman hadn't kicked him out of bed and down onto the floor was a miracle in and of itself.

"Sorry," Kit murmured. Truth be told, he wasn't all that sorry about it. Roman looked completely different from this angle. His eyelids were heavy, and the stubble on his chin didn't look styled professionally. His typically-gelled black hair was now free of any product and wily strands twisted in every direction. He looked handsome even right after waking up.

Fuck off, Kit thought to himself.

"I should probably get ready to leave," Kit said. He scooted to the edge of the bed and sat up. As he moved, the covers pulled away, revealing Roman's perfectly-sculpted chest. Kit felt a blush creeping up his cheeks, but he couldn't look away. His eyes moved lower and lower until they came upon the trail of hair leading to the waistband of Roman's boxer briefs. He swallowed hard.

"Kit," Roman said, amused. "Go get ready."

"Yes sir," he said, snapping himself out of the trance. He was already embarrassed with himself having demanded cuddles from his boss. Sporting a hard-on after clearly ogling his near-naked body would mean certain death.

Kit grabbed his clothing from the ground and hurried to the bathroom. The headache was dull and irritating, but it was nothing he wasn't used to. He washed his face with water and took a moment to catch his breath. Whatever had happened last night was no big deal. They didn't hook up. They didn't kiss again. The only thing close to intimacy besides this morning was the way Roman held him.

"Shit," Kit murmured, laughing at himself. The way Roman had held him in his arms was something he wanted to feel again and again. He had to keep it together for now, though. Roman had taken care of him, treated him like a person instead of an assistant. Hell, he probably even broke Jaylen's finger. Before, Kit thought that the hottest thing he'd ever seen was this straight guy he'd been crushing on in his English class making eyes at him, but now… Now Roman calmly putting Jaylen in his place had taken that spot.

By the time Kit had himself together, Roman stood in the corner of the room, pushing down the sheets from the beds into a nice little pile. Kit stopped in his tracks.

"Are you… doing the cleaning lady's job for her?"

Roman looked over his shoulder and smiled. "Maybe."

"You're something else," Kit said, shaking his head.

He gave the room one last once over before he walked to the door. He motioned for Roman to follow him. On their way to the elevator, the pang of emptiness finally hit him. He'd dropped seven hundred dollars on that hotel room, and he hadn't even gotten laid in it.

That following Wednesday, Kit arrived at the office at his regular time, coffees in hand. He'd left the house a little early so that he could talk to Michelle at the shop about what was going on in her life. Ever since that party, the two of them had started talking and getting to know each other better.

It also didn't hurt that Kit knew Michelle was interested in Chad. Chad was currently more interested in hooking up with guys, but he'd seen the way they'd looked at each other at the party. There was something there, and he wanted to help facilitate the interactions they had together.

Plus, it was easier focusing on *their* relationship than the one he had with Roman. Well, the lack of one, as it were. Ever since their night at the Mandarin Hotel, Roman had reverted back to his old ways. In his office, it was more of the same old gig; Roman would make a slick comment about Kit's job performance, and Kit would return with a jab of his own. But when Roman spoke to him in front of everyone else, there was something different about his behavior.

He nearly ignored Kit during their team meeting on Monday, and Kit tried to be understanding. At the end of the day, he was merely an assistant, and he didn't have much to offer when it came to working with clients or consulting with cameramen. Kit hadn't let that bit get under his skin as much as the other instances.

On Tuesday, Kit had left the seating area to speak with Roman, only to find that he and Yolanda were in the middle of a conversation. He stood patiently and out of the way, but still Roman gave him a nasty glare and made a comment under his breath. Yolanda, amused by Roman's reaction, did the same, making a joke about him almost being a piece of furniture around the office. It took everything Kit had not to offer to help lay her edges and add some concealer to the middle part of her new wig.

Walking into the office that Wednesday had Kit on edge. He wasn't sure what kind of petty remark Roman would make today, and truth be told, he wasn't even sure if he could hold his tongue this time. Whatever was going on with him wasn't his fault, and it wasn't fair for Roman to take it out on him. He placed the coffee down on the table and grabbed two of the cups, walking around the room and handing them out to everyone. He placed Yolanda's down, and she looked up from her computer screen.

"Did you not get those little cardboard cup-holders? Tsk tsk."

"Your wig strap is showing," Kit said. He turned

on his heels and walked back to the kitchen, positive that Yolanda was frantically checking to see if the adjustable straps actually were showing or not. Today was not the day to test him.

Kit delivered Roman's coffee as well, though his efforts were thankless. Before leaving, he stopped and turned around. He wasn't sure what had come over him, but he was going to blame it on the look of disinterest Roman had just given him.

"Hey, Roman?"

"Yes?"

"Don't insult me again." The words had a mind of their own.

Roman looked up from his notepad and raised an eyebrow. He placed his pen down slowly before sitting back in his chair. "Excuse me?"

"I wanted to tell you yesterday, but I didn't want to bring it up in front of Yolanda. Don't talk to me the way you did yesterday. I'm not your slave, and you don't pay me enough to allow myself to be insulted and demeaned like that. And while we're on it, don't let anyone else here talk to me that way, either. Especially not Yolanda."

Part of Kit wanted to bolt for the door and never look back. The way Roman's gaze settled on him had him terrified. He wouldn't let himself show it. Sure, they'd already talked about how Roman was an asshole at work, but it had never been like this before. Roman didn't look at him like he was worthless.

Roman didn't let other people join in on his critiques, like a pack of bullies.

Kit may have had a thing for Roman, but he wasn't going to let himself be treated like this just because Roman was *sometimes* nice to him.

"Is there anything else you'd like to get off your chest?" Roman asked simply.

Kit was fully prepared to lose his job over this, and at the moment, he didn't care if that happened or not. He couldn't let someone punk him like this. He may have hated the people he'd been raised by, but that was one thing he wasn't brought up to be. He was nobody's pushover.

"I just want you to remember," Kit said finally. "You may be my superior, but I'm inferior to no one. Enjoy your coffee." He turned and closed the door, squeezing his hands into fists to keep them from shaking. "Fuck," he whispered to himself. He'd most certainly screwed everything up. Roman was going to fire him and he'd be out of a paycheck.

The rest of the day proved that statement to be false, however. Roman didn't come out of his office until seven. He marched to the elevator wordlessly, ignoring the quizzical looks. Roman was usually the last to leave, packing up at eight o'clock. The fact that he was heading home early made people wonder what exactly was going on.

"That's weird," Barbie said, looking over Kit's shoulder as Roman disappeared into the elevator. "I wonder why he left in a hurry."

Kit didn't respond. He had a feeling it was about what they'd discussed hours ago. Before the awkward silence grew any longer, Barbie launched back into her story about how she and Kevin went two days without speaking to one another.

After work, Kit hailed a cab and climbed into the back. He gave the driver directions to Bria's apartment then put his head back on the seat, sighing. Today was a whirlwind of confusion, and he was just glad to be out of the office. Ten minutes into the cab ride, his phone rang.

He looked over Roman's name and frowned. "Hello?" he answered.

"Where are you?"

"I'm on my way home."

"I need you to turn around and pick up some paperwork for me," Roman said.

Kit rolled his eyes. "I'm off the clock, Roman. I'm not your errand boy anymore."

"Turn back and bring me the papers on my shelf. I need those, and I need to talk to you tonight too."

His stomach clenched. He wanted to talk? Well,

there was no doubt in his mind now that he was getting fired. Kit weighed his options, then sighed. "Bye." He hung up and asked the driver to turn around and let him out back where he'd picked him up.

Once they were back at the office, Kit told the driver to wait there and he'd be right back. By the time he returned, he had a stack of papers in one hand and his phone in the other.

He read the address Roman texted him to the driver and muttered, "Unemployment, here I come."

14
KITTEN

Roman was a liar. The address he'd sent Kit had been accompanied with a promise that it would only be a minute's drive. In reality, Kit sat in the back of his taxi for thirty-five minutes, impatiently tapping and tapping his foot against the backseat. This was the thing that bothered Kit the most about Roman.

He never cared whether Kit was doing something at home. He never bothered checking to see if he had plans outside of work before he requested Kit's company. Instead, he just *expected* that he had nothing on his agenda besides doting on Roman hand and foot.

At this point, it was getting ridiculous. He needed to go to HR, or unionize, or... something.

Kit had half a mind to put in his two-week notice and be done with the situation.

Before he could entertain the idea any more than he already had, the taxi pulled up to the curb outside of Roman's house. Kit paid and climbed out, looking at the gorgeous building before him. He wasn't all that huge on architecture, but he could appreciate something like this. It was modern—clearly built in this century—and a combination of dark wood and stone. Windows covered the building. He'd bet money the place was even more beautiful in the morning, when sunlight could stream in and illuminate the entire house.

Kit headed down the steps near the curb and followed the stone path up to the front door. He adjusted the papers in the crook of his arm as he walked, careful not to drop any as he passed the small birdhouse. The last thing he needed was Roman telling him to go back to the office and print out all the papers he'd gotten dirty or wet.

Kit raised his arm to knock on the front door, pausing when he noticed that it was slightly ajar. Was he walking into a crime scene? A horror movie? Slowly, he pushed the front door open, and entered. He closed the door behind him, then locked it.

"Hello?" he called out.

This is how white girls get cut the fuck up in movies, he chastised himself.

He waited until he heard a movement in another room further inside the house. He straightened up his back and continued forward. For a moment, he was worried he might find something terrible inside. What if he found a dead body? What if Roman was a secret hitman, and he'd walked in on an interrogation?

To his relief, he found Roman sitting in an arm chair in the living room, still dressed in his work clothes. He'd unbuttoned the top buttons on his shirt and loosened his tie, exposing just a peek of his chest hair. In his hand, he swished around a glass of something honey brown.

"Here," Kit said unceremoniously. He stalked towards the man and tossed the papers in his lap. Roman kept his gaze on the lit fireplace, wordless. Kit scowled. "This is where you say 'Thanks for not ignoring me like any other person would have.'"

Roman peeled his eyes away from the fire and looked Kit over slowly. "Thank you, Kit."

He was stunned. He hadn't actually expected Roman to thank him. "Yeah, you're welcome. If we're done, I need to get home. I had plans tonight. I mean, I don't expect you to care since I'm pretty much just your mule at this point, but..."

"Are you done?"

That dismissiveness was *really* starting to grate on Kit's nerves.

"I'm not done, no. I want you to apologize for this past week. I want you to say you're sorry for being a fucking *dick* to me. And I want you to apologize for being nice to me over the weekend, only to turn around and spit in my face when we got back to work." He stared Roman down, shaking his head a bit in hopes that would garner a response.

Roman took a long drink from his glass and set it down on the end table. He pushed himself up from the chair. Kit couldn't tell whether he was trying to intimidate him or what, but to prove that he was serious about expecting an apology, Kit stepped forward and set his jaw.

"Say you're sorry."

"I didn't mean to—"

Kit pushed his chest, causing him to step back just an inch. "Say it. Don't talk your way out of this, and don't give me some bullshit spiel you'd give one of your clients. Look me in my face and apologize for treating me like shit."

A grin pulled at Roman's lips, and he didn't bother hiding it. "You—"

"Roman."

"I'm sorry," he said finally. He stood up taller. "I'm sorry for acting that way these past few days."

"Why?"

"Because clearly it upset you, and I don't want to do that to you."

"No," Kit shook his head, "I mean, why did you act like that? I thought we were getting somewhere. I thought we were making progress. After we spent that night at the hotel, I thought we were... I don't know how to say it, but I just thought you were actually..."

Roman tilted his head. "Actually what?"

"Actually interested in me! I thought we'd go back to work and have this secret between us. No one else would know that we'd slept together at the hotel. We'd look at each other and just *know*. But then you went and started dogging me in front of Yolanda, of all people. You know she hates me—"

"She doesn't hate you, Kit."

"Well, whatever it is, we don't get along, and you were literally making fun of me in front of her. I should have reported your ass to HR, if we're being honest. But I didn't, because I care about you. I *like* you, Roman. And I thought you liked me too."

"Kit," Roman sighed, shaking his head. "That's why I was an asshole to you. I don't *want* you to like me. I wanted you to hate me, that way you could go back to doing your job and it wouldn't make things more complicated. But I actually..."

"You actually what? Like me too?" Kit stepped closer again, closing the gap of space between them. He looked up at Roman with a persistent smirk, well aware just how hard the man was trying to keep his face neutral. The corners of his mouth twitched, dangerously close to letting his true feelings surface.

"You should go, Kit. I made a mistake asking you

to come here tonight." Roman finally brought his gaze back to Kit.

"Fine," he said. He turned to storm off, but Roman caught his arm and pulled him back, pressing him up against his chest. Before Kit could protest, Roman leaned in for a kiss. Just like at the restaurant, Kit's world felt off balance. He grew lightheaded, and every hair on his arms stood in attention.

Roman backed Kit against the wall beside the fireplace, knocking over a picture frame from the mantel. He deepened the kiss and let one hand wrap around Kit's waist, pulling him flush against his body, no room to escape.

Breathlessly, Kit gripped the fabric of Roman's shirt and pulled away for a moment. "Can I?" He dragged his fingers over the buttons, looking up for approval. Roman nodded, then pressed his lips against Kit's once more. As their mouths worked together, Kit began undoing each of the buttons on his shirt until he reached the last.

"You don't know how fucking hard I was when you left my office earlier," Roman panted.

"Why?"

"No one's ever talked to me like that. I do the demanding, and I do the yelling. No one at that office has a spine the way you do, and it's so goddamn sexy."

Kit bit his lip and gave a small, giddy laugh. "You

thought it was sexy?" he asked, reaching up to run his hand over Roman's chest.

"So fucking sexy," he repeated. Roman tugged his shirt off and tossed it to the ground.

"Take off your pants," Kit ordered, his eyes darkening. If Roman liked him being bossy, telling him what he wanted and how he should be treated, then he could do exactly that.

Roman nodded and undid the buckle on his pants. He began to slide it out when Kit reached forward and tugged it roughly, tossing it to the side. Roman stilled as Kit began tugging down his zipper. The sound could just barely be heard between panting breaths.

Roman stepped out of his pants and pulled Kit closer. He guided the younger man's hand from his chest to the front of his boxer briefs. "You feel that? How hard you make me?"

Kit squeezed the bulge, a twinkle in his eye. "I think I can make it harder," he said. He pushed Roman back into his armchair and climbed into his lap. His kisses were deliberate, over his shoulders, along his throat, and down his chest. He eased down to his knees before nuzzling between Roman's legs, cheek pressed against his inner thigh as his eyes remained on Roman.

"Fuck, Kit," Roman breathed.

"That's the plan," he winked. Kit dragged his

tongue over the fabric of his underwear, slow, torturously slow. Roman groaned, his hand falling onto the back of the other's head. He added pressure, wordlessly encouraging more.

Kit's fingers inched up his thighs while he mouthed over the bulge. He wanted this to be painfully measured. He wanted Roman to grow impatient with him. When he was sure the man might explode from frustration, he grabbed the elastic of his boxer briefs and tugged them down. Roman lifted his hips to aid in sliding them off, then kicked his foot to the side, discarding the last piece of clothing.

Kit marveled for a moment, taking in the sight. He was beautiful, not too long but more than enough to satisfy. A thick vein ran from the base to the tip, one that Kit traced with the flat of his tongue. The action drew out another drawling moan from Roman.

He teased the slit, swirling his tongue mercilessly, circling him around and around. Roman hissed out a breath, his grip on Kit's hair tightening. Kit tilted his head, angling himself so that he could meet Roman's eyes, before he took him into his mouth.

The taste was thick, slightly salty but not unpleasant by any means. Kit worked him deeper into his mouth, eyes trained upwards, making sure Roman could see him. He needed Roman to know who it was that was doing this. Who was bringing him this level of pleasure.

"More," Roman insisted.

Kit obliged. He took a slow breath through his nose, then inched his cock deeper down his throat. His tongue stroked the underside, soaking him, coating him as best he could. As he sucked, Kit made sure to give his balls the attention they deserved as well. He pulled his head back when he'd reached the base, watching the strings of saliva connect him to Roman.

"Goddamn, kitten."

Kit raised a brow. The nickname was new. "You like that?"

"I love that."

Kit dragged his tongue over Roman's length, the praise music to his ears. He returned his lips to the head, paying special attention to all the sensitive spots. He'd just gotten into the groove when Roman pulled his head back by his hair.

"It's my turn," he said.

Without another word, he pushed Kit onto his back, into the fur rug on the floor, and hovered over him. His fingers were fast, unbuttoning Kit's shirt and sliding it over his shoulders. He kissed his way down to his belt, discarding the rest of his clothing soon enough. When it came to his underwear, Roman jerked them free, rough and impatient.

Kit closed his eyes and parted his lips when Roman took him into his mouth. The man was even more skilled than him, twisting his head and flicking his tongue in ways that made Kit whimper. He grabbed fistfuls of the rug, his back arching.

"Ah," Kit gasped, relieved when Roman pulled away from his length. That relief was short-lived. A moment later, Roman pushed his legs back and pressed his tongue against his hole. Kit's eyes opened and he shuddered. He took Roman by the hair, pushing him forward, rolling his hips against his tongue.

Roman worked up a pattern, spending a few moments on his ass before he returned to his cock, relentless with his pleasure. Kit could have easily climaxed then and there. The feeling was warm in his stomach, and paired with the softness of the rug, he was in heaven.

Kit didn't know how much time had passed, but it felt like forever that Roman pleased him. When Roman pulled away, he wiped at his mouth and leaned forward for a slow, tender kiss. Kit pulled him close, fingers threading through his hair.

"I'll be back," Roman said, standing and disappearing for a moment. Kit stared up at the ceiling, catching his breath. He needed to calm down before he came way too early. He closed his eyes and counted to twenty. By the time he finished, Roman was back and tearing a condom wrapper open with his teeth. He took a seat next to Kit and rolled it over himself.

Kit took the bottle of lubrication from his hand and straddled him. "You want me on top?" he asked, capping and uncapping the tiny bottle in his hand.

"Don't disappoint," Roman warned.

"I won't."

Kit slicked up Roman's length, then applied a bit to himself, working a finger inside. He lined himself up with Roman, then began easing backwards, carefully taking him. The sting was present, but he pushed through it, forcing himself to stretch enough to accommodate him.

"Jesus, Kit," he groaned, reaching up to grip his ass. He dug his fingers into Kit's skin, massaging him.

Kit smiled through the burn, regaining his focus. In no time, he bottomed out, fully situated in Roman's lap. He took a moment to breathe and grow accustomed to the feeling before he began to rock forward. He felt empty, and when he thrust back, so full.

Kit built up a slow pace at first, steady and constant. Roman's hands roamed over him, down his chest and around his length. He stroked Kit as the younger man rolled his hips. His lids were heavy, and he looked up at Kit with clear effort.

"That's so good, kitten," he murmured.

Kit placed his hands flat on Roman's chest for leverage. That compliment was nice, but he suspected Roman could give him more. To test this theory, he began to move faster, snapping his hips backwards each time he felt the head of Roman's cock come close to sliding out. He watched as Roman's face contorted, his eyes squeezing tight.

"This is mine," Kit said. He took Roman by the chin. "Say it. This dick is mine."

"It's yours," Roman groaned.

"Whose?"

"Yours, Kit. It's all yours."

He leaned forward to kiss Roman, nipping at his lip as he sat upright again. He didn't slow his pace, his movements growing rougher with Roman's admission. This was his, and he was going to ride it all the way home.

Kit took over for him, stroking himself. His head fell back, and he bit down on his lip, a moan bubbling in his throat. He felt on fire, hot all over, a bead of sweat running down his back. Just as he found himself in the zone, Roman's grip on his hips tightened.

"I'm close," he panted, nails digging into Kit's hips.

"Fuck me, Roman. Make me take it."

Roman planted his feet into the rug and began thrusting up, meeting Kit's downward motion. They moved in synchronization, drawing one another to their orgasms like magnets. Kit came first, his muscles twitching in a spasm as he emptied himself on Roman's chest. Words escaped him, and for a moment in time, he could only communicate in high-pitched whines and whimpers.

Roman followed him, his hips flurrying in a mad dash to bring himself across that finish line. He ground himself against the younger man, grunting, breathless by the time he came down from his orgasm. Kit held his face between his hands, staring at the beauty and pleasure that had washed over him.

Roman had said it himself. This was his. Roman was his. One round wasn't enough for Kit. He needed more, and he planned on working Roman all night long. He wouldn't stop until they were both utterly, totally, and completely spent.

15
SHOW ME YOU'RE MINE

Kit's eyes parted slowly, and he let out a long yawn when he sat up. He didn't immediately recognize his location, but when he looked around a second time, he recalled what had happened the night before. He and Roman had taken things to another level. They'd crossed a line he was so happy to finally be over. It still felt unreal, in a way.

On the pillow beside him, he found a note from Roman.

"Didn't want to wake you up. You can get cleaned up and have breakfast if you'd like. When you leave, use the spare key on the kitchen table to lock the door."

The last line was Kit's favorite part.

"You have the day off."

Those five words were about as good as the orgasms from the night before.

He stretched and padded his way across the tiled floor, a chill running through him. He needed warmth, and he needed it badly. He grabbed his clothes from the night before and hurried off to the bathroom to wash up. To his surprise, the water in his shower came down from the ceiling. He felt like a completely different person by the time he dried off.

Kit made himself a bowl of cereal and scrolled through his phone while he ate. He made sure there was a car that could come pick him up, then sent a text message to Chad. With the day off, they could hang out again. It had been a while since they'd had a day to just kick back and have fun. Chad was fine with hanging out, and even asked if Michelle could come along. Kit's brow went up at the implication. He made a mental note to ask more about that situation when they were all together.

The ride back to Bria's apartment was quick and painless, and he bounded through the door the moment he was done paying the driver. Kit headed to the small hallway closet and grabbed a few items that were clean, quickly changing in the bathroom when he was happy with his selection. As he stepped back into the living room, he heard his sister's voice.

"Kit, come here for a sec."

"No bad news, no bad news," he said to himself. He poked his head into the back room. "What's up?"

"Trish's show opens in two weeks. I need you to

look through your schedule and tell me when you're free so I can get our tickets for that date. You can invite your friends if you want, too." Bria looked at him in the reflection of her vanity mirror. He nodded, and couldn't help but smile with her.

Bria didn't have to say that she was proud of Trish for Kit to know how she felt. The way her voice sounded giddy when she mentioned that the musical would be opening in a few weeks made that perfectly clear to him.

"Uh, let me check and see what my schedule looks like, but I shouldn't have any problems going to see the production. Are you excited?"

"I'm so excited," she grinned, placing her makeup brush down on the table. "I never doubted her, but she really surprised me. Pulling this off in only a few months... That's amazing to me. She's just... You better go before I start getting *really* gay, Kit."

He laughed and nodded, leaving her to get back to her makeup. Twenty minutes later, Chad was outside of his place. Kit told Bria that he'd be back later. He ran downstairs and nearly tackled Chad with a one-armed hug.

"Damn, someone's in a good mood," Chad laughed, shoving Kit off of him.

"It's hard not to be when I got the whole day off!"

"That's true. We need to celebrate this occasion. What's the plan for today?"

Kit thought to himself. "We could go to the mall and get into our typical mess. I'm thinking Manhattan?"

"Manhattan sounds good, I'll text Michelle to meet us there," Chad said. As Kit waved down a taxi, Chad quickly sent his message. "Seriously though, what's got you in such a good mood?"

Kit chewed on his bottom lip, debating whether he wanted to get into this with Chad right now. He knew, without a doubt, the second he told Chad that he'd neglected to share the fact that he and Roman had kissed, Chad would freak out. They told each other everything, from their sexual conquests to their meals for the night. Hopefully he'd be able to understand why Kit had kept the information from him in the first place.

"Hello, Earth to Kit," Chad said, climbing inside the taxi.

"I'm gonna tell you something, but you have to promise not to get mad, okay?"

"You had sex with my older brother?"

"Ew," Kit cringed. "Your brother, no offense, looks like one of those Fuggler toys."

Chad snorted, "Damn right he does. Don't let him come near you."

"No, I didn't mess around with Casey. Um… Okay, so remember how last month I went to that bougie ass restaurant and all the food was trash? I think I told you it was boring and ain't nothing happen, but, yeah, something *did* happen."

"Aw shit, what happened?"

Kit sniffed and glanced out the window. Dragging this whole thing out was going to end up being more painful than just being up front about what happened. Rather than delaying, Kit shrugged and said, "Roman and I ended up kissing in the bathroom."

"Shut the fuck up," Chad nearly shouted. The taxi driver glanced back at them with disdain on his face.

"I don't even know how it happened, bro! We were arguing about something, and he eventually just grabs me and starts kissing me. And I'm not even gonna lie, I was really into it. You saw him at the club, he's fine as hell."

"I'd let him insert whatever he wanted into me," Chad nodded.

Kit gave him a disgusted look before he laughed. "He started acting mad weird after that. Didn't want to talk about it, always icing me out whenever I tried to bring it up. Some real dick moves, you feel me? That's why I didn't bring it up to you. I didn't want to talk him up and make it seem like we were going through some relationship-type shit and then have to turn around and tell you never mind. That's why I talked to Michelle."

Chad blinked. "Michelle knew?"

"She didn't know *everything*, just that I had a thing for some guy and we'd kissed. She told me to make it obvious that I was interested in him. Make him see me, treat me like an actual person and not just something he can ignore and pretend he didn't kiss. And it worked, because…"

"Did you fuck him? I swear to god, Kit, if Michelle knew before I did…"

"Well, she can't know because it happened last night, but…"

"Shut the fuck up!" Now Chad was shouting. The driver sighed and shook his head.

"I'm dead serious."

"Nope," Chad shook his head. "Nah, you're fucking with me. You did not go over there last night and fool around with that man." When Kit simply smiled back at him, Chad fell back into his seat dramatically. "Fucking legend status right now. Tell me *everything*."

As quietly as he could, Kit shared the details of his night with Roman, making sure to include the fact that Roman had surprisingly been into him taking control and claiming what was his. By the end of it, Chad looked like he'd just watched someone take off flying.

"I don't know what work is gonna be like tomorrow," Kit sighed. "Do I walk back in there like nothing happened, or do I play all sexy secretary-like?

Get a pair of glasses, wear a button-up with most of the buttons down, show off the titties?"

"You go in there and you remind him of what happened," Chad said confidently. "Dude, I can't believe between the two of us, *you're* the one that ends up sleeping with your boss!"

Kit couldn't believe it either. "All you have to do is get a job and show your boss what you're working with," he said, looking at his friend pointedly.

"I mean, you're not wrong. I'm just saying… I'm usually the one that gets into this scandalous ass mess, and you beat me to it. My little kitten's all grown up."

Kit felt his cheeks burn again. That word, *kitten*, now took on a completely different meaning than it had before. He couldn't help but think of fingers in his hair and the way Roman's voice sounded, low and suggestive.

The entire ride to the mall, Kit relived flashes of the night he'd had. He tried his hardest not to show it, but it was obvious from the smile on his face that he was thinking about all that they'd done. Thankfully they didn't have to wait much longer before they were outside of the mall. They found Michelle leaning against a wall, her hair tied in a messy bun.

"Hey, you two," she said, hugging each of them. "I was starting to wonder if I'd been stood up."

"We wouldn't miss this for anything. Especially not

since Kit has some interesting news to catch you up on," Chad said.

Although he hated having to explain what had gone down for a second time in an even more public setting, Kit was glad to see that Chad wasn't holding this against him. He didn't want his best friend being mad at him for not confiding in him immediately, especially when it came to something like this.

The three of them floated through the mall, shopping and talking about everything that had been going on in their lives. Michelle had just got her paycheck, and she was ready to binge on all the newest arrivals in Forever 21. Once they were both done grilling Kit about how nice Roman's house was, how much money he made, how long his dick was, and what the interior décor was like, it was Kit's turn to ask them about their business.

He decided to cut right to the chase and ask whether or not the two of them were hooking up.

"Uh, duh," Chad said, as if Kit had asked if he inhaled oxygen and exhaled carbon dioxide. Chad glanced in Michelle's direction as she paid for all her new clothing. "We're not serious or anything, so don't get weird about it. We've just messed around. I've also been texting this guy I met online all day, if that shows you how laid back we are about this. I just really like hanging out with her."

"I'm glad! She seems dope," Kit smiled.

He didn't want to get his hopes up, but ever since they'd graduated, Chad hadn't had much luck with people sticking around. All anyone in New York ever wanted to do was bust a nut and leave, and while Chad pretended he was about that life too, that wasn't how he was deep down. Kit knew his friend preferred companionship over constant random flings. He only hoped that this might be something that would benefit Chad in the long run.

"Oh, that reminds me," Kit said suddenly. "Trish's doing that whole all-women *Grease* production, and I was wondering if you and Michelle would like to go."

Michelle brushed a strand of hair from her face as she walked towards them. "I would love to," she said enthusiastically. "I'm all about supporting my fellow ladies."

"I'll only go if you invite Roman," Chad said, smirking. Kit glared at him, halfway tempted to pop him upside the head.

"Roman?" Michelle looked lost.

"That's his boss's name. Roman," Chad explained.

Kit's cheeks grew red. "I can't invite my boss to go as my date to the show. That's how you make things messy, dude. No way."

"Come on," Chad whined. "Call him right now and tell him to come. Rich dudes like that love musicals, plus maybe you can give him a handy in the middle of it as a surprise." Kit widened his eyes at the volume Chad had said that at. "Oh, and you can even tell Bria that this is you paying him back for treating you to that three-hundred-dollar dinner, just in case she gets suspicious. I'm assuming you haven't told her."

"I'm not inviting—"

"Then I guess me and Michelle will have to see a movie instead," Chad said, crossing his arms over his chest and looking at Kit smugly.

"You're a bitch," Kit said, yanking his phone from his pockets. He took a few steps backwards, his eyes still on Chad. "You're a snaky little bitch, you know that?"

Kit couldn't believe he was actually inviting Roman to a date. Sure, he might be the biggest fan of musicals, but there was a difference between a Broadway production of *Hamilton* and a local theatre group's performance of *Grease*. He doubted Roman would give him any other response besides an incredulous laugh.

"Yes, Kit?" Roman answered.

"Soooo, I have a question. Is there any way I can request the night off sometime in the next two weeks?"

"What for?"

"There's this huge musical that I'm required to go to. It's a family thing." Kit glanced in Michelle and

Chad's direction. Michelle watched him carefully, and Chad could barely hide his excitement.

"I suppose you can have the day off," Roman sighed.

"Perfect. I'll make sure you don't have any meetings or anything on that day, either."

"Why would you move my meetings around?"

Kit winced. "So that... maybe... we can go together? Look, I know you probably don't care about some dumb musical—"

"Correct."

"—but I think that it'd be nice to have you there with me. You took me out to eat at the fanciest restaurant I've ever been at. You made me your plus one at a party with celebrities I follow on Instagram. The least I can do is treat you to a musical." Kit made sure to exclude the fact that Bria would probably be able to get their tickets for free, and no one would have to spend a dime.

"I'm busy, Kit."

"Roman, please. I just want to treat you. Come see the musical for me. Show me you're mine." Kit bit down on his thumbnail, grinning like a fool. The silence that followed was confirmation that throwing that comment in Roman's face was effective.

"Fine. I'll see you tomorrow." The line went dead.

Kit slipped his phone back in his pocket and turned around to see Michelle and Chad waiting impatiently for his answer. All he had to do was nod for the two of them to burst into a round of applause. Kit couldn't deny that he found himself a bit more excited to see the musical now.

Being around Roman tended to have that effect on him.

16
SWEET THING

Since he'd started working at Yellow Fall, Kit's wardrobe had shifted from graphic tees and jeans to button-ups, slacks, and jackets. It was a slow and reluctant change, but he'd quickly realized how much easier it was not having to look like he was a model for the male line of Fashion Nova clothing. He could pick something simple, understated, and be out of the door and on his way to work. That was the case for most days.

This one in particular wasn't most days. It was the first day back at work since he'd had sex with Roman. It was the first day since that night that he'd be face to face with the man who'd blown his mind—among other things—all night long.

He woke up an hour early that morning, ready to head back into the office and show out. He wanted

Roman to know that despite the night they'd shared, he wasn't going to let that cloud his judgment or affect his work. Something told Kit that this kind of coolness, this nonchalant aura, would be well-received.

Once Kit had pieced together his clothes and posted an Instagram OOTD, he showered, shaved, and took special care to deep wash his face. Soon he was smooth, styled, and ready for anything. Bria stood in the kitchen, stirring her pot of organic hot breakfast cereal and humming along to the Tegan and Sara song playing from her phone.

"You look fancy today. Does Roman have a meeting with the big boss today or something?" she asked when he stepped out of the bathroom.

"Or something," Kit smirked.

"Well, good luck with that! And thanks for picking up dinner last night, I don't think I told you that."

He shrugged. "It's nothing."

"It's something, Kit! I'm so proud of you for sticking with this job as long as you have. I was worried that you'd get bored of it, or you'd get upset and quit, but you've stuck around, and you've really helped us out around here. Trish might've needed to take on another job if you hadn't started at Yellow Fall."

"Nah, no need for that," Kit said. He reached around Bria and grabbed an apple and a banana. "I'm glad I can help out. It's really shitty feeling like you're mooching off someone else. I wanna contribute as best I can. Plus, I'm still saving up for an apartment of my own. I hear there's an opening coming up on the second floor."

Bria's eyes lit up. "Wait, you want to move into this building?" She put down the spoon and rushed over to give Kit a hug. "I thought you'd want to move across the city or something. I know I act like you're annoying and stupid, but I don't want you being that far away. If you're a few floors down, though…"

Kit laughed and returned her hug. "I thought you might like that. I don't want to be that far from you either. Who else is gonna get my groceries?"

Bria swatted the back of his head and returned to the stove. "You're a butthead. But I'm excited."

"Good, I am too. I gotta head to work, but I'll text you if I hear anything else about the apartment, okay?"

"Alright, have a good day!" Bria waved over her shoulder as Kit headed downstairs.

Now that he had a little bit more money in his pocket, he was finally able to skip the subway every other day. Given that he looked this nice, he decided he was going to splurge and arrive at Yellow Fall without having ran there from the subway station. He hailed a taxi relatively easily, gave his directions, and sat back to eat his breakfast in peace.

That thirty-minute drive to work was enough time

for Kit to go over the coffee orders of all his coworkers multiple times. He'd worked there long enough to generally know when Barbie was in the mood for a caramel macchiato and when Damien was in the mood for hot chocolate instead of coffee.

He headed into the shop and greeted Michelle with his usual list of orders. While she prepared them, she said,

"Are you nervous about work?"

"Why would I be nervous?" Kit asked, smiling coyly.

She lowered her voice and said, "Last time I checked, most bosses don't know how their employee's ass feels in their hand!"

"To be fair," he started, "I'm not just an employee. I'm his *ass*istant."

"I can't believe you," she groaned, rolling her eyes. She gathered up all of the drinks and placed them in the cardboard carrier. "I wanted to ask you, you're not weirded out by me and Chad, right?"

"No? Why would I be?"

"I dunno, I've just been in some weird situations where someone will think I'm stealing their best friend from them. They think whatever we're doing in bed is going to take away from their friendship. You know how people are. They never leave the high school shit back in high school."

Kit could see where she was coming from. "I

guess if you're insecure, you'd be afraid of that, but I've known Chad for years. He'd never let someone come between us, even if that was what you were trying to do. I should honestly be thanking you, I kind of feel guilty for not being able to hang out as much."

"Okay, good," she breathed, laughing nervously. "I was kind of worried about that. But if you're cool, I'm cool."

Kit nodded. "Cool. I'll see you later, yeah?"

"Definitely," she said.

Kit carried the drinks across the street and headed up to the sixth floor as usual. When the elevator doors parted, he met the eyes of everyone in the office. Roman stood at the front of the room, stopping mid-sentence when he saw everyone looking in Kit's direction.

"Sorry, sorry, guys," he said with embarrassment.

Kit hurried to the kitchen and put everything down on the table. While Roman finished up with the team meeting, he silently adjusted the amount of sugar in Roman's coffee. Having made it for nearly three months now, it was almost automatic. He stirred until the sugar was dissolved, then moved on to Barbie's cup. She also liked plenty of sugar.

And because it was a good day for Kit, he didn't bother entertaining the idea of adding too much to Yolanda's cup. Today was her lucky day, it seemed.

"Does anyone have questions?" Roman asked. He

surveyed the room, pausing to allow anyone to raise their hand. When no one did, he said, "Great. Let's get to work." He glanced at Kit, jerking his head towards his office.

Wordlessly, he hopped up from his seat and grabbed Roman's coffee, hurrying to the room in the back. Kit closed the door once he stepped inside. "What's up, boss?" he asked, handing the coffee over. Roman placed it beside his rolodex and leaned back in his chair.

"Thank you for this," he said.

Kit's eyes widened. "And I didn't even have to make you say it. Character development, Romy."

"If you could never call me that again, that would be great."

"But I think it's kinda fitting," Kit said, rounding the desk to sit on the edge of it. "I mean, unless you're comfortable with me calling you Daddy at work."

Roman nearly spit out his coffee. "Kit, what did I tell you about keeping things separate at work?"

"I know, I know," he sighed dramatically. "'I don't talk about relationships or act like a human when I'm at work,' I get it. I'm just fucking with you, don't be so tight. That's my job. What did you want to talk about?"

"Well, I wanted to tell you that we both need to stop messing around and get down to business. Ari's breathing down my neck about figuring out this money situation. It's not a huge loss that we're taking, but he's anal."

"Same," Kit smirked. Before Roman could shoot him a dirty look, he added, "I'm *kidding*. What do we need to do to figure this all out? I can't promise that I'll be able to Nancy Drew this situation, but like I said, I want to help."

"Well, right now, Ari has the tech department trying to find some kind of paper trail back to the person doing this. I won't pretend like I understand anything they tell me, but I trust they'll figure something out. In the meantime, I'm considering doing personal interviews with everyone here."

"Like, *here*, as in this department? I doubt anyone here would need to steal, that's chump change compared to what most of you all make, isn't it? Like, you're probably making six figures every year, right?" Kit couldn't see anyone trying to steal a few hundred dollars here or there when they were being paid so much.

"You can never underestimate someone, Kit. Oftentimes the greediest are the ones with the most money. Look at the man some people call our president."

Kit clicked his tongue in agreement. "If that's the case, you should probably start investigating Ari as well."

Roman took another long drink of coffee. "Excuse me?"

"Like you said, if everyone is a suspect, then that should make Ari a suspect as well."

"You can't be serious."

"Um, deadass. I don't know much about how this business runs, but I do watch a lot of Shondaland shows, so I kinda know how to be shady. Ari had to fire his whole team before you and everyone else showed up. I'm sure he took a huge pay cut trying to replace everyone. How far of a stretch would it be for him to feel entitled enough to take money here and there?

"I mean, he busted his ass to keep this thing running, anyone would feel like they were owed at least that. Plus, he's the one that pointed it out to you. Classic case of pointing the finger and shifting the suspicion on someone else."

"Careful with what you say, Kit," Roman said, tapping his chin with his index finger, "Someone might think you yourself are the one stealing."

"You think if I knew how to hack and launder money, I'd be working here still? I had an apple and a banana for breakfast this morning, Roman, don't try me."

Roman chuckled and reached for his cup. Before he could grab it, Kit snatched it up and drank a good amount. He placed it back in Roman's hand and smiled. "Too sweet."

"I like sweet things," Roman shrugged.

"Oh yeah?"

"Yeah."

Kit glanced at the opposite wall, looking through the two-way mirrors. Everyone outside seemed to be working hard, none the wiser about Kit and Roman's interactions. He smiled, then slinked forward, trading his seat on the desk for a seat in Roman's lap.

"Kit…" Roman sighed, looking out at the other employees as well.

"They don't know," he assured him. Turning his head by his chin, Kit made Roman look at him instead. "Plus, you said you like sweet things. Am I not a sweet thing?"

"Sweet as you may be, you know my rules. I should throw you out of my lap."

"But you won't," Kit said. He straddled Roman and played with his green silk tie. "You can pretend that you don't like the whole PDA thing, but I know you do. I can feel it down here." Kit's hand snaked between his legs, teasing the front of his slacks.

"You're so sure of yourself."

"Because in the short time that I've known you, I've picked up on all your little tricks. You pretend like you hate me, but that's a lie. You don't like my attitude, but you like when I boss you around and give you lip. You're not as complicated as you think, Roman Li."

Roman's eyebrow cocked up. "Is that right?"

"It's right like a Conservative."

"That's enough puns from you, Kenneth. What are you doing tonight?"

Kit shrugged. "I don't know. What do you want me to be doing?"

"I want you to have dinner with me at my place. We'll order takeout, watch a movie, maybe other things."

"If you think I'm cheap enough to get freaky for a box of chow mein… you're right. I'll need to tell my sister I won't be home tonight, but I should be free."

Roman tilted his head. "You have a sister."

"And a mom and a dad too," Kit smirked. "There are a lot of exciting things you don't know about me yet." Slowly, he leaned in and pressed his lips to Roman's. The kiss was a combination of bitter and sweet, a byproduct of the coffee they'd both shared.

Roman slid his hands down to Kit's lower back, holding him. "I want you to tell me about these exciting things tonight."

"We'll see. I should probably get back out there. People might start to wonder."

"I'm inclined to let them wonder," Roman challenged.

"No you aren't."

He knew Roman, well enough to know when he was about to get himself into a bit of trouble. And if Kit gave in and let this go any further, trouble was certainly on the menu. Reluctantly, Kit stood up and made his way to the door. He began to open it, but paused. "Let me know if you need anything else, Romy."

"You're fired."

"If you say so, Mr. President." Kit loved the laugh Roman gave him.

He took one last look at him, then returned to the seating area in the office, impatiently waiting for work to be over.

17
DON'T DISAPPOINT US

Trying not to let his mind wander towards thoughts of dinner with Roman proved to be a much more difficult task for Kit than he'd thought. He couldn't help but find himself daydreaming about spending more time alone with Roman at his home, especially considering everything that had happened the last time he'd come over. To keep from fantasizing too much, Kit threw his energy into helping other people around the office.

Barbie needed to know which of the three catchphrases she'd come up with was Kit's favorite. When he settled on one, she quickly typed up the phrase and centered it on the pamphlet, smiling when she looked it all over. Once Kit was done helping Barbie out, he even ventured over to Yolanda's neck of the woods to see what was going on.

"I don't have any spare change, Kenneth," she said, not bothering to look away from her computer as she continued sketching.

"No need to be so hostile. I was just coming over to see if you needed help with anything. Roman's schedule is pretty blank today and I figured I'd make myself of some use."

For a moment, she ignored him, zoned in on her drawing. Kit took note of the amount of times she changed the color scheme of the lizard. No matter how many times she switched up the colors, she couldn't decide on a combination she liked.

"Kit, you can clearly see that I'm working on something, please leave—"

He didn't bother letting her finish before he said, "Orange, green, and yellow."

"What?"

"Make the body orange, the eyes yellow, and the spikes green."

She was reluctant at first, but eventually Yolanda added the colors to all the places Kit had indicated. She stared hard at the picture, bouncing her leg up and down. Finally, she shrugged. "It looks nice."

Kit knew he wouldn't get anything more than that, and he decided to take the win and go.

For the rest of the day, Kit made himself more available to the people around him, even going so far as to actually call a few of them coworkers. To his surprise, nobody seemed bothered by that word, either. It was nice to feel like he was part of the team rather than just some kid in the background.

At lunch, he received an email from his calendar app telling him to update it otherwise he might lose his data, and he didn't even hesitate. Most of the time he let those notifications sit for days until finally breaking down and updating. Considering this was work-related, he figured it was best to stay on top of things. He patted himself on the back for being so proactive.

It wasn't until nearly nine o'clock that Roman finally stepped out of his office, done for the day. Kit had almost fallen asleep on the sofa waiting for the man to finish up, and without anyone else in the office to keep him company, he'd turned to his favorite podcast. Conveniently enough, that particular episode was about relationships with older partners.

"Are you ready?" Roman asked, loosening his tie.

"That's funny coming from you," Kit said. He pushed himself up from the couch and stretched out his legs. "I've been ready for the past hour."

"I was on a conference call with some clients in LA, otherwise we would have been out of here sooner. I did order dinner, though. You said chow mein would make you do some freaky things, right?" he grinned.

Though he tried to pretend he was upset over

having to wait so long, Kit's resolve broke and he smiled. "I did say that, yes."

"Perfect. I ordered plenty. Let's get going." Roman gestured for the elevator. Kit followed him downstairs and then to the parking lot behind the building. Kit was surprised to see that he drove to work every day given how terrible traffic could be.

He buckled himself in, and while Roman backed out of the parking lot, Kit reached for the radio. Roman glanced at him. "If you put on some bullshit, you're walking home," he warned him.

"The level of disrespect, Roman… I have the best musical taste of everyone I know."

"Small social circle, then," he retorted.

It took all Kit had not to slap his shoulder. To prove him wrong, he scrolled through his playlists until he found the one that won over most people. No matter their preference of genre, the majority of the people he played it for were swayed.

Roman made a quick stop at the Chinese restaurant to pick up his order, then turned and headed towards his home. Kit took notice of the drumming of his fingers on the steering wheel, unable to keep from laughing softly. Not even Roman was immune to his musical selection. Fifteen minutes later, the two pulled into Roman's driveway.

Kit carried the food while Roman unlocked the door, holding it open so Kit could enter first. They both paused to remove their shoes and leave them by the front door. Kit watched Roman start for the table before he decided to carry the food over to the living room. By the time he put down the bags and took a seat on the fuzzy rug in the middle of the room, Roman had turned around to stare at him.

"What are you doing?" he asked, his arms crossed over his chest.

"I'm picking the most comfortable place in the room to eat." He shrugged and removed the sleeve covering the cheap wooden chopsticks.

"That rug cost two thousand dollars, Kit."

"I guess we better be careful then," he winked. While Roman glared at him, Kit opened up the container of orange chicken, expertly lifting a piece out with his chopsticks. Back in college, he and Chad had practically lived off of Chinese food. He was a master when it came to using chopsticks.

Roman, clearly weary, sighed and took a seat across from Kit. He leaned back against the couch and groaned as he stretched. He settled down comfortably, then asked, "How are things at home?"

Kit was caught off guard by that question. Roman never asked him about his personal life unless it was to tell him to cancel whatever plans he'd made that day. "Uh—things are pretty good. I'm saving up some money to move out of my sister's apartment soon. I'm sure she's tired of having to share a place with her brother *and* her girlfriend. I should be out of her hair in a few weeks. I was supposed to be gone earlier, but after what I spent on that room at the hotel…"

"That's thoughtful of you. Could your parents help with any kind of moving expenses?"

"I'm not close with them," Kit shrugged. He gave a strained smile and focused on mixing around his noodles for no reason in particular. "It's nothing serious, they just always had issues with my boyfriends."

This wasn't a complete lie. While the reason he and his parents didn't get along was a lot deeper than that, they did always have a problem with him talking to guys at school. Considering they were both highly active in their local church, having two gay children made them look like the worst parents in town. People whispered about them behind their back. They figured the two of them must have done something horrible to be cursed with not one but two sinful children.

"I have to admit, I'm not a fan of your boyfriends either," Roman smirked.

Kit laughed. "You've only met one. Normally I have good taste."

"I don't know about all of that. How is that one ex of yours? Still bothering you?"

Kit shook his head and said, "Nah, he's gone. He actually blocked me on every social media website.

Which actually pisses me off because I'm the only one allowed to do that since he cheated on *me*."

"At least he's out of your hair. Now you can focus on better things," Roman said.

Kit narrowed his eyes at the man. "Is that jealousy I'm detecting?"

"Do you really think I'd be jealous of *that*?"

"I think you'd be jealous of the fact that I was giving him any kind of attention when I was with you. I think you got really protective over me when he grabbed me. I think you liked when I told him off and kicked him to the curb. So yes, I do think you'd be jealous of him—even just a little bit."

Roman stabbed at a piece of chicken and pushed it past Kit's lips, shutting him up. "You talk too damn much, kitten."

Kit glared as he chewed. After he swallowed, he crawled across the rug until he was sitting next to him, back against the couch. "C'mon, Romy. Just say it. Say you were jealous of Jaylen, but now that he's gone, you get me all to yourself."

"I invited you over for dinner, not for an emotional evaluation."

"But you know it's true," Kit insisted. He thumbed over the front buttons on Roman's shirt absently, a devilish look in his eyes.

Roman sighed. "Maybe I was a little jealous. But

when he put his hands on you, I just got mad. I don't tolerate that."

"I like your hands on me more anyways," Kit said, shrugging.

A silence fell over the two of them as they ate. As much as Kit liked the flirty playfulness of their banter, he wanted to get to know more about Roman. "Tell me about your family."

"Why do you want to know?"

"Because I told you about mine. I want to know more about you."

"My parents have both passed away."

"I'm sorry."

Roman shrugged. "That's life. When they were around, they were the strongest people I ever knew. They moved from Taiwan to America when my mother was pregnant with me. After she had me, my father stayed home to raise me while she worked. She understood more English than he did, otherwise he would have done it in a heartbeat."

"She sounds like a badass," Kit said.

"Yeah," Roman laughed, "She was. My folks were also huge on gambling. I don't know how they did it, but they managed to win damn near every time they went out. Eventually they got bored of the casino and wanted something a little more risky. The next step was trading stocks. When I tell you they hit it big, I mean it. In less than ten years, we went from near-poverty to them paying for all four years of my private school up front."

"Holy shit," Kit exclaimed. The only thing he knew about the stock market was that if given the chance, he'd probably do some insider trading. Given the situation with Yellow Fall's financial issues, he didn't plan on admitting that aloud…

"They always knew when to put money on something, when to give it all of their attention. Thirty years ago, people didn't expect Alainment Enterprise to grow much more than it did. It was just this small entertainment company, but now look at it. I'm sure you've heard of The Danby?"

"Who hasn't? It's like The Hilton, but even more bougie."

"During the construction of that hotel, my parents knew they were onto something, so they invested in the company."

"Your parents are *both* badasses," Kit said, correcting his previous statement. It was impressive how much two people could accomplish with just a little faith in themselves and each other.

"They were something special. They died a week after one another. My father was sick for a long time. He passed away at the hospital. I know it's cheesy, but I'm pretty sure my mother died of a broken heart. They'd been through so much together, and without him, she wasn't able to go on."

The tone of Roman's voice changed. The smile in his words was gone, now replaced with something much more somber. Kit could tell that he was getting close to something he didn't really want to bring up, but he was unable to think of anything to say to stop Roman.

"Before she passed, she told me they'd given me everything I needed and that I couldn't fuck it up." He laughed at himself. "Her last words were, 'Don't disappoint us.'"

Kit could see everything falling into place now.

The way Roman held himself the way he did. The way he wanted to put forth the best foot he could. His sudden, uncontrollable anxiety when it came to his appearance and his presentation. He didn't want to ruin it. He didn't want to ruin all of the hard work his parents had done.

Their legacy.

Rather than saying anything, Kit took Roman's face in his hands and kissed him. It wasn't the passionate, clothes-ripping kiss from nights before. This one was softer, as if Kit had never done this before. As if, if he pressed too hard, Roman would fall to pieces in his palms. There was a tenderness to it that Kit surprised even himself with.

He hadn't kissed many people like this before.

Roman held him close, breaking the kiss and running his nose down the side of Kit's neck. Kit had intended to come over, eat a little bit, and then jump right into fooling around, but there was something much more satisfying about this—about being held like this.

"I think your parents would be proud of you," he said quietly.

"I don't know."

"Well, I do." Kit wasn't certain about a lot of things in life, but he knew for a fact that if Heaven existed, Mr. and Mrs. Li would be smiling down on their son, beaming with pride because of all his accomplishments.

After a moment of peaceful silence, Kit reached for the food. "We'd better not let this get cold," he said.

Roman wrapped his arm around Kit's shoulder and grabbed the television remote. As they ate, they watched reruns of *The Fresh Prince of Bel-Air*. It was the best date Kit had been on in years.

18
HASHTAG DID THAT

THE ONLY THING HARDER THAN ACTING NORMAL around Roman in public was behaving when they were in private. Over the past week, Kit had fought to keep all of his flirty comments to himself. Sure, Roman might not have a problem with them, but at the end of the day, he'd been right. They were at work. They were in a professional setting. It was important to make that distinction and stick to his guns about acting right.

On Friday, Kit sat in the kitchen with Barbie, absently scrolling through his Twitter timeline as Barbie went on about her review of the latest animated movie she'd seen with her kids.

"I'm not normally one for kitschy movies like this, but the animals could all sing really well and I was invested in finding out who was gonna win the contest. It was cute, though, I enjoyed it."

"That's good!" Kit said. He placed his phone down and took a sip of his coffee. "I haven't watched an animated movie in years, but that's probably because I'm too embarrassed to go into a kid's movie by myself."

"Oh please, no one looks at you any different, pumpkin. I love whenever I see someone by themselves. They just want to see a good movie, there's no shame in that. My favorite is whenever a group of boys your age comes in. It's cute that they're still in touch with the kid inside everyone," she smiled.

"I'll keep that in mind! Maybe my friend and I will go see one sometime, then. He's a big fan of Disney."

"We'll go see one together, how about that?"

"That's the perfect plan," Kit said. He was about to say something when Barbie held up a finger and quickly unlocked her phone. He watched her tap around for a moment before she said,

"It'll have to be a matinee or something, most of this paycheck is going towards buying my way out of my lease."

Kit's eyes went wide. "You're moving?"

"Just across town! I haven't told you, but Kevin and I have pretty much split up. He still lives with me, because it's hard to move out when you mooch off someone, but when I break the lease and get a new place with the kids, he'll be out on his ass. My mama always told me fighting comes with relationships, but I'll be damned if I let some out-of-work loser call me all kinds of names in front of the kids."

"Go off," Kit grinned. "I'm so happy that you're leaving him, he sounds like a real asshole. Are you okay, though? I'm sure getting a divorce takes a toll on you. If you need anything, you know you can call me, right?"

"I appreciate it, baby. But mama's got it." She winked at him and pushed herself up from the table. "I have way too much work to finish up. Talk to you in a little bit?"

"Definitely," he nodded. Kit watched her toss her cup and return to her desk. He could see the change in her behavior. When he'd first joined the Yellow Fall team, Barbie had been sweet but just a bit of a pushover. The way Roman had talked about her being fired for just spilling coffee on herself clued Kit in on the kind of soft person she was. That tenderness was still there, but she seemed more confident in herself.

Kit sat back in his chair and opened his own bank app, nearly choking when he saw his paycheck. He'd been expecting a lot given the amount of time he'd spent at work, but seeing an extra seven hundred dollars almost caused a spit take with his coffee. This had to be some kind of error. There was no way he was seeing the correct number.

Once he'd gathered himself, he marched into Roman's office without knocking.

"I don't know why I bother with a door anyway," Roman said without looking up from his computer.

"I think there was a bit of an error with my paycheck?"

"What do you mean?"

"I mean I have an extra seven hundred dollars that came out of nowhere. Given everything that's going on with someone stealing money from Yellow Fall, I don't want Ari to get the wrong idea about me."

Roman pressed a few more keys before looking up at Kit. "That's not an error."

Kit blinked. "So… you meant to give me that much money?"

"Yes."

"Roman, I know that we're like… doing whatever it is we're doing, but I can't take this money. No shade to any sugar babies out there, but that's not what I'm about. I earn my own money, I don't need anyone giving me anything. Especially not my boss. You know what this looks like, right?"

"Kit—"

"It looks like I'm sleeping with my boss and making extra money from it!" Kit couldn't believe that he was the one trying to keep things professional. He'd never been that person before, let alone that kind of person with someone like Roman.

"If you're done accusing me of paying for sex, I'd be happy to explain where that extra money came from."

Kit crossed his arms and raised an eyebrow. "I'm listening."

"Earlier you told me that you purchased that room at the Mandarin Oriental. I asked Ari, and he told me that we should have charged that to the card as it was a business expense."

"But it really wasn't a business expense. I bought that room because I wanted to sleep with you," Kit said.

"Obviously I left that part out. Either way, I rearranged some things, Ari approved of the hotel expense, and now you have your money back. If you were smart, you'd use that money to help pay for your first month of rent."

Kit didn't know what to say.

It was obvious that Roman wanted to help him, and he'd even gone as far enough as to talk with Ari and get the job done. There were too many emotions for Kit to process in that moment. Excitement that he'd gotten his money back and he had enough to actually pay for his own place. Confusion about why Roman would do such a nice thing. There was even a touch of something else that he couldn't explain or put a name to. All he knew was that it made his heart skip a beat and his smile grow wide.

Kit crossed the room and leaned down to kiss Roman. It was soft, and Roman smiled when it ended. "Are you going to take my advice or not? Go make that call."

"Yeah, yeah," Kit said, walking to the door. "Thank you, Roman. Really."

"You're welcome, kitten."

Kit headed down to the lobby to make his call in private. He tapped his foot impatiently as the phone rang and rang. Finally, Donny, the landlord, answered.

"Hello?"

"Hey Donny, it's Kit, Bria's brother. I called earlier about wanting to rent that apartment next week? Would there be any way for me to actually stop by today and pay now? I did a little reorganizing with my finances and as it turns out, I've got just enough."

"Hell yeah that would be fine. Stop by whenever you can tonight and we'll get all the paperwork filled out."

"Perfect," Kit smiled. "I'll see you tonight."

"See you then. Have a good day, buddy." Donny ended the call.

It took all Kit had not to throw his hands in the air and do a happy dance. Elation zipped through him like electricity. For a moment, he wore the biggest, happiest smile, still in shock that this was actually happening. He took a deep breath, shook out all the jitters, and headed back upstairs to finish the day.

Donny's office was a mess of papers and trash, but the man seemed comfortable with it. Impressively enough, he knew where everything was. His madness had method, it seemed. Donny slapped down the paperwork and slid a pen towards Kit.

"I'm sure you already know how everything goes, right?" he asked.

Kit nodded and reached for the pen. "Yeah, I've heard Bria and Trish talking about all the rules plenty of times." By talking, Kit meant complaining. There were a lot of rules to the apartment building, but Kit couldn't have cared less. All he wanted was the key to his new place. He could live with stupid rules.

"Alright, next you'll sign this right here." Donny handed him another sheet of paper. "You have the money order, correct?"

"Mhm, right here." Kit gave him the slip and quickly scribbled his signature down. "I just wanted to make sure, but I'm allowed to paint, right? Nothing too crazy, but I'm lowkey an interior designer now, so I want this placc to look grcat."

"Kid, you can paint whatever you want on the walls as long as you know you'll have to paint them back before you move out." Donny opened his drawer and placed the money order inside, locking it once he was done.

"Perfect. Keys now?"

"Hold your horses. One last thing." Donny placed his last piece of paper in front of Kit. "We don't allow subletting, and anyone staying over longer than a month must be on the lease."

Kit started to sign when he tilted his head. "I've been staying with Bria for like, four months. I never had to sign the lease."

Donny smiled. "Bria's the best tenant I have here. Plus, you're her family. Most people around here would say otherwise, but I'm actually not a dick all the time."

"I appreciate it, Donny." Kit signed his name and placed the pen down beside the paper. "We all set now?"

"All set, buddy. Here you go." He handed over the key to Kit's apartment and went back to organizing his papers. "Now get outta here."

"Don't have to tell me twice," he laughed. Kit took the key and left the office. He punched in the floor number and waited impatiently for the elevator to come down to him. By the time he made it to the door of his new place, he was buzzing eagerly. Kit twisted the key in the lock and opened the door.

"Surprise!" Bria said. She tossed a small handful of confetti over Kit's head.

"Hey!" he laughed. "What are you doing in here?"

"Donny called and told me you managed to pay for the first and last month's rent. When were you gonna tell me?" she exclaimed.

"I was gonna tell you later tonight once everything was said and done. It was a surprise, but you beat me to it!" Kit noticed the bottle of peach sparkling wine and two wine flutes on the counter. Bria looked back as well.

"I got those to celebrate. You want some?"

"Hell yeah I do!"

Bria crossed the room and managed to pop the bottle of wine without spilling too much. She poured two glasses, then took a seat on the floor in the living room. Kit plopped down beside her.

"Cheers," he said, clinking his glass with hers. He took a long sip then leaned back on his elbows.

"I can't believe my baby brother's all grown up. I knew it was coming, but I'm still kinda sad."

Kit nudged her. "Don't be sad. I'm still gonna need someone to take care of me. Remind me to buy groceries, take the trash out, all that stuff. Plus, I have no idea what to do about furniture."

"Oh, shut up," she laughed. "You designed an entire office with Alma Middleton. I'll still help you pick out some cute furniture, though."

There was a silence in the air that was broken by Bria sniffling. Kit turned towards her. Bria wiped her eyes with the sleeve of her shirt. "Why are you crying?" Kit asked. He slipped an arm around her shoulder, pulling her closer. "It's okay."

"I know it's okay," she said quietly. "That's why I'm crying. I'm just feeling a lot right now."

"Like what?"

"I'm proud of you. When you first started looking for a job, I was a bit unsure whether you'd be able to make it out there. I know you've got a smart mouth and you think you're a thug," she laughed. "But you surprised me. You're doing well for yourself. You're making responsible decisions. You're acting like a grown up. But I'm also sad that you're not going to be around as much."

"I'm only a few floors below you, Bria. I'm not going anywhere. I need you as much as you need me."

She turned to look at him, smiling tenderly. "Yeah?"

"Of course. You're really all I have out here. I mean, Trish is great, and I could have stayed with Chad, but I wanted to be back with you. You've always been there for me when I needed you. You're like my sister and mom and dad mashed up in one person. Unfortunately for you, you're stuck with me."

Bria snorted. "How terrible." She sighed and looked up at the ceiling. "Remember how Mom and Dad said we'd never make it out here?"

"Yup. They said when we were homeless and hungry, not to come crawling back. And I also remember what you told them back."

"Oh lord."

"My soft-spoken, timid, *kind* sister told them, 'You can suck my asshole.'"

Bria cracked up. "I was angry, okay? It was the first thing that came to mind."

"Hey, I'm not kink-shaming you or anything," he laughed. Bria slapped his shoulder and shook her head, stifling her laughter. "I'm not at all surprised. We were better on our own than we ever were with them."

"Damn right. They're probably pissed that we made it without them. Those two gays hashtag did that."

"We hashtag did that," she said in agreement.

19
YOU NEED IT

Kit ran the roller over the wall one more time, making sure that there were no white spots showing through the paint. After trying to redecorate his bedroom years ago, he'd learned that he needed to be more careful and intentional when it came to painting. He didn't want a patchy job for his first apartment.

Bria looked at their work and smiled, wiping her forehead with the back of her hand. "Does this look good?" she asked.

"It looks perfect."

He'd talked to Alma again and decided that he wanted something deep to help compliment the furniture color. He'd gone with black wood for the coffee table, entertainment center, and dining table set, and to match this, he'd picked a latte brown color to paint the wall. Once everything was dry and he could set the dining table up against the accent wall, it would all come together.

Bria started to say something when there was a rambunctious set of knocks at the door. "I got it," she said. As she hurried off to answer the door, Kit bent down and carefully folded up all of the plastic they'd put down on the carpet.

"Welcome to adulthood, beyotch!" Chad exclaimed, raising his hand. The six-pack of beers clinked inside.

"I'm a big kid now," Kit cheered. "You can put those in the fridge if you want. Hey, Michelle!"

Michelle gave a little wave and gestured to the large gift box in her hands. "I got you a little something!"

"Girl, you know you didn't have to do that for me!" he said. Michelle handed over the box and shrugged.

"I just wanted to congratulate you on your first place. It's a big deal, even if you pretend like it isn't! I remember the first place I moved into had a bedbug problem, but I was still proud of myself for actually getting out of my folks' house and on my own feet. Open that, hurry!"

"Yeah, don't act all modest now," Bria teased.

"Fine, fine!" Kit stuffed the floor covering in a large trash bag and wiped his hands off. He carried the box over to the coffee table and took a seat on the futon. "This better not be anything insane, I'm gonna have to get you something in return."

"No way, this is your celebration," Michelle said, waving that statement off.

Kit tore off the wrapping paper and cut open the brown box. Inside, he found the *Star Wars* lamp he'd been lusting after for the past six months. "Holy shit, Michelle!"

She clapped happily. "Do you like it?"

"I love it! But I can't accept this. This lamp is two hundred dollars online! How did you even know I wanted it?"

Michelle gave an obvious glance towards Chad and winked at Kit. "I had a little helper! And seriously, it's no biggie, all I have to do is work Uber another extra day and I'm good. I'm the biggest *Star Wars* geek myself, so I might even get one for my bedroom."

Kit looked back at the lamp and shook his head in disbelief. "Thank you so much, Michelle." He rose from the seat and gave her a tight hug. "I really appreciate this."

"You're welcome!"

Kit turned to Chad. "Where's my gift, you bum?"

"Hey, I brought beers!" Chad said indignantly.

Bria chuckled. "I'm gonna get out of your hair, Kit, but if you need anything, call me, okay?"

"Definitely," he smiled. "Oh, don't forget your key." After Donny had given him his keys, he'd made two extras. One was for Bria and the other was for Chad.

"Ah, almost forgot," she said. She scooped up the key and disappeared out the door.

Once she was gone, Kit looked at his two friends and said, "Soooo, what's on the agenda for today? I just went grocery shopping, but I haven't received any of the plates or silverware that I ordered, so we're gonna be rocking paper plates and plastic cutlery."

"Just like the old days," Chad said. "I can order a pizza. I mean, it's no *Star Wars* lamp or anything, but hey, I'm a modest man."

"You're a cheap ass bitch, that's what you are," Kit replied. "Pizza sounds good."

"While he's ordering that, I'm gonna set up my laptop and find something on Netflix to watch," Michelle said. She carried her bag over to the TV and took a seat in front of it, hooking the laptop up to the television.

While they got situated in the living room, Kit dipped out of the room and headed to the bathroom to wash off some of the paint. He scrubbed his hands together, looking at himself in the reflection. There was something different in his eyes. He hated to be *that* guy, but he couldn't help but think that something different was happiness. It had been a long time since he'd been this elated, and considering everything that he'd worked towards these past few months, he deserved a little bit of happiness.

Kit returned to the living room and spent the rest of the night with his friends. The pizza man showed up, and he seemed quite interested in Michelle. Kit was half tempted to invite him into the house and see if he wanted to watch this trashy show they'd found on Netflix. Before he could, Chad jumped up and paid the man, ushering him out of the doorway once he'd handed over the pizza.

Kit took notice of how close the two of them had gotten. They'd claimed they were just friends, but watching the two interact, it was obvious that they were really into each other. Whether or not they were going to act on it and make this relationship official was the true question. And when he wasn't thinking about their potential to become an item, his mind wandered to Roman.

He wanted to spend this night with Roman as well, but he doubted the older man would get along with Chad and Michelle. Kit wasn't as vulgar as them, and Roman could barely handle the jokes *he* told. Still, he longed for someone to hold him the way Chad held Michelle.

"Kit," Chad said, waking Kit from his sleep.

He blinked a few times. The clock said that it was just past eleven. "Huh? Did I fall asleep on you guys?"

"Kinda," Michelle giggled.

"Sorry, it's been a long day for me."

"It's fine," Chad said, shrugging. "Michelle and I are gonna head out though." The look Chad gave Kit told him everything he needed to know.

"You guys have fun. Thanks for the pizza and the lamp." He sat upright and stretched out his legs.

"No problem," Michelle said.

Chad led her out of the door and turned back to Kit. "I'll catch you later, okay?"

"Later!"

Kit rose from his seat to lock the door behind Chad. Before he headed to the bathroom to wash up and get ready for bed, he put the leftover pizza in the fridge and cleaned up the beer bottles.

Afterwards, he showered, washed his face, and brushed his teeth. He was ready to climb under the covers when his phone rang. The sight of Roman's name on his caller ID made his heart jump.

"Hey," he said, yawning.

"Did I call at the wrong time?" Roman asked.

"No, no, I was just getting ready for bed. What's up?"

"I was calling to see how that apartment renovation was going. You told me yesterday you were going to paint an accent wall. How did that go?"

"It went good! My sister helped out with it, so we got it done in no time. The hardest thing I did today was set up all my furniture. I pushed my bed around at least five times before I found a place that I liked." Kit rolled over onto his side and stretched out, stroking the pile of cool pillows on the other side of the mattress.

"You should have called me. I would have come over and helped set things up," Roman said lightly.

"It's okay. I don't know if I'm ready for my sister to meet you like that. I haven't exactly told her that we're kind of together."

"There's no 'kind of', Kit. We're seeing each other."

Kit hated how his stomach flipped hearing Roman say that. It made him want to bury his smile in his mountain of pillows and laugh like a child. "Okay." That was all he could muster.

"I do expect an invite over there soon, otherwise I just don't see how we're going to christen the new place."

"Ahhh. So, *that's* why you wanted to come over. Fair enough. I feel like the little bonus you gave me gets you pretty much anything you want."

"Anything?"

"Mhm," Kit said. He played with one of the tassels on his pillow, waiting for Roman to say something else. There was a long silence, and though he had no way of telling, it just felt like Roman was cheesing on the other end of the line.

"I'll be redeeming my prize, soon. Now, to completely kill the mood, I wanted to confirm that this musical you're dragging me to is next weekend, yes?"

"Yep," Kit said. "And don't be so negative. You're gonna have a good time."

"I'm only teasing. It will be our first date, I believe. Our first non-work-related date, that is."

"It will be. I'm looking forward to it. I think you're gonna love the show," Kit said. He'd been to one of Trish's shows before, and she knew her stuff.

"We'll see. I'm going to take it up with you if it turns out that I have a miserable time there."

"You do that. If you hate it, I'll make it my personal mission to make it up to you."

"You're a dangerous one, kitten. You pretend you don't know the double meaning of the things you say, but you're actually far too smart for your own good," Roman said.

Kit laughed and rolled onto his back. "Yeah, well, I'm also too tired for my own good. I'll see you at work tomorrow?"

"Indeed, you will."

"Good. G'night, Romy."

"Goodnight, kitten."

After the phone call he'd had with Roman the night before, Kit was determined to make something happen today. He woke up extra early and went through his morning ritual with added intensity. He picked out the tightest slacks he had and undid one too many buttons on his dress shirt. He looked casual, but also like he might be attending a photoshoot soon.

At seven, Kit walked into the office confidently, immediately meeting eyes with Roman. With everyone else looking his way as well, nobody but Kit caught the hungry, lingering look Roman gave him. Kit was warm inside, pleased to know that the outfit was doing its job.

But that wasn't all of his plan.

After handing the coffee cups out to everyone, Kit 'accidentally' knocked off a pack of sugar. He bent down to pick it up, giving Roman the perfect view of the pants that cupped him in all the right places.

He was no Nicki Minaj, but in this get-up, the shape of his body was clear as day. It worked like a charm. Roman's grip tightened around his cup, and for a moment, Kit expected him to squeeze hard enough to puncture the cheap paper.

Roman cleared his throat, adjusted his tie, and got back to the meeting. Kit took a seat in one of the rolling chairs, swaying back and forth slowly. Being that he was the only one moving in the office, Roman's eyes continued to fall on him, but he never once broke his focus on the words he was saying. Kit had heard the spiel before. They were doing great, Ari was very pleased with the rate projects were moving at, yadda yadda.

Kit's final move came to light when he unwrapped the single bubblegum sucker he'd brought with him. He'd seen it at the bodega by his apartment this morning and he couldn't turn it down. Not when his goal was seducing Roman in front of everyone.

The mischievous gleam in Kit's eye only brightened when Roman tripped over his words, his eyes nervously flitting around the room, everywhere but the place they both knew he wanted to look. Yolanda made a face, narrowing her eyes at Roman. Even Barbie took notice of Roman's sudden bout of stutters.

Finally, Roman ended the meeting and everyone was sent off to work. Before Kit could even move, he heard Roman's voice.

"Kit. My office."

Kit rolled his tongue around the circumference of the sucker once before he said, "Yes, sir."

He made his way to Roman's office as slow as humanly possible. He wanted Roman to suffer as long as he could, drawing this out and leaving him in his office to stew. He finally leaned against the door frame. Roman stood in the middle of the room, his back to Kit.

"Close the door," he said.

Kit didn't need to be told twice. He stepped inside and did as instructed. "You needed to see me?"

"Have you lost your mind?" Roman asked, turning around to face Kit. "Do you know who could have seen what you were doing?"

Kit's smile never once faded. "Don't be so uptight," he said, taking a step closer to the man. "You liked it. You were probably trying not to tent your pants, huh?"

Roman's mouth was a hard line, but he didn't deny it.

"Exactly. You were thinking about me the entire time. Imagining you in my mouth instead of the sucker."

"You give yourself way too much credit."

"No, I don't," Kit said. "It's written all over your face." He stepped close enough to Roman for him to run the sucker over his lips. Roman stared at him darkly for a moment, then let his tongue slip out and clean his lips.

Roman reached for the candy and tossed it in the trash. Without a word, he yanked Kit closer, off balance, and kissed him. Between flicks of his tongue, Kit let out a noise of approval. Roman reached around to cup his ass, squeezing desperately.

"You really are dangerous," Roman said, spinning Kit around and pushing him against the wall. He tilted Kit's head to the side before dragging his nose up and down the side of his neck. His lips came second, peppering kisses down his shoulder, and Kit's knees nearly buckled.

"Am I dangerous?"

"Very. You like pushing my limits, don't you? You like pressing all the buttons you can and hoping I'll give you the response you want."

"Mm, yeah."

"I bet you even like the fact that there's only a thin wall between us and them."

Kit opened his eyes and looked through the two-way mirror. He saw Barbie and Yolanda talking on their way to the elevator, and Logan by the watercooler, filling up a disposable cup.

Roman slipped his hand around and pawed at the front of Kit's slacks. This elicited a sudden whimper from the younger man. "Do you like that, kitten? Seeing them out there while you're in here, pressed against me, feeling how much you turn me on?"

Kit couldn't form words. All he could do was nod and groan.

"You showed me I was yours last time. Now, you're mine."

Before Kit knew what was happening, he was pressed face down on the desk and Roman's hands gripped the back of his pants. He was impatient, fumbling to get them unbuttoned and down to his knees. Kit groaned again, quickly covering his mouth. His coworkers might not have been able to see him, but he was positive they could hear him if he was too loud.

Kit heard the zipper of Roman's pants come down, and soon felt the weight of his length against his ass, teasing him. Roman slapped it down, allowing him to feel the heat, the pulse of his arousal. The hot breath on Kit's neck sent chills down his spine.

"I'm going to fuck you here and send you on your way back out there. If you're too loud, I'll stop. Do you understand?"

Kit nodded, biting down on his palm.

"Good boy."

Roman reached across his desk for a few necessary items, quickly covering his cock with both the condom and a bit of lubrication. He snapped the bottle shut then snaked an arm around Kit, holding him tight.

"Open up for me," he instructed, pressing the head of himself against Kit. Kit winced and clenched his fist, breathing through his nose as Roman pushed inside. He wasn't as gentle as before, and Kit had a feeling he might enjoy the sting he was delivering. When Roman's length slid across that bundle of nerves inside of him though, he whimpered and writhed under his grip, the pain all but vanishing.

Roman didn't stop until he was flush against Kit's ass, buried to the hilt. He eased backwards, and with a quick jerk, stuffed himself back in, withdrawing a sudden, pleasant noise from the younger man.

"Fuck," Kit sighed. He reached back, digging his fingers into his skin as he spread himself for the man. "Take it, Roman."

"I will," he said, swatting at his ass. "Tell me it's mine." He reached forward, seizing Kit by the throat. "Tell me this ass is mine, kitten."

"I don't have to tell you," Kit challenged, looking back at Roman, his cheeks a deep red. "You already know it's yours. So fucking take it. Make it yours."

Roman let out a low noise, a mix of a growl and a groan, and began thrusting, faster than Kit was prepared for. He pressed his forehead to the wood and bit his tongue, taking each jab inside of him as best he could. He reached down and wrapped a hand around himself, pumping his fist in accordance to Roman's moves.

Roman made no noise except for soft murmurs of approval, clearly pleased with the way Kit took him. Without warning, he pulled out of him, flipped him onto his back, and slid back inside. Kit brought his knees to his chest, eyes up in awe as he pounded away at him.

Kit stared as Roman went harder, rocking the desk with each thrust forward. His lips parted, silent when he wanted to scream out in pleasure. Roman smiled and leaned in to kiss him. He pulled away only an inch, enough for Kit to feel his warm breath wash over him.

"Beg for it," he ordered, biting Kit's lower lip. "You need it, don't you?"

"So bad," Kit panted. "Since this morning. I've wanted it, wanted *you*. I need it, Romy. Fill me with it."

The man's face contorted, and he stood upright, steadying himself on the desk. Kit wasn't sure if he could remain quiet given the pace Roman moved. It was a flurry, the sound of skin against skin, the electric heat of Roman inside of him. Kit came hard, his eyes squeezing tight. He left a mess on his chest, just inches away from the shirt he'd pulled up past his stomach.

Roman's orgasm hit as he and Kit kissed once more. In a flash, he pulled out of the younger man and pushed him down to his knees. "Open," he ordered, tearing the condom from himself. Kit obeyed, eyes up, tongue out, waiting. Roman held his head steady as he pumped. In a matter of seconds, he coated Kit's tongue with his seed, shooting out enough to paint his lips and cheek.

When he was empty, he slapped the hefty weight down on Kit's tongue, encouraging him to clean off every drop. He sucked the last of him down, swallowing eagerly.

"Fuck," Kit groaned. He wiped the corners of his mouth with his thumb.

Roman tucked himself back into his pants, took him by the chin, and stole one last kiss. "Clean yourself off." He returned to his seat at his desk and picked up his pen, turning his attention back to his stack of papers.

Kit reached for the box of tissues on his desk, using a handful to wipe himself clean. He adjusted his clothes, making sure nothing was out of place. He wanted to say something, something poignant and smart, but all he could do was catch his breath. Finally, Kit made his way out of the office. Before he could get too far, he paused.

"Do you need me for anything else, sir?" he asked.

"That's all. Get back to work."

Kit smiled. Then he closed the door behind him.

20
STANDING OVATION

"Kit, I swear to god, I'm about to lose my marbles," Chad said from the bathroom. Kit paused, unsure if he'd heard his friend right or not.

"You're about to what?"

"Dude, come look at this." Judging by the urgency in Chad's voice, he needed help immediately. Kit climbed off his bed and poked his head around the corner of the bathroom, looking to see what it was that was going to make Chad lose his 'marbles.'

"Do you see this tuft of hair?" he asked. Chad pressed down the swoop of hair, only to have it come popping back up like it had never happened. "I'm about to start swinging," he said.

"Chill out," Kit said. He stepped up to the mirror and removed the small bottle of cream from the medicine cabinet. Without saying a word, he uncapped it and turned Chad to face him. In a matter of seconds, Kit laid Chad's hair down and smiled when it didn't shoot back up.

Chad turned his head and looked at himself in the mirror. "What the hell is that stuff? It smells amazing."

"It's something Bria made. Moisturizes and controls frizz, but if you put a little more than the regular amount, it keeps flyaways down."

"Damn, black girl magic like shit," Chad laughed. Kit snorted and shoved Chad out of the way.

"I have to get ready. You done?"

"Yep, I'm waiting on you, kid." Chad leaned against the wall and crossed his arms. "So, I do believe this is the first time I'm going to meet your bae, correct?"

Kit didn't want to be reminded of that. When he'd asked Roman to come along with him and Michelle, he hadn't considered the fact that Roman would actually have to meet his friends. He loved them to death, but they cracked dick jokes with the same amount of ease as they told the weather forecast for the day. He knew that they were going to embarrass him. Well, Chad was at least.

"Yeah, it is the first time you're meeting him, so don't be a fucking creep. No jokes about ass-eating, no jokes about politics, and no jokes about me and him having sex, got it?"

"Wow, this is censorship," Chad said incredulously.

"No, this is you not getting your ass beat because I have to explain what you meant when you said that my bussy pops."

Chad's offended facial expression cracked and he grinned wide. "I would make that kind of joke."

"I know you would," Kit laughed. "Especially since you don't have Michelle keeping you in check or anything. How is she doing by the way?" Kit looked at himself in the mirror, running his fingers through his hair. Given the length of it, it only took minimal effort to get the style he wanted to achieve.

"She's doing a little bit better," Chad said. "She said the doctor is letting her leave tomorrow, but he wanted her to stay there overnight. Food poisoning is a bitch, man. I told you, never eat street meat… unless you know his name."

"Get it out of your system now," Kit warned him.

"I am, I am. I'm gonna go raid your fridge. You finish getting ready." Chad rounded the corner and left Kit to handle his business.

This musical tonight was important for two very different reasons. The first one was that this was Trish's first time selling out all the tickets to her show. The performances she'd directed before this had all been relatively successful, but given the attention this musical had garnered in the past few weeks, the opening night was going to be packed.

The second reason Kit needed to nail this was because it was his first real date with Roman. There was no work involved. Roman didn't have to excuse himself to go mingle with potential clients, nor did *he* have to worry about saying too much to nosy reporters. He wanted this date to be a success, romantic in a way that meshed well with Roman's typical level of PDA.

Without stalling any longer, Kit quickly showered and got himself all prettied up for the night. He threw on a tooth whitening strip, and while he waited for that to be over with, he hopped into his clothes. Given the situation, Kit figured it was more appropriate to dress down. He pulled on his favorite pair of chino joggers, his black high tops, and a baby blue fitted button-up. He rolled the sleeves up for maximum Chill Factor.

Once he was fully dressed, he checked his phone. Roman had sent him a text telling him he was twenty minutes away. He checked the time and saw that he'd received this fifteen minutes ago.

"You all ready, Chad?" he asked, running into the living room. He nearly tripped over the basket of items Chad had left at his apartment. He'd been completely accurate in his assumption that his friends would start leaving more things over at his place once they got comfortable. In just under a week, Chad had a small basket to himself, and Michelle had a corner where she kept her makeup bag and a spare phone charger.

"I'm ready, Freddy. Let's bounce."

Kit didn't even have time to roll his eyes at the terrible sayings Chad used. He grabbed his coat, his keys, and his phone, and headed downstairs with Chad. Just as they made it to the curb, Roman's car pulled around the corner.

"Best behavior, Chad," he said under his breath, smiling when Roman stepped out and rounded the car to open both doors for them.

"Wow, he's a *gentleman*," Chad said, looking between Roman and Kit.

"I try to be," Roman replied. Once they were all in the car, he pulled his seatbelt on and plugged in the address to the theater. "You look nice tonight," he said.

"Thanks," Chad piped up.

Kit glared at him through the rear-view mirror before he said, "You do too." The t-shirt Roman had picked for the night fit him like a glove, emphasizing the dips and curves of his arms and the broadness of his chest.

Despite all odds, on the way to the theater, Chad managed to keep the conversation PG with only a few near-slipups. Kit was almost impressed with how calmly the two of them were behaving. It was as if Roman had let loose, and Chad had gotten a little more proper. Chad even managed to keep from mentioning the last time they'd met—that night at the club. Kit didn't need anybody reliving the spilled cosmopolitan incident.

Once they parked, Roman and Kit walked side-by-side up to the front of the building. Just as Kit opened his mouth to say something, a sports car decked out in holographic paint came shooting across the street, narrowly missing them.

"Jesus Christ," Kit yelled, his heart skipping a beat. Chad flipped the driver off and cursed until the car disappeared.

"Are you okay?" Roman asked, lowering his arm from in front of Kit's chest.

"Yeah, I'm fine. I hate this fucking city though," he said, catching his breath.

"Anyone who drives a car that tacky needs to get right with God," Chad mumbled.

"Amen," Roman agreed.

Once Kit's heart rate returned to normal, the three of them headed inside the theater. Bria stood outside in the lobby waiting for them. When she recognized them, she came running over, throwing her arms around Kit.

"You made it!" she exclaimed.

"Of course we did!"

Bria looked up at Roman. "Hi, I'm Bria. You're Roman, right?" She stuck her hand out for a shake. Roman returned the gesture.

"I am, yes. It's good to meet you."

"Likewise," Bria said, airiness in her voice. Kit recognized that lightness. Whenever she talked about how beautiful Trish looked, that voice came out. Swoony Bria always made Kit laugh. "Well, we'd better get inside and take our seats before the show starts."

Bria led them into the theater, stepping around people as she guided them to their seats. She sat on the far left, Chad sat beside her, then Kit, and finally Roman. Kit was grateful that Chad had picked this seat out of all of them. The last thing he wanted was his sister on one side of him and his boyfriend on the other, especially since she was unaware they were together.

All of the chatter in the room ended when the musical began. As Danny and Sandy came out onto the stage, it suddenly made sense why Trish had looked so hard to find the perfect Danny Zuko. The actress she'd gone with was amazing, and it was only the first scene of the musical. By the time they performed *"Summer Nights"* Kit considered leaving Roman and hitting up Danny after the show.

Soon, *"Hopelessly Devoted to You"* began, and Kit felt inclined to act. He inched his hand closer to Roman's until his fingers were wrapped around the other's. The moment after that was silent, and Roman sat unfazed. Kit's heart stopped. He'd made a mistake. This was too public. This wasn't what Roman wanted from him.

But then Roman took his hand back, giving him a tiny squeeze, and Kit could breathe again. He bit back a smile and turned to look at him. Roman stared back at him, that normal hardness now much softer. It was a simple look and an even simpler gesture, but Kit felt like he was in a musical himself. He wanted to stand on his seat and sing about all of the feelings he experienced any time he was around Roman.

"Okay, tell me I might have a shot at getting Rizzo's number," Chad said during Intermission. He flushed the urinal and headed to the sink to wash his hands.

"You might have to fight some of the other audience members," Roman said. "I saw at least two other guys drooling over her, and plenty of women as well."

"It's Gucci, I lift regularly."

Roman stared at him blankly.

"Translation: 'That's not a problem at all, I work out, and because of this, I will be able to fight off as many men and/or women I need to in order to secure a date with Rizzo,'" Kit explained.

"Ah, well, if you do, make sure to record it. You might go viral on that one site… WorldStar?"

Kit and Chad laughed at the same time. "I don't even want to know how you know about WorldStar," Chad said, shaking his head. "I'm gonna go get some snacks, I'll leave you two with some privacy."

Kit watched him go before he turned back to Roman. He slowly approached him. When he was close, he walked his fingers up the man's chest and sang, "You better shape up, 'cause I need a man, and my heart is set on you."

"I better shape up?"

He nodded, "You better understand. To my heart I must be true."

Roman took him by the waist and pulled him close, kissing him on the nose at first, then lowering his lips to meet Kit's. Sure, it might not have been the most romantic of places, but it felt perfect. He could have been kissing Roman as the Cloverfield monster spiked The Statue of Liberty's head at them and it still would have been perfect. With Roman, it didn't matter where they were. All that mattered was that the man he'd called a rude dickhead—among other things—had a soft side that he got to see regularly.

Before things could get too far, Kit broke the kiss and pressed his forehead to Roman's. "We should probably get back to our seats. I don't want to miss anything, and I don't want Bria to start to wonder about us."

"That's a good idea." Roman stood still, smiling

mischievously. If Kit wasn't mistaken, it seemed as if he were challenging *him* to be the first to make a move to the door and pull away from his embrace.

Kit took a deep breath, quickly pecked Roman's cheek, and walked to the door. It was hard pulling himself away and getting back out to the theater, but he managed to keep his eyes forward and return to his seat. Like before, he took Roman's hand in his, this time much more at ease about the gesture.

The play ended an hour later, and as Sandy and Danny drove off into the sky, the audience rose to its feet and clapped wildly. Through all of the cheering, Kit could hear Bria hooting and hollering. She only got louder when it was time for the curtain call. With each new actress appearing on stage, the crowd celebrated earnestly.

Trish stepped out onto the stage, and that's when Kit noticed tears streaming down Bria's face. He reached around Chad and rubbed her shoulder. Though her eyes were wet, she was smiling and clapping. Trish held hands with both of her assistants. The three of them raised their arms together, then bowed. When she stood upright, the look on Trish's face changed.

In the midst of everything, Kit couldn't see what exactly was wrong, but he felt the shift. He glanced to Bria. She wiped her eyes, pausing when she noticed that Trish was frozen in place. Bria whipped her head around and searched the audience.

"That was amazing," Chad said.

"Yeah…" Kit said, looking between Bria and Trish. He heard Bria gasp and saw her cover her mouth.

"Kit," she said, jerking her head to the side. He narrowed his eyes and turned around. He searched the audience until he met eyes with a woman staring back at both of them.

"Fuck," he whispered.

Roman squeezed his hand. "Who is that?"

Kit's mouth was dry. He felt lightheaded. His heartbeat quickened, and he was tempted to take off, running for his life. Roman reiterated his question.

"Kit, who is she?"

"That's my mother."

21
CHANGE ME

It was like an out of body experience. Kit was certain he'd been hallucinating, but as his mother Tonya approached him and the others, the realization was slowly settling in on him. His mother was here, and she was going to ruin everything. He didn't have to question it, nor could he muster up any kind of hopefulness to combat the gut-churning feeling that came with her presence.

As the audience started to leave, Roman helped Kit up from his seat. Having someone there holding onto him grounded his mind. He and the others followed the audience out of the auditorium and into the main lobby.

"Are you okay?" Roman asked, glancing at Tonya as she approached. Kit didn't say a word.

"There you two are," Tonya said, rushing towards

them and pulling them into hugs. Bria was the only one able to hug her back. Kit remained unmoved, his jaw set hard enough to hurt. "I was looking for you two all night. I need to talk to you in private." Her eyes slid to Chad and Roman, looking them over judgmentally.

"Excuse us," Roman said, stepping away from them. Chad glanced at Kit, and Kit nodded. Once they were alone, Tonya smiled at her children.

"God, you two have grown up so much," she said, reaching to touch Kit's hair.

He moved out of her way. "What are you doing here?" He couldn't even keep up appearances with the woman. Bria reached for his hand, lacing her fingers through the fist he'd been squeezing at his side.

"Why are you here, Mom? Is Dad with you?" she asked, more levelheaded and relaxed.

Tonya brushed her hair from her face. "I'm here alone for a few days. Your father wanted to come but he couldn't just up and leave work. I heard about Trish's performance and I wanted to show my support. Is that okay?"

"Would it be okay if *we* showed up to a special moment of yours without asking if that was okay?" Kit asked, venom dripping from his words.

"Kenneth, be realistic. You wouldn't ask us anyways," The dismissal in her response was enough to make Kit see red.

Bria gripped his hand hard. "Look, I don't think now is the time or place. This is Trish's moment, and I don't want you ruining it. How much was your flight here? I'll pay for your ticket back, okay?"

"I'm not leaving," she laughed in disbelief. "I came to spend time with you. I haven't seen either of my babies since—"

"You called me a homo in front of everyone the day I told you I was leaving to go stay with Bria," Kit said, finishing her sentence. He'd tried so hard to keep his composure, but his body was alight with energy. He wanted to break something and scream in Tonya's face and break down in tears.

"Kit—"

"No, Mom, don't pretend like you didn't say that, because you fucking *did*. You told me to go stay with Bria because you didn't want anybody knowing that you had a faggot for a son, too. I don't care why you came here, but I know that I'd rather eat shit than spend any time with you."

As he turned to leave, Tonya reached out and took hold of his arm. "Get your narrow ass back here. Look at me," she demanded. Kit reluctantly turned to meet her eyes.

"What?"

"I'm not saying that I didn't call you that. I'm not denying that your father and I ever treated you and Bria terribly. We did. We didn't do all that we were supposed to, and there's no way that we can ever make up for that or change what we did. All that we can do is try and make you and Bria see that we're trying to do better."

Kit pulled himself from her grasp and looked at her hard, eyes narrowed as he searched for any kind of deception. He knew how they worked. He'd been on the receiving end of their mind games one too many times to fall for the okeydoke all over again.

"I think we all just need a bit of time apart to cool off, okay?" Bria said. Kit knew it killed her having to play peacekeeper when she was just as mad that Tonya was here. Guilt pressed down on him.

"I want to take you all to dinner," she said, looking between the two of them.

"No," Kit said. "You and Bria and Trish can go, but I'm not going."

"Okay," Tonya said. "Is that okay?"

Bria nodded. "That's fine. And you can stay on my couch until Dad gets here. I don't know if I'll have room for both of you on my sofa, but we can figure it out later. We have to go find Trish now, though."

"Sure," Tonya said, smiling slightly. "Hopefully we'll be able to spend some more time with you, Kit."

"Probably not." He turned and left, heading towards Roman and Chad. He knew they'd been watching the conversation by the way they averted their eyes when he approached. "It's fine," he said, letting out a long breath. "I'm fine."

"Are you sure? Because I'll catch a case for throwing bows at your moms," Chad offered.

"No," Kit said. "No fighting. She's staying in town for God knows how long, it's whatever. I'm not dealing with her. If she or my dad tries to talk to me, I'm walking right past them."

"All jokes aside, man, I'm serious. If it gets too much or you feel like you can't handle them, I'm here for you, okay?" Chad pulled Kit into a hug, patting him on the back.

A swell of emotions raced through Kit. He could have very easily allowed himself to break down. His hands shook from the adrenaline, and his breathing still hadn't returned to normal. He was a mess just barely hanging together, but being held by Chad reminded him that he wasn't completely broken.

Kit pulled back from the hug. "Thanks, man."

"Anytime, fam. I should probably get going, though. I'm just gonna catch a cab home. You guys have a good night, and tell Trish I loved the show."

"Definitely." Kit waved goodbye as Chad headed outside.

Roman had been noticeably silent ever since the play ended. He offered Kit a reassuring squeeze on the shoulder and steered him out to the car. Even on the drive back to Kit's apartment, Roman kept his lips pressed together tight. The radio playing was the only thing that kept the two of them from riding home without a peep.

When they made it back to his apartment, Kit said, "Will you come up?"

"Of course." Roman unbuckled his seatbelt and climbed out of the car. On the way inside, he slung his arm around Kit's shoulder and pulled him closer.

Kit unlocked the door and kicked off his shoes, sighing heavily. Tonight had been a whirlwind of emotions. He'd been terrified that Chad was going to mess something up when he met Roman. He'd been excited to see the musical and all the hard work Trish had put out there. He'd been enraged enough to consider letting Chad actually beat up his mother. All he wanted now was to sleep for a few hours—maybe even a few days.

He collapsed on the sofa and folded into himself, hugging his knees close. His gaze remained trained on the wall while Roman tinkered around in the kitchen. Eventually the man took a seat next to him and handed him a mug of steaming tea.

"Thanks," he said softly.

Roman waited a minute before he said, "Talk to me."

"It doesn't matter," Kit said. He dropped his gaze to the tea in his hands.

"It does matter, Kit. The person I saw after the

musical wasn't the person I saw before. I don't know what it is or why, but you changed. I want to understand it." Roman moved closer and slipped his arm around Kit's shoulders.

"I hate them, Romy," he said through gritted teeth. Though he tried to fight it, his eyes welled with tears. "I hate them so much. She ruined tonight. She ruined Trish's night."

"Did she?"

"You don't understand, Roman—"

"I don't," he said, "So tell me. You said that we were a team. If someone's hurting you, I need to know about that. I need to know why you're mad so that *I* can be mad."

"I'm mad because when I look at them, I see how much I hated myself when I was in high school. I see how I took everything they said to heart. How I wished and prayed and vowed to whatever god they wanted. I see how they considered a therapy camp for me. I think of how alone I felt when Bria left to come here. I see the time I tried to…"

His voice cracked before he could finish the sentence. He wasn't even sure if he wanted to finish it. The time he'd spent at the hospital afterwards had been the worst time in his life, and every single second of that was attached to the faces of his parents. They were stains on his memory that he couldn't wipe away.

"I don't understand how… how people that were supposed to look out for you can even…" Roman struggled to find the words. Kit knew what he was trying to say.

"They never wanted to look out for me." The words were bitter. "My parents wanted to control me and change me."

Roman took the tea from his hands and placed it on the coffee table. He pulled Kit to his chest. "There's nothing about you that they need to change. Every aspect of you is endearing in some way or another. You are funny, and smart, and caring, and genuine. You are perfect the way that you are, and like Chad said, if either of them has something to say about that, they can come see me."

Kit cracked a smile. "Yeah, right."

"I'm serious. These past few months with you have been… They're something new to me, but something that I love. I love how you keep me on my toes and I never know what to expect from you. I love learning more about you every single day. You're the reason I wake up and don't hate going to work."

Kit hated how much that statement affected him. He hated that deep down, part of him really *needed* to hear that. In his head, he was a fully realized person that didn't need someone else's confirmation to make him feel good, and the fact that this wasn't the case made him feel like shit. It also made his heart flutter knowing that Roman cared that much about him in the first place.

"Thank you," Kit said, pulling back to look at him. He sat like this, staring over each of his features intently. He'd never said it before, but Roman was beautiful, inside and out.

"I'm here for you, kitten. I know you. You're strong. You'll be able to handle having your parents here for a while. They'll be out of your hair soon enough, and then you can get back to being the man I know you to be." Roman kissed Kit's forehead, then his lips.

As Kit leaned in to return the gesture, the lock on the front door twisted. Bria came walking in, shaking her head.

"I'm serious, Kit, I'm about to lose my mind dealing with—" She stopped when she saw Kit and Roman together, one hand covering her mouth.

"Oh."

22
F-BOMBS OVER FRUIT SALAD

Just when Kit thought his situation couldn't get any worse, it did. A wave of nausea crashed over him the moment Bria came shooting into the room. When she froze, he and Roman froze as well. This wasn't how she was supposed to find out. Not with him having nearly cried in Roman's arms, their lips pressed together.

"I'll be back," he said, hopping up from the couch and running to the door. Part of him wondered which god or goddess he'd pissed off for him to have such bad luck tonight.

Kit caught up with Bria outside of the stairwell. He'd considered going to the elevator, but knowing the kind of person she was, he knew she'd head to the stairs instead. She tried opening the door, but it didn't budge. She let out an angry sigh.

"Bria, can I explain?" he asked lightly.

She turned to look at him. "Explain what, Kit? I mean, it's pretty obvious what I saw in there. I should have known."

"You couldn't have known," Kit said, smiling slightly. "We were pretty discreet around people who we didn't want to tell just yet."

"I wondered why you invited him to come to the musical with us tonight," she said, practically tuning him out. "I thought you were just being nice or something, but that wasn't it. You guys were actually going on a date. And I had no idea. I'm such a dumb bitch." She gave a humorless laugh.

"Bria, c'mon. Are you seriously mad at me?"

She looked at him incredulously. "Of course I'm mad! For a lot of different reasons. The first being that Roman is your *boss*. Do you know what kind of power imbalance comes from a relationship like that? Do you know how many people in your exact situation have been taken advantage of by their superiors?"

Kit held up a hand. "Look, I understand that. He's like, seven years older than me, he's in a higher position for me, I get all that. But you don't understand him—or know him—like I do. He's not that kind of guy. When we're at work, we behave." Kit knew that was a lie, but he wanted Bria to know that their relationship had never once gotten in the way of their work day.

"If you're being honest, that still doesn't make me any less upset about the fact that you never told me you were seeing someone. We tell each other everything," she said, crossing her arms.

"I know we're close, and I love you with all my heart, but you're not entitled to every single thing about me. On top of that, I didn't even know if this was going to be a thing considering what happened last time."

"What do you mean?" She scrunched her face up.

"With Jaylen. I gave him everything. I loved him as much as I possibly could have, and he still fucked around behind my back with some bottlenecked bitch from Miami. I wanted to have fun, and I wanted to take things slow before I introduced him to anyone in my family. Aside from my friends, I didn't tell anyone else. But things have gotten pretty serious between Roman and I, and I'm starting to actually think this could be something real."

"Really?" Bria's angry demeanor slowly started to melt away. Kit could only hope they'd be able to end this conversation without her still being pissed at him.

"Yes, really. Roman is… He comes across like a huge asshole, he can be a nightmare to work with, but deep down, he's an amazing person. He's—he's sensitive, and supportive, and… he's *good*. Roman's a good guy, and I think after everything I've been through lately, I at least deserve that. I at least deserve a good relationship, like you and Trish have."

Kit hated how soft his voice had gotten. Moments before, they'd almost been in a shouting match, and now Kit was talking like he had a secret to share.

"I'm sorry," Bria said after a moment. "Tonight's been stressful, but I know that's not an excuse for how I acted. You're right, who you date and get closer to is your business, and I shouldn't have expected you to tell me every single detail about your love life."

She threw her hands up and said, "I guess I'm just making up this feeling that we're drifting apart. You have your own place, and you're becoming your own person, and I should respect that. And… if you say Roman's a good guy, then I believe you. But I'm gonna need to spend some time with him and talk to him privately if you guys are serious. I'm not gonna let another Jaylen walk into your life, break your heart, and walk out."

Kit smiled. He reached for a hug, squeezing Bria. "I love you."

"I love you too," she said.

"How come you're not at dinner? Mom said she wanted to take you guys out."

"Oh," she said, sighing. "She changed her mind at the last minute. She wants us to all go out for breakfast tomorrow morning. Please say yes, Kit. I really need you there, otherwise I might reach out across the table and strangle her. Trish wouldn't even try and stop me."

Kit snorted. "Nah, she'd let you choke the life out of her and then go right back to eating her food. I guess I can go with you guys."

"Thank you, Kit. But… try not to cuss her out anymore, okay?"

"Do you think she's really trying to make amends with us?" he asked skeptically. He had very little faith in his folks that they would actually own up to their wrongs and try to do right by them now.

"I don't know. But it's been almost six years since I've seen them. I'm going to try to at least give them a chance."

"I guess," Kit sighed. "I should probably get back to…"

"Making out with your boyfriend?"

"Shut up," he grinned. "Have a good night. And tell Trish her musical was fucking dope."

"I will. You sleep well."

Kit watched Bria head to the elevator before he turned around and made his way back to his apartment. It was as if an immensely heavy jacket had been removed from his body. He could breathe easier and stand up straighter now that the air was clear and everyone knew the truth about his relationship with Roman.

While he might not have known when he'd planned on telling Bria about Roman, he knew that eventually she'd find out. Now that the cat was out of the bag and everyone was on the same page, he could turn his attentions to the bigger problem at hand: his mother.

Rather than stress himself over her, he put the thought of her in the back of his head, saving it until tomorrow when they had breakfast. Kit opened his door and smiled when he saw Roman asleep on the couch. Quietly, he locked the door, kicked off his shoes, and snuggled up close to him.

Roman stirred awake. "Everything okay?" he asked, his eyelids heavy.

"Everything's okay," Kit said softly. "Go back to sleep, baby."

IN THE MORNING, KIT WOKE TO AN EMPTY COUCH AND a handwritten note on the coffee table. He rolled over onto his side and grabbed it.

"'I left early to go home and get dressed for work. Take the day off. Recoup. I'll see you tomorrow,'" Kit read aloud. If there was one thing Kit could get used to, it was the sporadic off days that Roman gave him.

He glanced at the clock on the wall and sighed. He had to get up and shower before Bria and his mother came beating down his door. After washing up and getting dressed, Kit met up with his family downstairs. Trish seemed irritable, and Kit imagined it had to do with the fact that neither of them probably slept well with Tonya's white noise machine playing all night. Even when he was younger, Kit always hated the damn thing.

At the restaurant, Tonya ordered a large bowl of fruit salad and pancakes for everyone. Kit bit back a comment about not liking people ordering for him. Bria had asked him to at least try to behave.

"So, Kit, Bria told me about your new job," his mother said, looking up at him.

Kit shot a quick, worried glance at Bria, unsure if she'd told their mother about his relationship with Roman. She shook her head slightly. Relief.

"Uh—yeah. It's nothing too intense, but the pay is really great. These past few months, it's been good to me. Helped me get off Bria's couch and into my own apartment," he said, cutting into his pancake.

"That's amazing! I'm proud of you. When I first finished with school, I didn't start looking for a job until Sallie Mae came looking for me," she laughed.

"Me and Sallie aren't on speaking terms," he said, smiling slightly.

"I tried to tell her that when I was your age, but she was a persistent one. I really am proud of you, though. Both of you. When your father and I last talked to you, we said terrible things about you two. Things parents shouldn't say." She grimaced, like reliving the past physically hurt her. "I want to tell you how sorry I am. I'm sorry for not being there. Not accepting you."

Kit dropped his eyes and picked at his plate. To keep himself from feeling any kind of emotion, he popped a piece of pineapple into his mouth and chewed. Bria cleared her throat.

"Thank you for apologizing," she said.

Kit knew what that meant. It wasn't *okay* what their parents did, but Bria was grateful for them recognizing their mistakes.

"How are you guys doing? How's Daddy?" Bria asked.

"Your father is doing amazing. He's been working a lot, so I don't see him as often as I'd like to, but I know he's trying to provide for me, so I understand. It does get lonely, though. That's partially why I came to see you both. Since you guys left, I feel like a huge part of me is mis—"

"Pass me that syrup, please," Trish interrupted, gesturing towards it impatiently.

Though he was trying to be a better person, Kit couldn't help but smile at Trish's rude interjection. She was doing everything he wanted to do, but couldn't. Bria handed her the syrup with a glare and then turned back to Tonya.

"What were you saying?" she asked.

"Just that being alone has made me realize how bad of a mother I was. I didn't appreciate you. I gave birth to you, and I let you both walk out of my life so easily." Tonya's eyes watered up.

"It was more like you pushed us out, Mom," Kit said.

Tonya nodded. "I did. And I shouldn't have. There's no number of apologies I could give you that would ever make up for what I did to you and Bria. I could cry for years and it would never be enough. I can never express how sorry I truly am. I fucked up."

Kit's eyes went wide at the same time Bria's did. Their mother didn't swear like that. Growing up, she'd popped them in the mouths for even saying "crap," and now she was, dropping F-bombs over fruit salad.

Bria didn't say anything. Instead, she placed her hand on Tonya's. Kit wanted to do the same, but he couldn't. His hand was made of lead, too heavy for his wrist to manage, and he swallowed hard. Despite the hell she'd put the two of them through, Kit's heart thudded harder seeing her cry.

"You have to do better," Kit said, throat dry and aching. "It won't ever be okay, Mom, but… it can be better. If you try."

Bria looked at him with a soft expression. She didn't have to speak. He already knew that she was thanking him for trying to forgive her. After everything they'd discussed last night, Kit wanted to be there for Bria. They were in this together. They'd *always* been in this together, whether their parents wanted them or not.

He turned his attention back to his breakfast. Maybe things wouldn't ever be fixed, but if they could at least get back on speaking terms with their parents, Kit figured that was something worth entertaining.

23
SUS

With all of the drama at home, Kit was glad to get back to work that following week. Tonya had been making an honest effort to be nicer to him and Bria, but Kit was the kind of person that liked his own space. He didn't need to call someone or stop by someone's place every single day. Tonya, on the other hand, did. She'd been over to his apartment more times than Bria. It was almost impressive how many different reasons she came up with for being over.

And when his father finally touched down in New York... Truth be told, Kit was way more nervous about being around his father. The animosity in the family had mostly been his mother's doing, but just as unnerving, his father had stared on with judgmental eyes. Tonya wore her emotions on her sleeve, but Dorian's poker face was unsettling.

On his lunch break, Kit found himself thinking about his family situation again. Barbie opened up her salad container and drizzled her dressing over it, her eyes on him.

"Everything okay, sweetie?" she asked.

Kit absently picked at his sub sandwich. "My parents are back in town, and we don't exactly have the best relationship."

"Oh my gosh, when did this happen?"

"This weekend," he said. Kit explained how Tonya had showed up at the musical, completely unannounced.

"I can't deal with people who show up without warning. Kevin's mother used to do that all the time and it drove me wild."

Kit nodded. "That's how I feel. Don't expect to get inside if you don't give me a proper heads up that you're stopping by."

"Ugh," Barbie said.

"What's wrong?"

She tapped away on her phone. "My son just texted me. He tried ordering lunch with my card and it was rejected. Ever since I kicked Kevin out, it's been... hard, to say the least."

Kit nodded sympathetically. "Do you need some help? I already paid my rent this month, I can lend you some money if things are getting tight?"

"No, no, I've got it. It's just hard for me to make

this adjustment. I started saving up before I told Kevin to leave, but it wasn't much. A little here, a little there, nothing too big. Not enough to live off of. But it's okay. I've always been a crafty one," she smiled.

Kit was so proud of Barbie. She wasn't the type of person to let a little struggle keep her down, and since he'd gotten to know her, he could see that no matter what was hindering her happiness, she always managed to conquer it. In a way, she was a maternal figure to him. She inspired him, she cared about everyone at the company, and she always found a reason to smile.

"I don't know if anyone's told you this lately, but you're a good mom, Barbie," Kit said.

"Aw, thank you, sweetie." Barbie shot him a beaming smile before digging her fork back into her salad.

The two of them finished up lunch together, chatting about all the plot twists of the primetime shows they watched every week. Kit was surprised to see that someone like Barbie, who could have very easily been unaware of certain issues, actually picked up on the subtle hints of racial commentary throughout the programs.

Before either of them could get too deep into their conversation about microaggressions and how the fandom treated characters of one race compared to another, Kit received a confirmation on his phone that a package for Roman had been delivered. He excused himself and hurried down to pick it up.

Kit thanked the receptionist and took the box from her. The light shake he gave it wasn't enough to help him figure out what was inside. He headed back up to the sixth floor and marched into Roman's office. He had been in there all day making a suspicious amount of phone calls.

Roman was just getting off the phone when Kit marched in. "This was downstairs. It's for you." He shook the box one more time before tossing it to Roman. He caught it and sat it down on his desk. "So, what've you been up to today? I feel like I haven't seen you all day long."

"It's only noon, Kit," Roman said lightly. He searched his desk for a letter opener.

"I know, but usually you have me running in and out of your office. Today you've just been on the phone."

"I've been making calls," he said absently. He removed the packaging inside the box, then let out a breath. "I forgot I ordered these three weeks ago." Roman pulled out five expensive looking ties and laid them down on the table.

"What are these for? You already have plenty of ties back at your place?" Kit had spent a few minutes going through Roman's closet while he ran out for food. He'd been shocked to see all the suits and accessories.

"They were a birthday gift for myself," Roman said, waving his hand. Kit was stunned. He watched Roman put the ties back in the box and return to work.

"Excuse me? Did you say it was for your birthday? Is… is your birthday today?"

Roman let out a long sigh. "Yes, it is my birthday. But if anyone else besides you finds out, I'm going to fire your ass on the spot, you understand me?" Roman looked at him hard. It was clear that he wasn't messing around.

"Why? Birthdays are fun!"

"No," Roman said, shaking his head, "Birthdays are *not* fun. They're work. Everyone wants to come down and see me, or throw me a party, or take me out. Family I haven't seen since this time last year. On any other day, they're nowhere to be seen. I wish people would just send a card and leave me alone."

Kit cracked a smile. Roman's grumpiness was cute. "I won't tell anyone, okay? It'll be our secret."

"Thank you. Speaking of our secret, I wanted to tell you that you need to clear your schedule for the first of the month."

Kit pulled out his phone and opened his calendar. There was only one week left in September, and most of that was already clear. He swiped to October and tapped on the first day of the month. "What should I put down?"

"Just write something like, 'Surprise.'"

"Surprise," Kit repeated. "What kind of surprise is it?"

"Well, I was going to tell you *then* that today was my birthday but I wanted to spend it alone with you and not have to worry about work getting in the way of that."

Kit put his hand over his heart. "You wanted to take me on a secret birthday trip?"

"And I'm going to, as long as you behave and nobody else finds out about this. The last thing I need is everyone getting distracted from their work because of something as unnecessary as throwing me a party."

Kit nodded. "I won't tell anyone. But it's going to cost you." He walked his fingers across the desk, inching closer to Roman. He leaned in for a kiss, smiling against Roman's lips. When he least expected it, he threw a leg over Roman's and straddled him.

"Kit," Roman sighed, shaking his head.

"I have to sing to you," he insisted. Roman started to argue but the look on Kit's face said it all. He wasn't going to be satisfied until he sang the stupid little song. Roman gave a conceding nod.

Kit took his time, and despite the fact that he was no world-renowned vocalist, he managed to stay in his vocal range and finish off strong. "Happy birthday,

Romy," he said softly. He stole another kiss before he placed his head on Roman's chest. Roman's hands slid up and down his back as they sat together in the silence.

Kit heard Roman's heartbeat skyrocket when there was a knock at the door. In a hurry, Kit jumped up and tried rounding the desk as quickly as he could. A moment later, the door opened and Yolanda stepped inside. She looked between the two of them and said,

"Roman, Ari needs to see you. It's probably about…"

"Ah. I should go see him," Roman said, glancing at Kit. Kit nodded. Roman rose from his seat and walked out of the room briskly. Now that it was just him and Yolanda, Kit stood up as well. He started to leave when she smiled at him and held up her hand.

"You know, Roman really does see something good in you," she said.

"That's good," Kit said. He was sure Roman could see a lot of things inside Kit.

"I wish I could say the same, though. I've tried and tried, but I just… don't get it. I mean, the office looks decent, but he didn't need to hire *you* to get that done. Aside from that, I'm not sure you do anything special that somebody else couldn't do."

Kit was just about sick of this. "Look, I'm not sure why you ever had a problem with me in the first place, but I'm tired of dealing with your bitchy comments and your smartass mouth, Yolanda. I don't know who the fuck you bullied and pushed around in the past, but I swear on every single three-dollar AliExpress bandage wrap dress you have in your closet, I am not the one nor the motherfuckin' two. I do my job, and I mind my own business. Maybe if you stopped worrying about what I'm doing, your edges wouldn't be the only thing looking up for you."

Yolanda crossed her arms and smiled at him. "You know what I think?"

"No, but I also don't give a damn, so."

"I think that you're the one who's been stealing money," Yolanda said. "When you're not here, I get to hear all about the money troubles that this company has going on. And it wouldn't surprise me if it was you. You just got out of college, and this is just some job to you. Who cares if you get fired? But let me tell you this, Kenneth. If I find out that you're the one fucking with the company I've given so much of my time and effort, I'll make sure you never get hired at any establishment that doesn't have a dollar menu."

She took a slow breath, then smiled. Kit shook his head slightly. "Is there anything else you wanted to wrongly accuse me of?"

"No, I think that's about it." She glanced at the ties on the table, thought for a moment, then added, "Tell Roman I said happy birthday." She turned on her heels and walked out back into the main room. Kit clenched his fists.

Not only had she gotten the last word, but she also knew something about Roman that he thought he'd been the only one to know. There was something seriously wrong with that woman, and Kit couldn't put his finger on it. He'd never been around someone who had so quickly disrespected and distrusted him upon their first meeting.

Kit looked out at the employees in the main room, talking and working in little groups. The mystery of the missing money was still in full swing, and Kit was getting more and more tired of having to deal with it each and every day. It could be anybody, really.

Logan's wife just had a baby, and he probably needed the extra money.

Patricia's washer and dryer had both crapped out at the same time, and now she was making regular trips to the laundromat.

Yolanda needed surgery to remove whatever was stuck up her ass, and Barbie had her thing with Kevin. Nearly everyone had a reason for taking money when nobody was looking. Kit swallowed hard.

If everybody was a suspect, did that mean it could just as easily be Roman behind this?

24
FRISKY FELINE

It wasn't until two in the morning that Kit finally fell asleep.

The night before, he'd been up getting his work done ahead of schedule, tapping away on his tablet until his vision went fuzzy and his eyelids grew heavy. Whether he was exhausted or not, he needed to get ahead of the curve and clear out Roman's email inbox. So, he spent all night putting on his business voice and replying to everyone that was waiting for a response.

Finally, when he was sure he'd end up using his tablet as a pillow, he logged off for the night and slid under the covers for some much-needed sleep. He was treated to a peaceful, dreamless night, and in the morning, he woke feeling refreshed and ready for whatever this mysterious date Roman planned had to offer.

Just as he finished breakfast, Kit's phone buzzed. Roman's text message informed him to be ready in an hour. Trying not to get too excited, he hurried to wash up and get changed into something comfortable. Roman's text said to dress casually. Luckily for him, his entire wardrobe, save for what he wore to work, was casual.

By the time he was done and ready to go, Roman had pulled up to the curb downstairs. He grabbed the gift box he'd wrapped last night, then headed down. He found Roman leaning against his car while he waited.

"Hey handsome," Kit said, pushing up on his toes to kiss the man on the cheek. "I got you this."

Roman chuckled in surprise when Kit thrusted the large box in his direction. "You know you didn't have to get me anything, right?"

"Oh please, what kind of boyfriend would I be if I didn't splurge on you? You better accept that gift too. I don't take presents back."

Roman placed it in the back of his car and opened Kit's door for him. Kit watched him round the car to the other side, and to anyone that knew what Roman was like on any other given day, it was clear to see how excited he was. Kit had never seen him this eager before, aside from the time he'd been writhing in Roman's lap. His smile was persistent, he drummed his fingers on the steering wheel, and he kept glancing at Kit out of the corner of his eye.

"So, where to?" he asked Roman.

"Like I would spoil the surprise. Just trust me, you're going to love it."

Kit wanted to nag until he knew where they were headed, but there was also fun in the mystery of the unknown. Roman could just as easily take him to some seventeen-star restaurant as he could take him to the subways to watch people twerk for spare change. He wasn't sure what to expect, and that was the enjoyable part.

Kit instantly recognized West Village when they entered the neighborhood. Back before he started working at Yellow Fall, he'd been to this side of town a few times for some parties.

Roman parked the car outside of a little pub called Frisky Feline. Kit couldn't say that he knew it, but if Roman thought it would be the perfect place to spend his birthday date, he'd go along with it. They walked inside, hand in hand, and it was in that moment that he realized why Roman had driven so far away from their usual restaurants.

Nobody from work would recognize them here. At Frisky Feline, they could be themselves and enjoy each other's company without worrying that they might get caught by a coworker. A warm feeling came over Kit.

Here, they could just be boyfriends, not a boss and an assistant.

They took their seats and ordered a couple of burgers and beers. Roman took Kit's hand in his and stroked over his fingers. "Thank you for coming out here with me," he said, looking into his eyes.

"You don't have to thank me, Romy. I'd want to spend your birthday with you wherever we went. We could literally just sit at your house and watch TV and it would be the perfect date. That said, this place is… It's really cute."

On the left side of the room, a few pool and ping pong tables were set up, and in the back corner, a collection of old school arcade games were nestled close together. It was the exact opposite of Roman, and he loved that this was where the man had wanted to spend their day together.

After they ate, they carried their drinks to one of the pool tables. Roman popped a mint into his mouth and started the game off while Kit watched, sitting perched on the corner of the table.

"Green stripe," Roman said, calling out his shot. He worked the stick between his fingers a few times before he let it shoot forward. With incredible precision, he pocketed the green striped ball like it was nothing. He sank two more balls before it was Kit's turn.

"I'm gonna pretend like I don't know how to play

this game," Kit said, rubbing chalk over the tip of his pool cue. "Why don't you come over here, get behind me, and teach me?"

With a mischievous smile on his face, Roman wrapped himself around Kit's body and bent him over the table, his hands on top of Kit's.

"Like this?" Kit asked, turning his head to look up at Roman.

"Just like that," he said coolly, his minty breath intoxicating.

Kit thrusted the cue forward exaggeratedly, letting out a little noise of effort. The orange ball rolled across the table and fell into the pocket. He laughed lightly. "You're good at working a stick."

"I'm also good at sinking balls, too," Roman teased.

This kind of banter continued between the two of them until the end of the game. Though Kit had begged and pleaded for Roman to let him win the game, the man was determined to be the champion, and before Kit could even get half of his balls, Roman tapped the 8 ball into the pocket. Kit reluctantly congratulated him on his victory, muttering to himself as he wandered over to the arcade games.

"Holy shit," Roman exclaimed. Kit looked at him curiously. "I can't believe they have this game. Me and my cousins used to spend hours at the skating rink playing this." Roman looked over the *Simpsons* arcade machine.

Roman had never been cuter, and Kit could tell this clearly had meaning to him. He slipped in the appropriate amount of quarters and said, "Let's play then!"

While they'd both been good when competing against each other, Kit and Roman were even better when they were on the same team. The two of them fought their way through Springfield, karate-chopping and side-kicking any enemy that got in their way. Kit hadn't heard Roman laugh this much in a month, let alone an hour. It was almost hard playing the game when all he wanted to do was sigh and listen to Roman laugh and jab at buttons in a frenzy.

Kit didn't want to leave Frisky Feline when it was time to go. If it were up to him, he'd spend the entire night there, trying to finally beat Roman in a game of pool. They hadn't even gotten to play ping pong, but Roman promised that the next time they came here, they'd try that game out.

Roman took Kit back to his house and helped carry the box inside. "Jesus, what'd you put in this thing?"

"You should open it and see!" Kit hurried after him, closing the door and flopping down on the rug in the living room. Roman took a seat on the couch and began opening the wrapping paper from one end, careful and concise. Impatiently, Kit grabbed the paper and tore it down the middle.

"Hey!"

"You were taking too long!" Kit said with a shrug. Roman shook his head and tore off the rest of the paper rather than prudently peeling it open. Inside was a pretty box filled with a variety of body care products.

"Jeez, Kit, you really didn't have to…"

"I know you pretend like it doesn't bother you, but I can practically feel the knots in your shoulders whenever we hug. All of this stuff is supposed to help you relax and decompress after all the hard work you do." Kit dug through the tissue paper and grabbed a purple bottle. "See this? This is a soothing lotion. There's also some massage oil and lots of bath bombs inside as well. Plus, this…"

Kit reached into the basket and pulled out a watch. He'd seen it at the store and knew Roman would love it. Perhaps it wasn't as nice as the Rolex he usually wore, but Kit hoped that the thought would count more than the price tag.

"This is amazing, kitten. Thank you." Roman leaned in to give Kit a hug.

"I'm glad you like it. I normally just get ties for guys, but you already bought yourself some, so I had to get a little more creative with it."

"Well, I love this. And I think that you should

show me how this massage oil works. What do you say?" Roman made his brows jump as he gave the bottle a little shake.

Kit tapped his chin for a moment. "Hmmm… I think I can do that. Go take your shirt off and lay down in bed, I'll find some nice, calming music and then I'll be in there in a minute."

Roman didn't need to be told twice. He tugged his shirt off and walked to the bedroom, slipping his pants off on the way.

"I hate you," Kit laughed.

"You love me," Roman replied.

Kit sat back on his haunches and looked over everything. For not knowing what exactly to get Roman, he'd done a pretty good job if he did say so himself.

He made a quick search through his playlists on his phone until he found one he used for sleeping. There were plenty of relaxing songs on there. Kit hopped up and hurried into the bedroom after Roman.

"Alright, let's get to it," he said. Kit cracked open the bottle of oil and warmed it up in his hands. With firm pressure, he massaged it into Roman's back. "How's that feel?"

Roman let out a groan of approval.

"Good," Kit said. He worked his hands up and down Roman's body, each little noise the man made acting as more encouragement. The music playing from his phone even helped Kit relax, and soon he fell into a groove. He dragged his fingers over Roman's shoulder blades, pressing hard to help relieve the knots he found just below the skin. When he reached his lower back, he switched to his elbow, rolling it in circles, gentler this time. The last thing he needed was to hurt Roman before birthday sex.

After he finished the massage, Kit leaned down to Roman's ear. "How was that?" he asked softly. When there was no response, he leaned to the side and saw that Roman was asleep. Kit smiled to himself and eased down onto the bed, cuddling up next to him.

"Happy birthday," he whispered.

25
FREE MONEY

As much as he loved getting to see Roman every day at work, Kit needed a break. Desperately. This past week had been the busiest he'd ever had, and he'd designed an entire office in less than a month.

Not only was there talk about hiring new people —and by association, talk about firing old employees —but there'd been a meeting Roman needed notes taken on every single day. Kit had scheduled his next three weeks down to the time he was supposed to eat and sleep. On top of all that, he'd kept up with the lives of his coworkers.

Barbie was proud to let him know that her second job was paying off pretty well and she might stick to it. Even Yolanda seemed nicer to him. When he offered to let her use his phone to test out how all of her graphics would look on a smaller screen, she didn't have anything snarky to say.

Come Friday night, he was done with it all. He headed home and collapsed on his sofa. Chad and Michelle were supposed to come over tonight, but he had a few peaceful hours to himself until it was time to meet with them. In his pocket, his phone buzzed loudly.

"What's up, Bria?" he answered.

"Hey, are you busy?"

He groaned. "Is it important? I was gonna take a nap before my friends got here."

"It's actually pretty damn important. Mom and Dad want to talk to you."

Here we go, he thought. He had no idea what they could possibly want or why they'd picked the worst day of the week to come over. "I'll be there in a second," he sighed. He turned his phone off and tossed it onto the other side of the sofa. "Fuck my life."

Kit rose from his seat and headed up to Bria's apartment. He didn't bother knocking when he realized the door was unlocked. Inside, he found his parents and sister sitting around the table. His mind immediately drummed up the worst scenarios. His mother was pregnant. They were staging an intervention into all the beer he purchased. Somehow, they'd gotten a hold of the thotty pictures he took for guys back at school.

"What's going on?" he asked.

Tonya smiled wide. "We meant to tell you we needed to talk to you earlier."

"It's fine," he shrugged. "What'd you need?"

Dorian glanced at his wife before he said, "Your mother and I were thinking about how we behaved the past few years. We made some bad decisions with you two, and that really shows. Bria and I were talking, and she told me how much debt she's in because of school. Your mother and I would have never let that happen had we not been so stubborn about you two."

Kit made a face. "So… What are you saying?"

"Mom and Dad said they want to help pay off our student loans, Kit." Bria's lips curled into a smile.

He wasn't sure he'd heard that right. His parents—the ones who'd kicked him out years ago for something he had no control over—were trying to flagellate themselves by paying off his loans from school? Not only was that ridiculous, but the idea that they thought he couldn't do it on his own pissed him off.

"I don't need your handouts, you know that, right? I have a job. I make money. I've been making payments since I started working at Yellow Fall. You can keep your charity money, I'm good." Kit didn't mean to sound so bitter, but he couldn't help it. The audacity of their implication was enough to bring out that side of him.

"Kit," Tonya murmured, "We're not saying that you can't take care of yourself. You have your own apartment. You're making good money at your job. You've been living on your own since you were eighteen. *Clearly* you can take care of yourself."

"Your mother and I know we could never change how we treated you and Bria, but we can change what happened to your debt because of what we did. Had we never abandoned you, neither of you would be in this situation. You'd be debt-free, a clean slate. We can fix that. It's nowhere near enough to apologize to you, but I'd like to think it's a start…" Dorian looked at Kit with pleading eyes.

He'd never seen his father with so much emotion on his face, nor had he heard Dorian speak this much in one sitting. Unsure, he looked at Bria. She bit at her thumbnail, silently watching the conversation unfold.

"I need a minute," he said. Kit stood up and walked out into the hall. He leaned against the wall and sighed. All he'd wanted to do was spend the rest of his night watching dumb movies with his friends and eating Doritos. He didn't need to add making financial decisions onto his plate tonight.

Bria stepped outside a minute later. "Kit…"

"Bria, what are they even doing? Do they really expect me to just be cool with them throwing money at us to fix the problem? That's some white people shit!"

Bria nodded. "I know. I agree. But I don't think they're trying to parent us anymore. They can see that we made it just fine without them, and they're probably just hoping we haven't cut them out completely."

"Why shouldn't we?" he asked. "The way they used to talk to us and treat us?"

"Let's look at this another way," Bria said. "You're fifty thousand dollars in debt. Do you know how many payments you'd have to make to pay that off? How many years you'd have to work at Yellow Fall before that was all taken care of? Even if you don't forgive them or *want* to forgive them, fifty grand is fifty grand. I don't take that shit lightly, and I know you don't either."

Kit wanted to argue, but she was right. They couldn't find that amount of money just lying around somewhere. His shoulders slumped. "I guess you're right. My thing is, I don't want to feel like I owe them something, y'know? Like, years from now, I don't want them throwing it back in our faces that they did this for us."

"That's a risk we just have to run," Bria said. "I don't want you feeling pressured, though. If you don't want this, you don't have to accept it. Just know that I'm not the kind of bitch to turn down free money."

It made sense. Bria had spent all summer taking

care of him and now someone was offering to take care of her. He couldn't be mad at that. He pushed himself up from the wall and headed back inside with Bria.

"So, what do you say, son?" his father asked.

"I'll think about it. Today's been really stressful, and I just need a breather before I make any other huge decisions. I hope you guys understand," he said. He hated how apologetic his tone was. He didn't need to apologize for being hesitant.

"Of course," Tonya said. "Take as long as you need. The offer's always on the table."

Kit nodded and glanced at Bria. She seemed relieved that he wasn't still so defensive. It was crazy to think that when she was his age, she'd been just as fiery as he was. Now that she'd calmed down, Bria had changed into the level-headed one in the family.

"Listen," he said, "I have to get going, now. I have company coming over. I'll talk to you later." He gave a small wave to his parents and made his way back to his apartment. He had a little bit of time left to get a quick nap in before Chad and Michelle were over, and he was going to use up every last second of it.

His friends arrived at eight that night. He heard the knock on the door just as he pulled the pizza out of the oven. He wasn't a chef by any stretch of the imagination, but he knew how to throw together a little pizza. It didn't hurt that he enjoyed flirting with the lady that made the dough and got it for a discounted price.

"Hey!" Michelle exclaimed when he opened the door.

"Hey, you guys, come in!" Kit stepped out of the way and ushered them inside. "I just finished making dinner. Chad, do me a favor and cut it for me?"

"Cut it, cut it, cut it, cut it," Chad sang, heading into the kitchen. "This pizza way too big, you need to *cut it*."

This was what Kit needed. Trying to balance work, dating, and his family was becoming increasingly difficult, and he knew that taking a break from it all and enjoying some time with his best friends would be good for him. Just like Roman had needed the massage oils and lotion to destress, Kit needed time off and hilariously shitty horror movies.

Michelle took a seat and stretched out her legs before she said, "How have you been, Kit? It feels like I haven't seen you in forever!"

"Work at the office has been keeping me busy all week. I seriously miss last week when all I was doing was filing paperwork and shit."

"Speaking of last week," Chad said from the kitchen, "How did your birthday date go with Roman?"

One corner of Kit's lips curled into a smile. That date had been on repeat in his mind since it happened. "It was perfect," he sighed, shaking his head. "We went to a bar, played some games, had food, then went home and spent some time there." Repeating it out loud made it sound lame as hell, but to him, it had been everything.

"You guys are seriously the cutest," Michelle exclaimed.

Chad looked back over his shoulder. "I'd be down for a double date if you would."

"I'll ask Roman what he thinks about that." Kit reached for his phone, but hesitated. Tonight was about the three of them getting together and forgetting about work. His text to Roman could wait.

Chad managed to carry three plates of food into the living room, handing one off to Kit and Michelle. Kit tore a bite out of his pizza and began scrolling through the movies on Netflix. There were plenty of bad "scary" movies there, and for a moment he couldn't decide. He eventually settled on a cheesy slasher flick.

"Here, can you take a picture of me, Michelle?" he asked. He handed over his phone and posed with the food. She had to take the picture twice because she couldn't stop laughing at his ridiculous face. When she was done, she handed the phone back to him.

"Here you go."

"Thanks," he said, wiping his greasy hands off. He took the phone and headed over to his Instagram. He knew Michelle didn't have one, so he didn't bother tagging her in the post. He did tag Chad, however, and he captioned the picture, *"Greasy bitch brigade."*

Halfway through the second movie, Kit felt his eyes get heavy. Michelle and Chad had gotten quiet as well, but he wasn't sure whether they were asleep or just paying close attention to the movie. Clearly the nap he'd taken before wasn't enough to keep him up for much longer, because the second he convinced himself he was going to "just listen to the movie," he was drifting off towards some much-needed sleep.

26
DISAPPOINTMENT

On Monday, Kit nearly fell out of the shower from dancing too much. The combination of his erratic movements and the soap on the floor wasn't the best, but he managed to catch himself just before he went tumbling out onto the bathroom floor. He didn't let that kill his vibe, either. Instead, he grabbed his towel and shimmied as he dried himself off.

This past weekend had been everything that he needed. Chad and Michelle slept over on the couch Friday, and on Saturday and Sunday, he'd stayed over at Michelle's apartment with Chad. Chad had just recently purchased a ton of new games on Xbox and Kit was more than willing to test some of them out.

Though he wasn't exactly *keen* on going back to work, Kit couldn't deny that he was excited to see Roman again. They hadn't talked all weekend and

Kit still needed to invite Roman out for a double date. He wasn't sure if he would be into it, but it wouldn't hurt anything to ask him and see.

At the coffee shop, Kit gave Michelle his usual Monday order and stepped to the side as the next customer moved forward. Michelle blended up the vanilla drink and looked up at him.

"So, don't be weird or anything, but I think Chad and I are getting pretty close to making this thing between us serious," she said. Kit could tell she was choosing her words very carefully.

"For real?"

"Yeah. When you went home last night, he stayed over a little longer and we had a long talk. It's kind of scary because I don't get this way about very many guys. There's only been one in the past that I really cared about, and he treated me like trash. Chad's the first guy since then to actually capture my attention and make me feel like I'm wanted."

Kit's smile widened. "Michelle, that's amazing. If you feel that sure about it, you should go for it. I know he can be annoying and frustrating sometimes, but Chad is an amazing boyfriend. I've seen the way he treats the people he's with. He's a good guy."

He wasn't just saying that to hype his best friend up, either. There were times when Kit wished the guys he'd been with gave him even a drop of the care and affection that Chad had given his boyfriends and girlfriends in the past. When he wasn't making sex jokes or crass comments about celebrities, Chad was capable of deep, meaningful conversations that could easily change Kit's opinion on something entirely.

"You think I should go for it?"

"Absolutely. He cares a lot about you, and clearly you feel the same way, so go for it. Love is in the air, Michelle!"

She laughed and rolled her eyes. "If he rejects me, I'm gonna have some choice words for you, you hear me?" She handed over his two carriers of coffee and winked at him. "Have a good day!"

"You too!"

Kit used his back to push through the doors of the shop and made his way to work, his thoughts returning to his friends. Had Michelle never invited him and Chad to that party months ago, he doubted the three of them would even be as close as they were now. There were times when he was skeptical about fate, but this wasn't one of them. Everything happened for a reason.

Kit headed into Yellow Fall and smiled at the receptionist, Jules. He'd asked Roman what her name was last week, and as he passed by, he greeted her by her first name. She looked shocked that anyone had even bothered to address her in that way. He knew exactly how that felt.

When he'd first started working at Yellow Fall, not

very many people talked to him. Aside from lunch with Barbie and verbal sparring with Yolanda, his other coworkers ignored him. Now, however, they talked to him regularly and made him feel like he was part of the team. Being acknowledged had a way of turning someone's day around, and he hoped he could give that to Jules.

Judging by the way the room felt when Kit walked onto the floor, Ari was in Roman's office. Barbie wasn't her usual chatterbox self, and Logan *and* his corny jokes were nowhere to be found. Kit didn't let it get to his mood, though. He placed the drinks down and handed them out to his coworkers, offering a bright smile to each of them. He turned to grab Roman's when his office door opened.

The look on his face froze Kit in his place. Roman's mouth was tight, his eyes were hard, and his silence was deafening. Rather than saying anything, he jerked his head towards the room. Kit looked around at the office. Everyone averted their eyes. Without a word, he swallowed hard and grabbed Roman's coffee, following him into the room.

"Close the door," Ari said.

"Sure." He did as he was told, then took a seat in the chair next to Ari. Slowly, he placed the cup of coffee on Roman's desk, beside an empty brown box. "So… What's up?"

Roman and Ari shared a look before Ari said,

"Kit, I wanted to ask you a few questions before I left for my trip."

"Of course," Kit nodded.

"Do you enjoy working for Yellow Fall?"

"I haven't had many jobs, Mr. Naser, but Yellow Fall has been the best place I've ever worked at. It's corny to say, but this place really does feel like a family." Kit glanced at Roman, unable to tell if he'd answered that properly by the look on Roman's face.

"I'm glad to hear that," Ari continued, "And you're comfortable with the company? The progress we've made?"

"One hundred percent. I had some family that was worried about me working here after the Grandeur campaign, but I know that you've gone above and beyond to fix that fiasco. I believe in Yellow Fall."

Ari nodded slowly, his splayed fingers pressed together as he listened. "My last question is if you think you're smarter than me."

Kit blinked. "Uh—what?"

"Do you think you're smarter than me?" he repeated. "Did you think I wouldn't find out about what you've been doing?"

Kit's stomach sank. Ari knew about him and Roman dating. Roman's expression told him everything. "I... I don't know what to say. We didn't mean to, but it kinda just happened. I know it's unprofessional, but I—"

"Stealing from me is more than just *unprofessional*," Ari said curtly.

"Wait, what are you talking about? I didn't steal from you." Now Kit was truly lost.

"Don't. Don't play stupid with me, Kit." Ari shook his head.

"I'm not playing dumb, I genuinely have no idea what you're talking about," he said. He looked to Roman for support but found nothing. Only that expressionless, granite stare.

"As I'm sure Roman told you, my tech team was looking into the theft. For weeks, there was nothing. Ask them. I was pissed that they couldn't find any trace of this person. I'd given up hope. Then, last week, we saw something interesting. Rather than seeing a large amount of money disappearing into any offshore accounts, we saw three hundred dollars deposited into your account."

Kit shook his head. "No, that's impossible. That wasn't me."

"It wasn't? But it was on your work tablet. The money was transferred directly into your account, from your own company card. Pretty sloppy considering how untraceable everything had been before that."

"Almost like it wasn't me that did it," Kit said,

narrowing his eyes. "Almost like you're accusing the wrong fucking person—"

"Enough," Ari nearly shouted. "Over the course of four months, you've taken seven thousand dollars from me. I've thought about it for hours, and pressing charges against you simply isn't enough. Roman is the one that gave you the job. Roman is the one that hired you. After the shitshow that was his last assistant, he promised me that he'd choose much more wisely. Evidently, he wasn't able to do so. That's why this money is coming from his salary. That's why I plan on putting your ass in prison. That's also why you're fired."

Ari stood and scooted the box over to Kit. "You have twenty minutes." He closed the door behind himself.

Kit sat in silence, staring at the box. This had to be some kind of joke. This had to be some mistake. He couldn't even take money from friends when they offered to pay for him at the movies. How the fuck would he have been able to take seven grand from Yellow Fall?

"I didn't take that money," Kit said, looking up at Roman. He hadn't said a single word the entire time. Even still, he kept quiet. "Roman, you believe me, right?"

"I trusted you, Kit."

He felt as if he'd just been punched in the gut. "You don't still trust me?"

"Honestly, *no*, I don't. The evidence is right there. I want to believe you, but I… I don't. Please tell me you didn't buy my gifts with money you stole from Yellow Fall." His eyes fell to the watch on his wrist.

Kit couldn't believe what he was hearing. "Roman."

"Tell me you didn't."

"I didn't," he whispered.

Roman stared at him for a moment before he said, "Kit, you need to pack up your things."

"No."

"Get your things and *go*. I'm not going to tell you again."

"Why would I listen to you? Apparently, you're not my boss anymore. I'm guessing that applies to you being my boyfriend, too?" Silence. "Thought so. Good luck doing your fucking job without me, Roman." Kit snatched the box from the table and threw it across the room.

"Kit."

"Don't 'Kit' me. You believe that asshole over me. I'm sitting here telling you I didn't take shit from this place and you believe him over me. But that's cool. No, it's totally fine. I understand why you didn't stand up for me. You didn't want to lose your job."

That was what it took to make Roman explode. "I *did* fucking stand up for you. The tech department talked to me on *Friday*! I tried calling you all weekend and you didn't answer me. I wanted to be ahead of this, not involve my boss, but when I showed up at your place, your sister told me you were out with your friends and she didn't know where they lived. I *tried*, but you ignored me. Were you out spending all that money you stole?"

"I didn't get a single fucking text, Roman." Kit pulled his phone from his pocket and swiped to unlock it. "*Look*. I didn't get shit from you. I didn't get a text, or a phone call, or a message." He all but threw the phone at him.

Roman shoved it back across the table. "I don't want to hear it, Kit. I called you. Multiple times."

"I'm sure," he said sarcastically. "Well, I guess this past weekend was a sample of the kind of silence I'll be getting from now on."

"Of course, this is all about you. I'm losing seven thousand dollars and you've made it about you," Roman muttered.

Kit laughed loudly. "Aw, you poor *thing*! You'll only be making two hundred and ninety-three thousand dollars this year, that must be *so* hard. Meanwhile I won't be able to pay my rent, I'll have to go live with the parents that spent eighteen years making my life a living hell, and I might even end up going to prison over this bullshit. But you're right, let's feel bad for the

Chief Creative Director at a million-dollar company."

"Grow up, Kit."

"Fuck you. I hope that when you realize that this wasn't me, you feel like the biggest asshole in the world. Because you are. And good luck with the next assistant you get, by the way. I hope this one does a better job than me, because you'll need it. I know you don't want to disappoint your parents or anything." Kit knew that the second the words left his mouth, he'd crossed the line. The flash of rage on Roman's face was indication of that. He felt sick, like he'd just stepped off a roller coaster, and his head throbbed with anger.

"You'd know about disappointing your parents, wouldn't you, Kit? You stood up to them like you were big and bold, but now you'll have to go crawling back to them. Any parent would be disappointed with that, I'd think," Roman said coldly.

Kit's smile held no humor or happiness. It contained the same chill of Roman's gaze. He turned and left the office, his nails digging into his palm. He didn't need to take anything home with him. What he needed more was to get the hell out of this place. To burn it down. To hide forever.

His journey to the elevator was the worst walk of shame he'd ever experienced. There was no way that everyone in the office *hadn't* heard him and Roman screaming at each other. They knew that he'd lost his job. They knew he'd "stolen" the money.

Kit managed to keep it together until the elevator doors closed. Then, he let himself fall apart. He stepped out when he reached the main floor and looked in Jules' direction. Her smile faded, quickly replaced with a look of sympathy.

He thought back to the first time he'd met her. The woman they'd both seen crying was like a secret they shared. Kit had been so sure that even if his interview went poorly, he would never let it show like that. Yet here he was. Letting Jules see him react this way felt like a disappointment in itself. He was getting good at that.

Kit wiped his eyes and marched to the door. He'd figure it out. He always figured it out.

27
NICER

It was almost seven at night, and Kit still hadn't gotten out of bed to turn the lights on. He hadn't eaten anything, or even looked at his phone all day. He was focused on one thing and one thing only. He needed to find a new job. His bills needed to be paid, and he didn't care if trying to find another job killed him. He wasn't going to go back to Bria's sofa—not after having tasted what true freedom and independence really felt like.

He finally found a decent offer working in customer service. He'd be able to work from home, which would save him money on subway rides, and it would also allow him to keep from having to socialize with anyone ever again.

When he got to the part of the application that asked for previous work experience, Kit grit his teeth and took a few slow, calming breaths. Arguably the worst part of being accused of stealing seven thousand dollars from his previous employer was knowing that he couldn't use Yellow Fall on his application. If he did, they'd call Yellow Fall and it would come out that he'd allegedly "stolen" all that money.

Kit was exactly where he'd started almost five months ago. He had no real experience that would be enough to put on his application, just a degree in business. He wanted to bury his face in a pillow and scream until he fainted, but he twisted the spare pillow in his hands, wringing it until his frustration subsided.

Fuck them, he thought.

That sentiment was what kept him going all day long. He wanted to prove to them that he could do anything. This wasn't the end of Kit Bayer. But as he passed up on more and more job opportunities, his confidence began to waver. He wasn't even sure who *they* were, and why he was trying so hard to prove himself to them. Were they Yellow Fall? His friends and family? Roman?

On the nightstand, Kit's phone buzzed loudly, startling him. He'd been ready to ignore it, but when he saw that it was Ira from the temp agency, he snatched it up.

"Hey, Ira, what's up?"

"Kit, hi! I hate that I'm calling so late, but I actually found a job that's right up your alley. I know you said that you didn't want to work as an assistant again, but how would you feel about working as the receptionist at a small company that's just starting up? They're looking for someone to stick with them for a long time, and they've informed me you'll have the usual benefits. Health insurance, dental, all of it."

Ira was slowly becoming Kit's favorite person in the world. "I can't even be picky right now. I'm more than interested in this."

"Perfect! I'm going to email you all the details and you can see for yourself if this is something you'd want to be part of."

"Thank you again, Ira. You're a lifesaver."

He laughed with embarrassment. "I try, really. You have a good night, okay? I'll talk to you soon!"

"You too." Kit hung up his phone.

For the first time in a week, he smiled. All he needed to do was believe in himself. He'd proven time and again that when faced with seemingly impossible tasks, he had a talent for persevering and showing the world what kind of person he was. Kit flopped back in his bed and sighed with relief. With the shitshow he'd just gone through at Yellow Fall, he needed a tiny bit of good news.

After a minute of lying in bed, he stretched out and grabbed his shoes from the floor. He'd spent the entire week cooped up in his apartment. He might not have it for much longer, after all. He needed to get out of the house and go for a walk. He needed to clear his head.

Kit headed downstairs and aimlessly walked through the streets, his music blaring through his headphones. His mind wandered through everything he'd been repressing since last week. He'd tried his hardest to block out the disappointment on Roman's face. He'd also tried blocking the anger in the low blows they'd both given.

Roman was right—in a way. There were really only two options left for Kit. He could either go crawling back to his parents begging for rent money, or he could bust his ass and prove to himself and everyone else that he wasn't a failure. Just three days ago Kit had accepted his parents' offer to help with his student loans. He didn't want to ask for anything more from them.

Kit scrolled through his phone, switching songs and reading through the texts he'd yet to respond to. Bria wanted to know if he needed anything, Michelle was worried about him, and even Chad—the person that rarely considered personal space—told him he'd give him some time to deal with things.

Eventually, Kit scrolled down to Roman's name. He opened the conversation out of morbid curiosity. He'd expected to find all their texts, but instead, there was nothing. Everything was gone. Not only that, but his phone informed him that the number had been blocked. His brows knitted together in confusion.

When had he blocked Roman's number? Was this why he hadn't received any of his phone calls or texts over the weekend?

Before he could go down this path of bottomless questions, he straightened himself up and closed his phone. There was no time for *what ifs* and alternate timelines. What he was going through now was his reality, and he had to deal with that first.

Kit's journey eventually led him into Chad's part of town. He stopped outside of the apartments Chad's parents had put him in, debating whether or not he wanted to be social with his best friend. He took a deep breath and decided he'd ignored everyone for far too long.

Shame washed over Kit as he knocked on the door of Chad's apartment. He should have done this earlier. He shouldn't have shut out the people he loved the most. As much as he hated that about himself, this was how he'd handled most of his breakups with people. With Jaylen, he had gone completely MIA, fading away from every social event until Chad had to hunt him down and make him explain what was going on. He wasn't going to put anyone he loved through that pain again.

"Dude," was all Chad said before pulling him in for a hug. He pulled away and looked Kit over skeptically. "How are you? Bria told me you were going through some shit, but she didn't specify. What's going on?"

Kit closed the door and shrugged. "Well, Roman and his boss Ari basically accused me of stealing all that money from the company."

Chad laughed loudly. "Are they serious? If you had money like that—"

"I *know*. I wouldn't be living where I'm living now if I knew how to do all this sneaky technology shit," Kit exclaimed.

Out of the corner of his eye, he saw movement. Michelle peered over the couch, a little disoriented. She rubbed her eyes and yawned, and when she finally recognized Kit, she ran over to give him a hug. Hers was much tighter than Chad's had been.

"I'm so happy you're okay," she said. "We've been worried sick."

Kit followed them into the living room and gave them both all the details about how he lost the job and how Roman was suffering from this as well. While Chad was willing to sympathize with Roman, Michelle's anger was apparent.

"He just sat there and kicked you out like he didn't care about you? Men are literally such shitheads!"

"Part of me wants to blame him for being so cold, but the other part... I still care about him. I said some really lowdown things about him, and he threw it right back at me. I'm just so tired of wasting my time with guys that don't treat me the right way," Kit said, putting his face in his hands and sighing with exasperation.

"You don't need Roman," she said, stroking his back. "There are a million and one men out there that you can easily replace him with."

Kit laughed bitterly. He'd about had enough of successful businessmen. With the way Ari and Roman had treated him, he was almost angry enough to call off all men regardless of their financial status. On the other end, he was ready to scam someone. This time he'd *actually* steal some insane amount of money.

"I'm sorry I didn't message you guys back," Kit said, biting at his bottom lip. He kept his gaze on the floor, unable to meet either of their gazes. That shame had returned. For a few days there, he'd allowed himself to think that nobody cared about him. He'd wallowed away by his miserable self. Being here now was proof that he'd only been feeling sorry for himself.

"Kit, you don't need to apologize for taking some time away to deal with this. Nobody here knows what you're going through. I mean, you and Roman were getting serious, and all of sudden he's firing you and accusing you of committing felonies," Chad said.

"Still, it feels like I—I let everyone down." Kit's voice was hoarse. He hated that he showed his emotions this way, especially in front of Michelle. She'd never seen him get like this before, and the last time Chad had been around for this, he'd been screaming and shouting about Jaylen.

Chad slung an arm around Kit's shoulder. "Let us down how? By dealing with your heartbreak the only way you knew how?"

"I let you all down because I shouldn't have done any of this! I shouldn't have gotten close to Roman this way. I let Bria down because I told her we weren't like that. There was no power imbalance with us. I let you guys down because I know how badly you all were rooting for me. I—I let myself down. I fell for another person that tossed me aside like I wasn't even important to him."

Kit's voice finally cracked, and he lowered his head, tears spilling out once more. Chad sighed and pulled him into his arms. While he held Kit, Michelle rubbed Kit's knee tenderly.

"Man, I love you, but you need to be nicer to yourself, Kit," Chad said softly. "Do you know anyone else that did what you did with such skill? You met every single one of Roman's challenges. You designed that office. You worked with some of the most influential businesses in New York. Hell, you even made someone like Roman give you a second chance after your interview! You did that, and the only person here that's even remotely trying to take that away from you is *you*."

Kit sniffled and closed his eyes. There was no room for him to argue with that. He was too hard on himself. He'd always been too hard on himself. Not only that, but he could admit that there were times when he walked around with a chip on his shoulder, like he had something to prove. He'd felt it when he moved out of his parents' house. He'd also felt it when he'd passive-aggressively cleaned up Roman's office.

"Look at me," Chad said.

"Yeah?"

"Everyone here is so proud of you. Your first job out of college and you were working somewhere plenty of people only dream of. Most people have to flip burgers or deal with soccer moms that are angry about their expired coupon being rejected at Macy's. But not you. You whined and you complained the entire time we searched for jobs, but you *still* went through with it. And everyone that truly cares about you is so fucking proud of you."

Kit's throat closed tight. He wanted to thank Chad for being so kind to him. He wanted to thank him for being the very definition of a true friend. All he could do instead was choke back another sob and hold Chad even tighter.

"Chad's right," Michelle said softly. "You're gonna find another guy, and another job, and soon all of this will be a memory. You can't hold onto this, otherwise it'll consume you and take hold of your entire life."

"I don't want that," Kit said, swallowing hard.

"It's the worst feeling in the world," Michelle murmured.

"We're not gonna let that happen," Chad said. "We're gonna show the world that Kit isn't the one to mess with. You may think you're going to show him up and hurt his feelings, but you've got another thing coming. He's a bad bitch, period."

Kit looked up at Chad through watery eyes. "You promise?"

"I promise."

28
BACK FOR US

Kit wasn't sure he'd ever studied this hard for anything in his life, not even for his finals during his senior year of college. The past twenty-four hours had been dedicated to reading up on every little bit of information he could find about Winston & Wolfe. If he was going to nail this interview and get the job, he was going to have to walk into that building with his head held high and all this knowledge tucked under his belt.

Winston & Wolfe was an insurance agency that had come up six months ago, and in those six months, they'd taken off. Unlike Yellow Fall, there was no previous scandal the company was recovering from. There was no risk if Kit worked there. In his eyes, this was a safe job, albeit a boring one. It didn't matter whether he liked it or not, though. He'd signed a lease. His landlord Donny had given him a chance. He wasn't going to blow it. He wasn't going to let the world see him fail.

So, Kit spent the entire day before his interview preparing himself. When it was finally time, he stood in front of the mirror and looked himself over. He wore a simple, understated outfit—something he'd never worn to Yellow Fall before. A black pair of slacks, a blue button-up shirt, and a gray tie. Call him crazy, but he felt like going into the new place with a little bit of his past on him would majorly jinx him.

With an hour left until his interview, Kit took a cab to the other side of town and walked the rest of the way. This was the most air he'd gotten in days, and it actually felt good. After his little breakdown in front of Michelle and Chad, Kit had promised to keep himself together and do better for himself. He wasn't going to wallow away in his own misery, entertaining the idea of giving up completely. He had friends in this, friends like Chad, that would do anything to help him, and friends like Michelle, that were ready to burn Roman and all of Yellow Fall to the ground.

It was finally time for his interview, and he cleared his throat while striding through the doors. The front desk was noticeably empty. "That's going to change," he said to himself, giving himself a mini pep talk.

A woman across the room giggled softly. "That's

the spirit," she said. "Are you here for the interview with Mr. Hendon?"

"I am, yes."

"If you follow me, I'll take you to his office." She ran her fingers through her long blonde hair and offered a reassuring smile. Kit could sense a nervousness about her, but also a touch of familiarity. He wasn't sure what it was, but he felt he could relate to her.

He followed her down the hall and towards the elevator. Inside, the two of them stood uncomfortably silent until he said, "So, do you work here?"

"I do. I'm Mr. Hendon's assistant."

"Ah, like my last job."

"Where did you work?"

Kit didn't want to admit it just in case they made some calls and asked around. If they called the wrong person, he could easily lose this opportunity as well. Instead, he coyly said, "I don't kiss and tell, sorry."

The woman nodded. "Fair enough." Kit couldn't think of a time he'd been on any longer of an elevator ride. The stifling silence continued until she said, "This is really unprofessional, so please don't tell him I said this, but he's going to attempt to bully you and scare you, so you have to be prepared for it."

Kit blinked. "Who, Mr. Hendon?"

"Yes. The only reason I got the job was because I didn't leave his office crying like everyone else did. He takes asshole to the fifth level, so get ready now. And don't let him trip you up with his mental challenges, okay?"

"Why are you helping me?" he asked.

"I'm tired of seeing people getting upset. If I can help them, I want to, even if it's only by letting them know what they're walking into."

It suddenly made sense. That familiarity. Roman had done the same thing to him. Unluckily for Mr. Hendon, Kit wasn't going to let himself fall for that trap a second time. He had this under control.

"Thank you for the heads up," he said, smiling slightly. The worry lines in her forehead softened.

When the doors opened, the assistant took him to Mr. Hendon's office and knocked. She poked her head in to tell him that his three o'clock interview was here, then stepped aside to let Kit in.

"Good luck," she whispered before closing the door.

Mr. Hendon mirrored the stock image of a businessman. He was stout with a heavyset frame, slicked back black hair, and a hard brow. He looked angry already, and Kit hadn't said anything yet. Determined to make an impression, though, Kit reached forward and stuck his hand out.

"It's nice to meet you, Mr. Hendon."

"You too, Mr. Bayer," Hendon said, shaking his hand firmly.

The beginning of the interview was quite routine. Hendon was looking for a receptionist, nothing more, nothing less. He wasn't going to ever get a promotion to become part of the team, he wasn't going to end up making close friends with anyone, and he certainly wasn't going to be irreplaceable. Hendon said this as if that was supposed to scare him.

The last job he'd worked at, Kit's boyfriend-boss had fired him and broken up with him in front of all of his coworkers and friends. Not making friends with anyone here actually sounded like a dream.

"I want you to tell me, right now, why you want this shitty job," Hendon said. The question was completely left field, and Kit needed a moment to think. He'd never been asked a question so bluntly, nor had he ever seen an interviewer so blatantly express their disdain for a position.

"I was going to come up with some kind of wistful and dreamy answer, but the truth is that I have bills to pay and I need this money. I know, I'm supposed to say that I 'want to be a part of a bigger thing' and talk about how being a receptionist has been my dream since I was a little boy, but I want this job so I don't end up homeless. I want this job because I have responsibilities and I made agreements with people that I can't back out of. Even if it means working somewhere where I'm isolated and I have no friends."

Kit shrugged and looked back at Hendon who sat

staring him down. If Hendon was looking for honesty, he'd surely gotten exactly that. Another long silence passed before Hendon nodded and pulled out his pen. He scribbled something on a notepad and glanced at the door.

"You can go."

"Alright," Kit said. He pushed himself out of the chair, almost tempted to laugh at his situation. When he reached for the doorknob, Hendon stopped him.

"Come in on Monday and we'll get your paperwork set up. Don't thank me, don't start crying, just get out of here."

Finally, Kit laughed. This entire experience was almost surreal. He'd basically shitted on this opportunity with his new boss and had still gotten the job. Mercury had to be in some kind of retrograde because none of this made sense. Taking Hendon's direction, he headed out without a word.

"To Kit getting another job!"

Tonya raised her glass and nudged Dorian to do the same. Kit looked at his parents like they were crazy before he laughed and finally joined in. He clinked his glass with theirs and took a long sip of the wine. Dorian set his glass of water down and said,

"I know you probably think that we're being

corny, but Kit, we're seriously proud of you. You've grown to be such a go-getter, and I think that's what makes us the proudest."

Tonya nodded enthusiastically. "You've become the person we always wanted you to be. Mature, responsible, and brave."

Their corny, sentimental words were only slightly cringey. He'd decided that tonight, he was going to let them have this and enjoy their praise. He'd spent so many years trying to earn that, and now they were willing to share it with him. He only wished Bria could have been with him. As great as his parents were treating him, she was still the biggest protector and provider in his life. He wanted her here more than anything. Unfortunately, she'd already made plans with Trish, but she'd promised to take him out to celebrate tomorrow.

"You know, I think this is the first family dinner we've had together in almost five years," Tonya said, looking between the both of them.

"It feels good, doesn't it?" Dorian asked. Tonya smiled softly, her eyes growing wet. She quickly swiped them away.

"Sorry, I don't want to get emotional," she said.

"It's fine, Mom," Kit said, reaching out to touch her hand. He gave her a squeeze.

"I love you," she said quietly.

"I meant to tell you earlier," Dorian began,

"We've set up the automatic payments for your loans, Kit. By this time next year, you're going to be a free man!"

This was the kind of good news Kit needed to hear. After a long deliberation with Bria, he'd decided to let their parents take care of his loans, and neither of them had made a big deal about it yet. He'd been waiting for the ball to drop, for one of them to say "Just kidding!" and change their mind, but Tonya and Dorian did nothing of the sort.

"I don't think I ever thanked you both really," Kit said. "But I want to now. When you first showed up, I felt like everything I'd worked to build was going to fall apart. I don't want to beat a dead horse because I know you both feel terrible, but you guys really fucked me and Bria up. What matters, though, is that you're both trying. You're trying to be here now. It takes a big person to actually admit that they were wrong. Especially you two," he laughed. Tonya joined in with him.

"I just want to thank you for being there for me and Bria. All we ever wanted was a family like this," he said, ending his little speech. This time, Tonya couldn't fight back the tears. She stopped them before they reached her chin, sniffling hard.

"It takes an even bigger person to forgive someone, Kenneth," Dorian said.

Maybe it did. His whole life, he'd been determined to prove them wrong, and in that determination, he'd found true happiness here in New York. No matter where he came from, this was his home. When Tonya and Dorian had arrived, he'd been sure they were going to destroy that. He'd lashed out at them. And now, here he was, actually having dinner with them without throwing drinks in their faces.

Dorian took a long drink of his water. "Your mother and I wanted to ask you something," he said, his tone slightly calmer. Tonya looked up from her food as if this was news to her.

"What's up?" Kit asked. He popped the last of his breadstick into his mouth.

"I need your help, Kit."

He glanced at his mother curiously, then back to his father. "Help with what?"

"Last month, I was having some back pains, and I couldn't figure out what it was. I went to the doctor to see if there was something bad going on, and he told me it was my kidney." Dorian's words hung heavy in the air. "Kidney failure, to be more specific."

"Holy shit, are you gonna be okay?" he asked.

"I don't know. My doctor said that it's extremely likely that I'll make it through surgery, but from the looks of the donor list, I might not be around long enough to. I'm a fifty-year-old man, and there are children on that waiting list. Who do you think they're going to try and help first? My only hope is finding someone that's willing to donate to me."

Kit was silent.

His smile faded away as the realization of the situation crept over him. He stared at his hands, watched how they shook, and squeezed them into fists. He was such an idiot. He was such a goddamn idiot.

"You didn't come back for us," he said slowly.

"Kit—"

"You didn't come back to fix the fucked-up things you did to us. You didn't want to pay off our loans because you felt guilty. You wanted to buy my fucking kidney from me." His voice grew loud enough to draw attention to their table.

"Dorian, you can't be serious," Tonya whispered.

"Kit, I did come back because I wanted to fix our family," Dorian said.

"I can't believe I actually believed that you were thinking about anyone but yourself. I told Bria earlier that you were finally becoming a man of God. You were finally righting all the wrongs you'd done. But all along, you only came back to take something else from me. Wasn't my entire fucking childhood good enough?"

Kit was shouting at this point. He couldn't have cared any less. "Wasn't it bad enough that you took so much from me that I tried to kill myself? Now you *literally* want me to cut myself open for you? You can go fuck yourself!"

He shot up from his seat, knocking his glass of wine to the floor. Dorian's eyes darted around the room.

"Kit, I'll die if you don't help me."

"Then die."

Shock settled on Dorian's face. Kit had never felt this much coldness towards a person. He wanted to drive his fists into his father's face until his hands broke. He wanted to scream until he could no longer feel anything but the rawness of his throat. He squeezed his fists and turned, shoving past the manager as he approached Kit. He didn't even grab his umbrella on the way out.

He had to get out of here. He had to get far away from these people. Outside, Kit checked his phone. He could barely see with the rain falling on the screen, but he saw that his sister had tried calling him four times.

"Kit."

Kit turned to find Roman standing across the street, drenched in the pouring rain. He took off towards him, narrowly avoiding being hit by a taxi. Kit threw himself into Roman's arms, sobbing, and for a moment, he forgot about their fight and everything that had gone wrong between them.

29
I ONLY WANT YOU

Kit didn't care if he was soaked through his clothes. He didn't care if he'd just humiliated himself in front of the entire restaurant, nor was he concerned with how his father would react after he'd just told him off.

All he could see was the anger that rolled through him like a violent storm. He'd given Dorian a second chance. After years of emotional abuse, he'd opened his heart to forgive him, only to be stabbed in the back. He couldn't believe he was this stupid.

Slowly, his tunnel vision disappeared when he realized who he was hugging and where they were. He pulled back and shoved Roman away from him, glaring up at him. "What are you doing here?" he demanded.

"I came to talk to you," Roman said, wiping the rain from his face.

"What, are you stalking me or something? How'd you even know where I was?"

"I went to talk to Bria. She told me where you were."

The missed calls on his phone suddenly made sense. Bria must have been calling to warn him that Roman was on his way to the restaurant. He wanted to be mad at her for not keeping her mouth shut, but he knew his sister and he knew Roman. She got flustered under pressure, and Roman knew how to persuade someone to do something for him.

"What happened?" Roman asked. He looked back at the restaurant.

"You don't get to ask me questions, Roman. You're the one that broke up with me, remember? What was it that you said? That everything about me was endearing and you never wanted me to change? Am I suddenly endearing again because you and every other person at Yellow Fall thinks I stole seven grand?" Kit knew that his anger was coming from another source, but he couldn't stop it. If he could, he would've yelled at every single person who'd ever wronged him. Instead, he settled for Roman.

"That's what I wanted to talk to you about." Roman didn't even seem to flinch at Kit's volume. He stared back with hard eyes, determined.

"Roman, get the fuck out of my face, honestly."

Kit started to turn but Roman caught him by the arm. Kit shot him a warning look and Roman's hand fell to his side. "I need to apologize."

Kit stared back, unsure of himself. He'd spent so much of his time trying not to think about Roman that seeing him suddenly turn up was an overload. He wanted to slap him and kiss him and tell him where he could shove his apology. He raised an eyebrow expectantly.

"Okay," Roman said. His hardened mask fell and Kit watched him struggle to get his thoughts in order. "I… I called you. The entire weekend, I called you, because I couldn't believe what the IT department was telling me. You couldn't have done this—"

"I didn't."

"Please let me finish."

Kit sighed. "Fine."

"I couldn't see you doing something like this. But I let Ari get in my head. He wanted this done and dealt with, and you were an easy answer. You were the new employee that got so accustomed to spending Yellow Fall money with the first project I assigned to you. You were fresh out of college and looking to make some quick cash. You were believable. And when you didn't answer my calls, I—I thought about my ex. She put this fear in me that I couldn't trust anyone again because they'd always let me down, just like she did."

"That has nothing to do with me, Roman. I'm not her."

"And thank God you're not," Roman said. "But for a second, I thought you were. And I'm a fucking idiot for thinking that. Do you want to know why I know that this wasn't you?"

"Aside from me telling you point blank that it wasn't me?"

"Yes."

"How?" Kit looked at him cautiously. Roman was already on thin ice with him.

Roman smiled sadly. "I looked over that information again tonight. The day you sent me those emails and the day money was withdrawn from Yellow Fall's account was October first. You were with me, celebrating my birthday, not a tablet in sight. You spent the entire day taking care of me. Showing me what it felt like to have someone in my corner. You were there for me, and… and I was convinced that you'd betrayed me."

Roman's eyes darted away. Kit wasn't sure if he was looking at tears or rain rolling down Roman's cheeks, but his heart tugged and he wanted to touch him. He didn't care whether it was holding his hand or wiping his eyes, but he longed for that contact.

"I told Ari about us. I told him that we'd been seeing each other, and that you were at my house the night this happened. You were with me all night.

You weren't even on your phone, let alone your tablet."

"You put your job on the line," Kit said quietly.

"I don't care. I don't care if Ari's pissed, or disappointed, or even if he fires me. None of that shit matters because without you being there, it's a fucking job. I can get hired anywhere. There are a million and one jobs out there that want me. But there's only one you, and I only want *you* to want me again."

It was Kit's turn to look away.

"You were my teammate, Kit. You were the one person I could depend on more than anyone else. And I fucked that all up, and there's nothing else I can do but beg for you to see how stupid I am and how much I need you. I'm sorry for saying that shit about your parents. For embarrassing you in front of everyone in the office. For even thinking for a second that you were anything less than an honest and *good* person."

Kit finally met his eyes again, shaking his head. "You're so stupid."

"I know." Roman stepped closer, tentatively placing his hands on Kit's hips.

"You got me fired because you believed someone else over me."

Roman nodded. "I did." He pressed his forehead to Kit's.

"And you hurt my feelings."

"I'm sorry." Roman kissed Kit's nose. This close to

him, Kit could smell that familiar cologne that he wore, and he took in a deep breath.

"I'm sorry I said that you couldn't do anything without help from someone," Kit said.

"It's okay. I deserved it."

"Kinda."

They stood together, hugging in the rain, shivering against one another. Try as he might to not feel something, there was a spark of warmth in Kit's stomach. Finally, they parted and Roman looked him over. "What happened? Why were you crying?"

Part of Kit wanted to tell Roman right then and there. He wanted to see Roman Hulk out and kick his father's ass. He knew Roman would do exactly that, too. Jaylen had only touched Kit and Roman nearly broke his finger. If he found out what Dorian was asking of him, he'd do much worse.

"Can we talk about this somewhere where it's not pouring?" Kit asked.

Roman nodded and waved his hand at a taxi pulling around the corner. When it stopped at the curb, Roman helped Kit inside. He pulled the younger man into his arms, offering a bit of warmth despite being wet from the freezing rain.

For most of the ride back to Roman's home, neither of them said anything. Kit couldn't even muster up a joke. All he could do was lean against

Roman, shivering from the cold. He stroked his hair softly.

"We need to figure this out," he said. Kit suspected he was talking more to himself than anyone else. "I'm sick of this shit."

"*You're* sick of this," Kit smirked.

"I mean—"

"I'm just teasing. This person is fucking with everyone, not just me."

"Maybe not, but it's clear they're targeting you. When you can, I want you to change all the passwords and make sure everything is secure."

Kit nodded. "I'm always careful with those things. I've got all kinds of numbers and shit in my passwords. I've even been staying up to date with updates, like with the calendar app. I didn't want to lose all your shit like the email said."

Roman's hand in Kit's hair stopped, and he tilted his head. "What email?"

"I got an email saying that I had to update the calendar app on my tablet, otherwise I might lose all the things that I'd planned."

Roman shook his head. "I'm in my email every single day, I didn't get a single one about updating that app."

Kit looked out the window in confusion. He clearly recalled being told he had to update just in case he lost all of his information.

"Do you still have the email?"

Kit reached into his pocket and pulled out his phone. He navigated to his mailbox, then handed it over. Roman mumbled out the words, shaking his head again. "No, I didn't get anything like this. You said you downloaded this on your tablet?"

"Yeah, a few weeks ago."

"Then that's probably how this person got access to it. Through this update that you downloaded. Your tablet was compromised, and they were able to transfer the money into your account."

Kit's face fell. "I keep all my information on this thing. My bank account number, the company card number, all of it."

Roman nodded solemnly. "They knew what they were doing. They knew they could pin this on you."

Kit had never felt stupider. He'd fallen for the okeydoke, tricked by a spam email that would've cost him a job had it not been for the fact that Roman recognized the dates matching up. He wanted to knock himself upside the head and throttle whoever had tricked him.

"I'm such a fucking idiot."

"No," Roman said, "This person is just a whole lot smarter than us. But they'll fuck up. They'll do something so simple, so stupid, and we'll find out who they are." He tightened his grip on Kit, and the younger man simply nodded, leaning against him.

When they made it to Roman's place, Kit started up the shower and leaned against the opposite wall, letting his head hang. He wasn't sure if it would be appropriate to ask or not, but he really needed a massage to help alleviate some of the tension in his back.

Roman entered the bathroom with two fluffy towels and laid them down on the counter. He met Kit's eyes in the mirror and smiled solemnly. "You can tell me what happened at the restaurant when you're ready," he said.

"I don't want to think about it right now."

Roman nodded. "Your parents?"

"Yeah."

"Well, they're not here. Out of sight, out of mind." Roman peeled his clothes off and tossed them into the basket by the door. When Roman discarded his pants, Kit finally looked away. He didn't want to seem like a creep.

"You're getting in too, right?" he asked.

Without a word, Kit removed his clothes and stepped into the water alongside Roman. He hugged himself and stood to the side, allowing Roman to slip under the stream first. Roman's hands ran through his hair and over his body, lathering himself up. He looked back at Kit.

"Kit…"

"I know, Roman." He didn't need to hear it again.

He knew that he was sorry. He knew that he felt bad about what he'd done. Roman had said it plenty of times already.

"Tell me what I have to do. Anything. Anything at all, Kit, I swear to God."

"I don't know… You just have to show me," Kit said, pulling his eyes from the tiled floor. "Convince me that you're sorry. Because words don't do anything if your actions don't match."

Roman thought for a second, then stepped closer, backing Kit against the wall. He placed a hand on either side and looked down at him. "Can I tell you something?"

"What?"

"I cried a lot when you were gone."

Kit had a hard time believing that. That must have shown on his face because Roman continued,

"I did. At first it was because I thought that you were the one who really did this. Then it was because I ended up not being bothered by that. I'd never felt that way before. The fact that I could look at someone that—I'd thought—had hurt me, and still want them in my life… It's a scary feeling, Kit."

He didn't need to tell Kit that. He'd already experienced that feeling way too many times in his life.

"I was scared that I could be hurt by someone and still want them back. Common sense tells you that you pull away from pain, but I wanted to embrace it and bring you back to me. And then even worse, that turned into me realizing that I'd royally fucked up and I'd lost you forever."

"You didn't lose me forever," Kit said, rolling his eyes.

"It felt like it. It was like I'd finally replaced the hole my ex left and you were gone all of a sudden. I couldn't sit around and wallow in that. I took it upon myself to go look into this 'evidence' that the tech department found. It didn't dawn on me before, but you said it in my office that day. It was very convenient that the one time this scheme was messy, it was connected to you. The timing also correlated with you not getting any of my calls. Those two things don't happen by chance."

"Which is what I told both you goofy bitches," Kit grumbled. "This person probably got into my phone, too. When I tried reading through our old texts, they were all deleted and your number was blocked."

"I'm sorry, kitten. I should have listened."

"Yeah, you should've listened to me over Ari. Ari didn't dry hump you in your office, *I* did."

Roman cracked a smile. "I know."

"So… you really believe me? No bullshit, you're not just saying that?"

"Kit, I'm going to figure out who the fuck tried framing the man I love if it's the last thing I do."

Kit blinked in surprise. For the smallest of

seconds, he considered pointing out what Roman said, but he held his tongue. He'd known Roman felt this way about him for a long time now. He wouldn't have put up with Kit's bratty behavior and spoiled personality if he didn't love him.

"What are you gonna do when you find out who it is?" he asked, looking up at him and dragging his fingers over Roman's abs.

"I'm going to kick their ass. They're going to wish they'd fucked with someone dumber than me—which, I know, probably doesn't exist."

Kit laughed and placed a finger over his lips. "Shush," he said. He leaned in to replace his finger with his mouth, kissing Roman slowly. Though it was only a kiss, the rush to his head was unparalleled. He molded himself against Roman's body, closing the small amount of space between them.

"Promise me we'll talk about any other problem," Kit said, breaking their kiss after a moment.

"I swear."

Kit looked into his eyes, searching for a hint of deception. There was none. "Okay. Now, take me to your bed and show me just how sorry you are."

30
THE BEST PARTIES

"I'm scared, Romy."

"Of?"

"Of everyone thinking that I'm some Joanne the Scammer type bitch or something."

Kit sat in the bathtub with his back against Roman's chest, his knees held close. Monday morning had come much faster than he'd anticipated, and now he was seriously regretting not enjoying the weekend. Over the past two days, he and Roman had talked about everything. Their goals, their future, and how they'd made it a whole week without seeing each other. Roman admitted he'd nearly broken down and called Kit—even when he still thought that he'd been the one stealing. He was too far gone into this relationship.

Though he'd been embarrassed, Kit finally

managed to tell Roman that he wanted his job back. He explained how he'd been interviewed by someone a lot like him, and how he was a hot commodity. If Roman didn't make the decision now, he'd be working for them instead of Yellow Fall. He also told him that he'd need Ari to personally address him and clear his name. Roman didn't hesitate to make those calls and get the ball rolling.

"Kit, I promise, no one is going to think that. I already sent out the email that you'll be coming back, and if anyone makes a smart comment about you, they'll have to deal with me." Roman wrapped his arms around Kit, sloshing the warm water. He kissed the part of Kit's back that wasn't covered in soapy bubbles.

"Anyone that says anything bad about me?"

"Anyone," Roman said.

"I hope Yolanda has some more job applications then," he smirked.

"She'll leave you alone, Kit. Your name is cleared. Out of anyone, you're the one that's the least likely suspect. I can't see you framing yourself. Then again," he murmured, "I couldn't see you as a thief, either."

Kit slapped Roman's arm around his waist. "Fuck you," he cried.

"Mm, which position?"

"We should finish getting washed up," Kit said,

glancing at his phone on the edge of the tub. The screen read 6:30.

"I don't want to get dressed, kitten," Roman whined, clearly making fun of Kit's pouty drawl.

Kit rolled his eyes and stood up, bubbles running down his back and thighs. He offered Roman his hand, and he took it. Not without pausing to marvel at his backside, of course. Kit released the water in the tub, then turned on the shower, helping Roman clean spots he couldn't get on his own. Ten minutes later, they were both cleaned and standing in Roman's closet.

"We don't have time to run back to your place and make it to work on time, so you can wear any of the things I have in here," Roman said.

Kit felt his stomach do a flip. With Roman's admission to Ari—and presumably everyone else at work—they no longer had to hide the fact that they were seeing each other. It may have been against professionalism, but it wasn't illegal. That was good enough to Kit.

He walked through the large room, looking at all of the expensive shirts and ties Roman had collected over the years. He grabbed a white button-up that looked to be his size, pairing that with the slacks he'd been wearing at the dinner with his parents.

Ugh, he thought.

He'd tried avoiding thinking about his parents for

the past two days, and aside from telling Bria why their father could blow him from the back, he'd managed to do exactly that. He knew they were going to have to talk in more detail about it later, but right now, he was perfectly content never speaking of his father again. For all he cared, he didn't have one of those.

Kit pulled on his outfit and looked himself over in the mirror. The shirt was still a little too large for him, but it wasn't anything too noticeable. He fixed his tie and looked back at Roman. Roman sat on the bed, dressed, simply watching him.

"What?" he asked, taking note of Roman's small smile.

"I'm just really happy."

Kit reached for his hand, lacing his fingers through Roman's. "I am too."

"We should get going," Roman said. He grabbed his coat out of the living room and gestured for Kit to follow him to the garage. They both buckled up and pulled out of the driveway. Kit called Mr. Hendon's number and left a voicemail telling him that unfortunately he wouldn't be able to take the job. He wished the man good luck with finding the right fit for the job, then hung up.

"I need you to stop at the coffee shop before we get to work," Kit said.

"Don't worry about it," Roman replied, waving

his hand. Kit made a face, but didn't say anything. If any of his coworkers got mad about their missing coffee, they could take it up with Roman.

They reached the parking lot, and Roman paused to send a text. He held out his hand for Kit. For a second, Kit wasn't sure what he was doing. He'd grown so accustomed to hiding their relationship that he couldn't imagine holding hands with Roman as they walked inside. But here Roman was, waiting patiently for Kit to take it. After the disbelief wore off, Kit did.

When the elevator doors parted on the sixth floor, all of Kit's coworkers stood nearby yelling, "Surprise!" Barbie threw a handful of confetti into the air above Kit and Roman.

"You guys," Kit whined, immediately taken over by a swell of happiness. When he left the job, he'd been sure that everyone that he considered a work friend was done with him. Seeing how enthusiastic they were to have him back made him emotional.

"I'm so glad my baby's back," Barbie said, pulling him into a hug and rocking him side to side. "I missed you so much, Kit. No one else here listens to my boring stories the same way you do."

He laughed. "I can't wait to hear all the boring stories you have left."

Barbie patted him on the back, then ushered

everyone over to the cake on the table in the kitchen. Kit's eyes went wide, and he looked back at Roman.

"You didn't have to do all of this," he said quietly.

"I didn't. They did. This was Barbie's idea."

Kit turned back to Barbie and watched as she cut into the chocolate cake. "Now, I know it's only 8, but I told everyone to skip breakfast because we have it all here." She gestured to the counters behind her that were filled with all kinds of breakfast food, from bagels to sandwiches to little boxes of cereal. "I'm only cutting you a piece because I know how big your sweet tooth is," she teased.

"Thank you, Barbie," Kit said, unable to keep from cheesing again. It all made sense why Roman hadn't bothered stopping to pick up coffee. His coworkers had probably asked for permission to set this up in advance and he knew that they were going to be providing all the food and drinks anyway.

Kit had never really believed anyone could make friends with people at work. He'd heard stories from Bria and Chad about being close with people, but this wasn't exactly the best place to find his lifelong bestie. When one got fired, especially in his low-level position, that was generally the end of things. But now it made sense. These people genuinely enjoyed having Kit around. They didn't get annoyed with him or only act nice to him at work. Logan, Patricia, Barbie, *all* of them seemed to care about him more than he'd ever thought they did.

It felt like a family. A work family.

Even Yolanda seemed less tense than usual. She didn't have anything smart to say to him, and Kit would've wagered that was because he was no longer a suspect on her list. Having his relationship outed by Roman proved that there was no way he'd actually taken the money; therefore, she no longer had a reason to suspect him. That by no means meant she went out of her way to be nicer to him than before.

"Welcome back," she said. Her words were short, but her tone was no longer angry. Still, she lacked any kind of warmth for him. Kit was completely satisfied with that. He didn't need to be friends with Yolanda.

Roman poked his head out of his office half an hour later. "Kit," he said, waving him over.

"Be back in a bit," Kit said to Barbie and Logan, heading into Roman's office. "What's up?"

Roman placed a large stack of papers on the desk in front of him, as well as a pen. Kit took a seat and looked it over.

"What are these?"

"The paperwork I had you initially sign back when you first started working here. Since you were let go, you have to redo all of that. But," he said, smiling, "Once you sign on all those dotted lines, you'll officially be a Yellow Fall employee again."

Kitten

For being back on the job, Kit didn't get much work done. He suspected this was Roman's doing, and that he was giving him a day to get readjusted before they went back to their usual roles. He wasn't complaining, either. It gave him plenty of time to get caught up with his friends. Logan's wife was well taken care of, which Kit was so happy to hear. One day his wife would bring the baby up to the office to meet everyone. Not only that, but Barbie's financial issues had resolved themselves when her eldest son proudly announced that he'd gotten his first job.

By the time the work day was over, Kit was sure he'd spent a majority of the time chatting with his friends. He poked his head into Roman's office while everyone headed for the elevator. "Hey, Romy, I have plans with my friends. I'm gonna catch a ride over to their place."

"That's fine, I was going to stay here and work anyways."

"Cool," Kit said.

"Love you," Roman said, flipping through his papers.

Kit was still taken aback by the coolness of his tone, but he said, "Love you too." He headed down to the street and managed to get a taxi without much struggle. Usually the drivers had attitudes, but this one was sweet as could be. She told him all about her collection of cat statues, all the way to Chad's apartment.

The apartment was unlocked when Kit made it to his door. "Hey, I'm here!" he called out.

Michelle poked her head out from the kitchen and waved. "Hey!" She wiped her hands on the apron around her waist and gave him a quick hug. "How was your first day of work?"

"God, I really don't know if I'm gonna last there long," he sighed dramatically, laughing when Michelle did. "Where's Chad at?"

"He went to the store to pick up some onions. I thought he had some, and you can't make burgers and onion rings without them."

"Do you need any help?" he offered.

"No, no, you always cook for us at your apartment, let us treat you this time. Besides, I wanna hear all the gossip about your first day back. Spill the tea."

Kit took a seat at the bar and let out a deep breath. He didn't even know where to begin. "It was seriously one of the best days I've had in a long time. I don't know if Chad told you about what happened with me and Roman a few days ago…"

"Just that you got into it with your folks and you found him outside waiting to talk to you." She sprinkled seasoning salt over the beef patties like an expert.

After that, she grabbed the knife and quickly began chopping up potatoes.

"Yeah, that's pretty much exactly how it happened. He found me and apologized for treating me like dirt. He told me all about how his ex was shitty and kind of the worst person ever, too."

"Shit," Michelle gasped, pulling her hand back suddenly. Kit didn't realize she'd cut herself until he saw the blood on the knife.

"Damn, let me get you a bandage." Kit jumped up from the bar and hurried into the bathroom to grab the medical kit Chad kept underneath the sink. Inside, he removed the peroxide, cleaning swabs, and a Band-Aid. When he returned to the kitchen, he helped Michelle clean off the blood from her finger.

"I didn't bleed on any of the food, right?" she asked, looking over her shoulder at the potatoes.

"Just the one you were cutting, but that's fine. I can take over, okay? Now, this might sting a little." Kit poured the tiniest amount of peroxide on the cut, watching it bubble and fizzle in the wound. It wasn't deep at all, thankfully. Michelle winced, but she managed to keep quiet.

Kit wrapped the Band-Aid around her finger and smiled. "All better!"

"Thank you," she murmured finally. "I'm such an idiot."

"Nah, just clumsy." Kit cleaned up the mess on

the counter and tossed the bad potato, grabbing a new knife to cut the rest of the food up with.

"So, what else happened? Distract me so I don't end up bitching about this cut," Michelle laughed.

"Well, today was good because when I got there, one of my coworkers had thrown me this huge party. She got everyone to pitch in and they got me a cake and everything. It was one of the sweetest things anyone's ever done for me."

Michelle held a hand to her heart. "That's the sweetest. Barbie's parties are always amazing."

"If they are, I hope I'm invited to all of them," he laughed.

While Kit seasoned the fries and got them put into the oven, Michelle hopped onto the couch to look over everything they had on Netflix. Good food and a horror movie had become their thing. Kit washed his hands and leaned back against the counter, smiling to himself.

Then he frowned.

How did Michelle know who'd thrown him the party, let alone that Barbie's parties were nice? He'd never mentioned her by name to either of his friends, nor did he talk about anyone else from work except Roman. Kit looked at Michelle, and his stomach fell.

It all slowly came to him.

Roman's number being blocked on his phone after she and Chad had stayed the night. Her bragging that she'd been smarter than everyone at her old computer job. The lamp she bought him that was far too much for any barista. Her knowledge of Yellow Fall employees by name.

Michelle.

It was her.

31
SADIE

Kit ran. He couldn't even bother coming up with a decent excuse other than Bria sent him a text about their parents and he needed to go. Michelle had looked at him with suspicion, but she didn't say anything.

Kit took off, flying down the stairs and bursting through the door. When he reached the curb, he waved for a taxi and caught his breath.

Why? This didn't make any sense. Michelle was his *friend*. Friends didn't do this to each other. They didn't get each other fired. They didn't steal thousands of dollars and try to pin it on someone else. He'd trusted her, and she did this.

He knew where he was going. Roman was still working late at the office, otherwise he would've given directions to the man's house. Instead, the cab driver sighed and headed towards Yellow Fall, clearly irritated with the drive he'd have to make. Kit couldn't be bothered to care about the driver's feelings given his current situation. All he could think about was why Michelle had done this.

The driver stopped at the curb, and Kit tossed his money, ignoring the angry shouts from the driver. He pushed through the doors and jabbed at the elevator button, his heart racing. Finally, the doors parted and he was inside. The ride up to the sixth floor had never been slower in Kit's life. When he stepped out, Roman was in the middle of a conversation with Ari, but that didn't stop Kit from saying,

"It was Michelle."

Both men turned to look at him in confusion. "What?" Roman asked.

"Michelle's the one stealing the money," he panted.

"Who is Michelle?" Ari asked, looking between the two of them. "How do you know?"

Kit still hadn't completely forgiven Ari for accusing him of stealing, so he ignored the man's question. "Roman, it's *Michelle*. I was at Chad's place helping her cook and I mentioned the party today. She knew Barbie's name. I've never said it—I've never even talked to them about my coworkers—but she still knew Barbie's name."

Roman's brows turned downward, like he was

trying to piece it all together. "How would your friend from the coffee shop know Barbie?"

"I don't know!" Kit exclaimed. "I just know that she specifically said her name, and the only way she could have known about the parties is if she knew what happens here at work. Do either of you know if she maybe worked here or something?"

Ari scratched his chin. "No, I don't recall a Michelle."

"I don't either," Roman murmured.

"Well, don't you guys keep a record or something? Can you see if anyone named Michelle *did* work here? Because that would explain a lot." Kit didn't wait for their answer. Instead, he headed back to the elevator.

"Where are you going?" Ari asked.

"Tech department," Roman said, answering for Kit. He waved Ari over with him, and when they were all inside, Kit pressed the button for the third floor.

He could barely sit still. He was full of adrenaline and nerves, sick to his stomach but desperate for information. He needed to figure out what was going on. There had to be some kind of explanation.

Part of him rationalized that this was just some weird mistake. Maybe he *had* mentioned Barbie before. Maybe there'd been another party that he forgot about, and he told Michelle and Chad about it. It was a stretch, but a part of Kit didn't want to believe that someone he was so close to could have done something like this to him.

When the doors parted, the group of three made a beeline for the young man sitting at his computer. He looked up, and when he saw Ari, fear crossed his face. "Evening, Mr. Naser," he said, clearing his throat and sitting up straighter.

"Evening, Sam. I need you to pull out the database of all our employees at the company."

Sam nodded and began typing at his computer, skillfully clicking through branches of folders until he found the proper document. "Okay, now what?"

"Search the name Michelle," Kit said before Ari could open his mouth. Sam did as he was told.

The program sorted through all the names of current and past employees of Yellow Fall. There were only three instances of a woman with that first name, then someone with the middle name. Sam's eyebrows went up, and he clicked on the last one.

"Sadie Michelle Schreiner," Kit said aloud. He looked between Sam, Ari, and Roman, deducing that their silence was because they knew something he didn't. "Who's that?"

Ari gave Roman a hard look. "Sadie was Roman's previous assistant. And his ex-girlfriend."

Kit felt like he'd been punched in the gut. He thought he might really double over and start heaving. This was too much for him. "What?"

"I'll let Roman do the explaining. Right now, I have some calls to make. I'll see you tomorrow, Sam. Good work, Kit." He patted Kit on the shoulder and left the three of them alone. There was a heavy silence after his departure.

"Come with me and I'll explain it, okay?" Roman said quietly. Kit nodded and took his hand when Roman reached for him. "Thank you, Sam," Roman said over his shoulder.

Roman led him out to the lobby of Yellow Fall. Kit was at a loss for words. Flashes of Michelle and Roman together made his stomach twist—from jealousy or disgust, he wasn't quite sure. All he knew was that he felt like he'd been hit by a car that didn't bother slowing down.

"I need you to tell me everything," he said finally, looking up at Roman.

He took a moment to collect his thoughts. "Michelle became my assistant last May. She'd moved here from some small town and she was looking for a job that wouldn't take up her time every single day. Jesus, she was a computer science major," he said, laughing humorlessly. "I should have known when you told me about that update."

"Ari said you two were dating?" Just saying that made Kit irritated.

"We did date. She was the ex I'd told you about. The one that fucked me up. At first, she was amazing.

She was funny and sweet and all of that, but as the months went by, she got more and more possessive. She started acting different. Sadie became controlling, and manipulative too. She constantly pretended to be hurt or sick, just for my attention."

Kit thought back to the time she was supposed to go see Trish's musical but had called out because she was sick. But the truth was, she wasn't, at least not in that sense. She had known Roman would be there, and if he saw her, her cover would be blown.

Roman shook his head. "She threatened to hurt herself if I didn't give her what she wanted. Finally, I'd had enough. I wasn't going to suffer through it when I could get rid of her if I just fired her. So, I did. Yolanda and I were ready for her to come back with claims that I assaulted her or press charges for sexual harassment, but she never did. She just kind of… disappeared. I haven't seen her since April of this year.

"That's why I was so wary to hire you at first. It had only been a few months since she and I split up, and I was worried I might end up with another crazy ass assistant. In a way, I was right."

Kit, despite everything, smiled. "You were."

"I don't know why I didn't expect something like this from her. She was gone for so long. I'd let myself think she was gone for good."

"That bitch pretended to be my friend," Kit

muttered. "When you and I were, y'know, going through our thing, she sat there with me and comforted me when I was crying. She dated my best friend, and for what? Just so she could get revenge on you for breaking up with her?"

"That's how Sadie works," he said, placing his hand on Kit's shoulder. "She gets close to you and makes you need her. She gives you nice gifts, and she treats you like someone she's known her whole life. She invites you out, she makes you feel important, and then when you're finally hooked, she decides she wants more. She's never satisfied with what you can give her. She'll always want more from you."

Kit's head spun. Never in his life did he think someone close to him would be this out of her goddamn mind, but he couldn't argue with Roman. He'd dated her for months before he got free from her grasp.

Kit's phone rang. He pulled it from his pocket and looked down. He tensed when he saw who was calling. "Hey, Chad," he said.

"Hey, dude, where the hell are y'all at? Michelle sent me a text saying you got here, and now you guys are gone and she's not answering her phone."

"Look, Chad, I can't explain this right now, but you need to stay away from Michelle, okay?" Kit looked at Roman, who nodded.

Chad laughed. "What?"

"This isn't a joke, dude. This is serious, you have to believe me. Just go somewhere else for a while. Shit, go hang out with Bria or something. Just stay away from Michelle."

"Why? What's going on?"

"You remember how I couldn't tell you why you needed to get out of that convenience store back in 2014 because I knew you'd freak out if I said someone walked in with a knife?"

"Yeah?"

"It's that serious," Kit said. "Stay away from her, at least until I say it's okay."

"Uh… okay, fine. But you better explain this when you get here." Chad hung up the phone.

Kit knew it wasn't a very compelling case. "Because I said so," never satisfied anyone's curiosity. But the truth was, he didn't have time to explain this over the phone. If Michelle wasn't with him, she could be anywhere. He didn't think she was dangerous, but he'd seen too many movies like this. He knew people could simply snap, and if she knew she'd been caught stealing thousands of dollars, she might just lose her shit and try to hurt someone.

He scoffed. He'd like to see her try.

Kit turned to Roman. "What's Ari gonna do?"

"He's probably filing a police report right now. There might be a warrant for her arrest by morning."

"Good," Kit said, covering his face with his hands.

"This is too much. I just wanted some burgers and onion rings and they got my Black ass in *Fatal Attraction*."

"Come on, let's go get some food and we'll wait this whole thing out." Roman pulled Kit closer and draped his arm over his shoulder, walking through the front doors with him.

They crossed the street, talking about nothing in particular. Kit opened his mouth to make a joke when he saw Michelle at the same time she saw the two of them. She stood on the other side of the street.

"Kit!" she exclaimed.

"Keep walking," Roman said, putting his head down and continuing their stride.

"Kit! Roman! I need to talk to you guys! I need to tell you something!" Her voice was hoarse, rough like sandpaper. Like she'd been crying. "Stop ignoring me, goddammit!"

"Roman…" Kit whispered.

"It's fine. She's not going to do anything, not in public."

Michelle hurried to keep up with them. "Listen, I know you think you know what's going on, but I need to explain. Please, just let me explain. Kit, you need to get away from him."

Kit looked at her like she was crazy. "What?"

"He doesn't care about you. He doesn't care about

anyone. All he can think of is himself, and what other people can give him. Isn't that right, Roman? You probably told him all about how 'crazy' and 'obsessive' I was, didn't you? Did you tell him how you were all ready to tie the knot with me? How you were going to walk me down the aisle and give me a baby? That's all I ever wanted, and you told me you would give me that."

Roman scoffed under his breath. "None of that matters anymore, Sadie. You should go before the police show up." He pulled Kit closer and quickened his speed.

"No, you wanted a family with me because you knew all I ever wanted was that. You think I stole all of this from you because I wanted it for myself? No, I stole it because I needed it. Because I finally got the family I'd always dreamed of."

Kit stopped in his tracks and turned to face her. "What are you talking about?"

A knowing smile formed on her face, and she stepped away from the curb. "I needed the money for this." As she hurried towards them, she put a hand over her stomach. "I needed the money for my baby. Chad's baby."

Roman's head snapped up at the same time Kit covered his mouth. He barely processed what she'd said before the screech of tires and the flashing of headlights registered. The car connected with

Michelle and she collided against the windshield, shattering it.

The car came to a halt, and she rolled down from the hood. Her bloody, battered body hit the ground with a heavy thud.

32
I'M FREE

Kit had never seen anything more horrific in his life. He'd watched graphic videos online, and even witnessed a few disgusting videos Chad had challenged him to sit through, but this was something else entirely. He knew Michelle. She'd been his friend. And now he wasn't sure whether she was dead or not.

His head spun.

He grabbed for Roman, clutching the sleeve of his shirt in his fist.

The sound of a woman's scream finally broke him from the trance. Kit struggled to dial for an ambulance, nausea rising up his throat. He tore his eyes from Michelle's body. If he didn't, he was going to lose it.

The driver stepped out from the car with tears in

his eyes, visibly shaken. Kit wanted to tell him that it wasn't his fault, but his throat was sealed shut. He could only croak out that they needed the paramedics, *quickly*.

All around them, people stood in shock. A father held his son close to him, covering the boy's eyes and turning his head away from the accident. Two women clung to each other, silently sobbing. Then there was Roman.

"Roman," Kit whispered, shaking him.

"She... she's pregnant?" His voice was thin.

Kit had no words. He stepped closer to Roman, wrapping his arms around him and burying his face in his chest. Kit shivered, tears wetting the front of his shirt. Roman buried his face in Kit's hair.

The ambulance arrived faster than Kit had ever seen, and Michelle was loaded onto the stretcher. Kit wasn't sure what that meant, and nobody would tell him anything. Was she still breathing? Was she okay? Just as they closed the doors, Roman spoke up.

"You need to call Chad," he said to Kit. Roman turned to hail a cab, and Kit pulled his phone from his pocket. Chad picked up on the third ring.

"Tell me what's going on, Kit," he said. "Why am I hiding out from Michelle?"

"You need to get to Lenox Hill, Chad. Michelle was in an accident."

Kitten

Chad couldn't sit still. He walked back and forth, pacing around the small waiting room. Kit wanted to tell him to sit down, but he couldn't. He knew that Chad was still reeling from everything that he'd just learned about Michelle. Not only was his girlfriend the one that had been stealing thousands of dollars from her old employers, but she'd admitted to being pregnant. Kit could only imagine how sick he'd feel if he was in Chad's shoes.

Roman took Kit's hand in his and gave him a squeeze. Throughout the entire wait here in this suffocating room, he'd been quiet, keeping to himself and his own thoughts. It pained Kit to see his best friend and his boyfriend both in so much agony.

Dr. Richards stepped into the room, her soft brown eyes on the three of them. "Mr. Gillespie?" she said. Chad stopped in his tracks and spun around to face her.

"Is she okay? Please, god, tell me she's okay," he begged.

"Ms. Schreiner is in stable condition, yes," Dr. Richards said, holding up a hand to calm him down. Chad collapsed in his chair and let out a choked noise of relief.

"What about the baby?" Kit asked.

The doctor's eyes fell. "When we first brought her

in, she was inconsolable. She said a lot of things. The police spoke with her, to get her side of the story, and... she said some very concerning things."

Roman crinkled his nose. "Concerning how?"

"She told us that she tried talking to you two, but he was livid," she said, gesturing to Kit. "She told them that you'd never liked her. You'd never been okay with their relationship. In fact, you were jealous of what she and Mr. Gillespie had. What disturbed me was that she implied that you pushed her into traffic."

Kit laughed in surprise. "What the fuck?"

Dr. Richards shook her head. "She said you were willing to do anything to keep her and Mr. Gillespie apart. You couldn't bear watching her steal him from you."

Kit felt his blood pressure rising. She knew what she was doing. Back at the coffee shop, she'd asked for permission, worried that he might feel this exact way. He'd said he was okay with her getting close to Chad.

"This is bullshit," Roman said.

"That's what I thought," Dr. Richards continued. "None of the witnesses at the scene could vouch for her. Each and every one of them said she ran across the street. And when we checked on the baby, there was none. She showed no signs of pregnancy."

Chad buried his face in his hands, a retching noise escaping him. Kit placed a shaky hand on his back.

"I need to talk to her," Chad murmured.

Dr. Richards cleared her throat. "Ms. Schreiner says that she doesn't want to see you."

Rage took over Kit. "That's bullshit," he nearly shouted. "She doesn't get to do this."

"I'm sorry," Dr. Richards said. "Sir, I can show you to her room if you'd like."

Roman nodded slowly. "Yes."

"We're going to figure this out," Kit said, assuring Chad. He bent down to give him a hug, one that Chad was too stunned to reciprocate.

Dr. Richards led Roman and Kit down the corridor until she gestured to the right room. She stopped Roman before he entered. "I'll leave you both to speak with her."

Roman said nothing. He walked into the room with Kit. Inside, Michelle sat in a small blue bed, stitches and bandages covering her wounds. Her right arm was in a cast, as was her left leg. She looked worse for the wear, but much better than what she looked like the last time Kit had seen her. Before, she'd appeared dead.

Michelle's bloodshot eyes slid towards the two of them. "I only want to talk to Roman."

"Come escort me out then," Kit said.

"Sadie… The doctor said that you weren't pregnant. Why would you lie about that?" Roman asked.

"She did it because she was desperate to get away

with all of this," Kit answered, stepping closer to her. "That was your whole game, wasn't it? You started working at the coffee shop so that you could meet the next assistant. You'd get all buddy-buddy with them, make them trust you, and then when you were done siphoning money from Yellow Fall, you'd pin it on them. That little email with that bogus update you sent me was pretty damn genius."

She glared at him. "None of that is true."

"Oh, fuck off with that, Michelle. Or, is it Sadie? Either way, you're a fucking snake. I can't believe I thought you were my friend. All that time I spent crying over Roman, you were probably loving it. Did it make you mad that Roman was mine? Is that why you tried lying to the police, telling them that *I* pushed you in front of that car?"

"It's what you deserve," she spat venomously. Kit could practically see her drop her innocent act. "I would've blamed Roman if I could, but he wasn't stupid enough to open an email like that. But you? You were perfect. Some kid from a shitty neighborhood, playing at being a grown up? I almost felt bad for how easy it was."

Kit didn't consider himself a violent person, but his fists clenched tight. "I fucking trusted you. Chad loved you, and you used him. Out of everyone, he deserved this the least, and you screwed him over too. What kind of piece of shit pretends to be pregnant for sympathy? Actually, I know. The kind that's desperate for a shorter sentence. I thought, just for a second, that you might have some mental health issues, but you knew exactly what you were doing the whole way.

"I've learned to spot abusers, and Roman can attest that that's exactly what you are. You're not crazy. You're not unhinged. You're a manipulative bitch that was mad that you lost your toy. And you almost got away with it. You almost pinned this whole thing on me. But you didn't. You decided to frame me the day Roman and I were together, for his birthday. You picked the day I spent the day taking care of him. Every single one of his needs. Massaging him, kissing him—"

"Shut up!" she screamed.

Kit was in her face immediately. "No, this is exactly what the fuck you need to hear," he spat the words at her. Before he could say anything else, Roman pulled him back, cupping Kit's face and forcing him to look at him.

"Please don't," he said, searching Kit's eyes. "Please don't. She's not worth it. She wants this. She wants to get under your skin."

"She used Chad," he said, shaking his head. His throat constricted and he felt his eyes grow wet. "She used me. She used everyone."

"I know, baby, I know. Don't look at her, look at

me, okay? Look at me. If you let her see you like this, she'll only get worse. Please be strong, for me."

"Okay," Kit said, squeezing his fists by his side. He had to think about something else. If he thought about Chad sitting in the waiting room crying over her, he might actually put his hands on her. Nobody hurt Chad. Nobody.

"I hope you know all the damage you caused, Sadie," Roman said after a slow breath.

"That's rich coming from you, Roman. You hurt me. You never loved me. You used me and threw me away when you were done with me," she exclaimed, her voice wavering. Tears formed in her eyes.

"I loved you completely," Roman said, shaking his head. "I gave you everything I had. My money. My love. My past. I gave it *all* to you, so don't project that shit onto me. I fired you because you wanted too much! You were manipulative and controlling and toxic to me and everyone around me. I had to let you go."

Michelle shook her head, tears falling. "No. I was good. I was a good person," she whispered.

"You weren't. You were a monster. You *ruined* my life. The second you left, I could finally breathe. I felt like I was a person again, not some *thing* for you to boss around and demean whenever you felt like I wasn't giving you enough."

"Please, stop," she sobbed.

"No. I never told you this, but maybe I should have. Maybe hearing this will finally help you understand that I never want you in my life again. With Kit, I'm happy. I know what real love feels like. I know what forgiveness feels like. I give, and he gives. Nobody takes too much from the other. *That's* what love is. You never loved me. You owned me. But this shit ends today, do you hear me?"

Michelle didn't say anything. She covered her face with her free hand, her shoulders shaking.

Roman kept his gaze on her. "This is over. You didn't ruin my life, but your own. Ari's pressing charges. Grand Larceny is serious. You'll be lucky if you're out of prison before you're thirty. And not only that, but I'm filing for a restraining order against you. We'll all have one against you. I've tried being kind, I've tried being understanding, but this is where that landed us."

Kit swallowed hard. He hadn't even thought about the punishment she'd receive for her crime. Everything that she'd done, from the hacking to the stalking to the stealing, was coming around to bite her. He wanted to feel sorry for her, but all he could think about was the path of destruction she'd left. The betrayal and the scheming. She deserved every bit of this.

"Sadie, *look at me.*"

Michelle wiped her eyes and looked up at him. "What?"

"Kit and I are going to leave now. Do not contact us again. Leave Chad alone, leave Kit's family alone, and leave the employees at Yellow Fall alone. This is me telling you that if you don't, I'm going to do something that I can't take back."

Kit didn't want to find out what that was, and evidently, neither did Michelle. She nodded and covered her face again, crying. Roman took Kit's hand and led him outside into the hallway. They walked for a few moments in silence before Kit stopped and pulled Roman back to him.

"Are… are you okay?"

Roman's eyebrows knitted together. "I'm free."

"Yes. You're free, Romy." Kit stepped into his arms and hugged him for the second time tonight, this time squeezing him tight. After a moment, Kit stepped back. "Are you sure I can't beat her ass? Because I would *love* to beat her ass."

"No, kitten," Roman sighed. "No beating anyone's ass. She got hit by a car. I feel like that's punishment enough."

Kit looked back out into the waiting room. Chad sat with his head in his hands.

"We should get him back to my place," Kit said.

"I feel bad for him," Roman murmured. "Sadie

actually felt something for me. She never had any feelings for him."

"He'll be okay. Chad's strong. One of the strongest people I know."

He bumped Roman's hand. Roman laced their fingers together, and as a pair, they walked back into the waiting room to take care of Chad.

33
PEACE OF MIND

It was no wonder people spent so much of their lives trying to destress and relax. In the midst of the hustle and bustle of workplace drama and interpersonal relationships, that level of peace was gone. Kit had only been a free man for a few hours, and his life had gotten exponentially better.

His dinner tasted better. Sex with Roman felt better. Most importantly, sleep was better. With all of the scandal and torment that Michelle had brought out of his life, Kit felt as if he were a new person. No longer did he feel he had to prove himself to his coworkers. No longer did he lie awake in bed, wondering if Yolanda would make a smart comment about him or give him a dirty look. The culprit had been caught.

The only thing left was to clean up the mess she'd left behind in her wake.

Chad hadn't said a word that night after they came home from the hospital. He'd nodded when Kit asked if he wanted to come over to his place and sleep on the couch so he wasn't alone, but aside from that, he'd been silent. He put his headphones in, pulled the blanket to his neck, and rolled over, facing the cushions. Kit wanted to reach out and touch him, but Roman stopped him. Chad needed time to process this. Nothing Kit could say would change that.

That night, for the first time in their entire relationship, Kit didn't worry about his standing with Roman. He had his job. They'd caught Michelle. They'd fessed up about their feelings and were finally able to have something real that nobody could threaten. It was enough to make Kit emotional. Before the two of them really got down to it, Kit considered keeping his head on Roman's chest and sleeping. Then he remembered how good Roman could make him feel.

Roman fell asleep soon after their romp, leaving Kit some time to think about everything. His mind wandered to his job. It wasn't an easy conversation to have with himself, but by the end of it, he knew what he had to do. It was best for everyone.

Kit woke before Roman. He yawned and stretched, heading out into the kitchen. At the counter, Chad sat with his head propped up in one hand, the other shoveling a spoonful of soggy cereal into his mouth. He looked up when Kit stepped out of his room.

"Hey," was all he said.

Kit sighed and shook his head. "I'm sorry, Chad."

"It's nobody's fault but hers. I keep telling myself that. This isn't my fault. I didn't do this to us. She did. And yet… I feel dumb as fuck. I should've known."

"You didn't see her in that room, Chad—"

"I didn't," he laughed bitterly.

"You didn't *want* to see her. She's got issues, man. She's not the person I thought I knew. She's not the person that comforted me when I was crying over Roman. She's not the person that cuddled and watched scary movies with you. That bitch is a figment of our imagination. She didn't exist. If she did, she'd be dead." Kit couldn't sugarcoat it. They never did that, he and Chad. It was open and honest and brutal if it needed to be.

Chad stared into his bowl, silent. His grip on his spoon tightened.

"'Michelle' doesn't exist. We knew someone Sadie made up. We were her pawns. We got played while she was trying to play a game with Roman and everyone at Yellow Fall. You have to treat this like Michelle straight up died, because she's never coming back."

"I know," Chad exclaimed. "I know. You're right."

Kit knew it was time to dial it back. He wasn't going to rub salt in a wound that hadn't even finished bleeding, let alone begun to heal. He rounded the corner and pulled Chad into his arms. "I'm sorry she did this to you." Kit felt the front of his shirt wet with tears.

"I thought I loved her."

"I know," Kit said in a softer tone. "It's okay."

Chad stayed this way for a while. When he finally seemed to be ready to let go, Kit stepped back and looked down at his breakfast. He carried it to the sink, washed it, and made him a new bowl of cereal.

"I'm not hungry," Chad murmured.

"Eat. You're gonna need your energy."

"Why?"

"Because tonight, we're gonna find someone that's throwing a party, and we're gonna get you white boy wasted. I don't want you sitting here and crying over some thieving ass hoe. You're stronger than that."

Chad sighed. "Kit, I—"

"Nope, I don't wanna hear it. When Jaylen broke my heart and made me feel like shit, you were there forcing me to cheer up and feel better. So, I'm doing the same for you. I won't stop until you're laughing and smiling and you're ready to let go of Michelle and find someone who loves you for you. That person is out there, and they might just be throwing a bomb ass party. You need to get negativity out of your life and invite positivity into it."

"You sound like you've been reading some of Bria's self-help books again," Chad laughed.

"Close. Those little inspirational posts on Facebook."

"Gross," Chad grimaced. "Fine. We'll go do something tonight. Get the negativity out and invite the positivity in. I should probably get going and shower up. I wanna clean all her shit out of my place before I end up breaking down and smelling her shirts, Tommy Wiseau style."

"I'll text you when I find a good party."

Chad placed his bowl in the sink and headed out the door. Now that he was alone, Kit smiled to himself. This wasn't going to be an easy road, but he knew that Chad was going to be just fine. They'd both been there for each other during shitty breakups. They knew what it felt like to be the one taking care of the other as well as the one being taken care of. Kit would be there through it all, just as Chad had been there for him after Jaylen and Roman.

Kit crossed his arms and leaned back against the counter. Maybe it was time to start taking control of his own life. While Michelle was out of the picture and his job was back to normal, there was still one thing lingering in the back of his head. His parents. He couldn't preach about improving his life and living better while also ignoring the fact that his father had basically offered to pay him to give up his body parts.

"Everything okay?" Roman asked, stepping into the kitchen. "I heard you two talking and I didn't want to interrupt. It sounded like it was important."

"It was, but everything's okay now. I just have to find someone who's having a party on a Tuesday night. I'll spend my day at work looking all over Twitter," he laughed. Roman nodded and stepped closer, placing a hand on either side of the counter beside Kit. He looked down at the younger man and smiled.

"We're late and you're already planning to skip work tomorrow to deal with your hangover. Tsk, tsk."

"Oh please, what's Ari gonna do? Fire me again?" Kit teased. "I figured out who stole seven grand from him, and now she's going to jail and he can spin this into an angry previous employee targeting him. Yellow Fall's gonna be in the papers and his company will be on everyone's lips for a little while. This time not for some terrible ad."

"You're really proud of yourself, huh?" Roman chuckled. He pecked Kit on the nose, then his cheek.

"I am! I did the damn thing."

"Yes, you did, kitten."

If Kit hadn't wanted to get back to work just to see the look on everyone's faces when he strolled in, he'd have allowed himself to give in to Roman's advances. They could have headed back to the bed for another round, waving Yellow Fall and Ari out of their minds. But Kit had a mission. He had things to do today, and he wasn't going to let Roman's stroke game get the better of him.

Roman headed into work first while Kit turned down at the street corner by instinct. He stopped in his tracks and looked at the coffee shop he'd been visiting since he started working. What if someone else was there to fill Michelle's role? What if he walked in there and befriended another person that wanted to break him and Roman up?

"Their coffee sucks anyways," he murmured to himself. Kit turned and jogged across the street, heading to another spot he was familiar with. This shop was much less personal, and maybe that was a good thing. At the moment, he didn't need any new friends. This barista made quick work with his order, moving around the small kitchen like he'd been working here for years.

"Have a good day," the man behind the counter said, his attention already on the customer behind Kit. Kit smiled.

When he returned to the office, everything seemed perfectly normal. His coworkers moved around the room with purpose, typed away at their computers, and murmured between themselves as they always did. Yolanda placed her drawing pen down and looked back at Kit as he carried in the drinks.

"That's new," she said, gesturing to the logo on the cups.

"Given everything, I figured it'd probably be best to try another shop out for a little while." He placed the cups on the table in the kitchen.

"Good thinking, Kenneth," she said, grabbing her cup and returning to her seat. Kit wanted to be annoyed with her calling him by his full name, but he knew she was only doing it because it *did* annoy him.

Barbie stepped out of the bathroom and her eyes went wide when she saw him. "Oh my gosh," she exclaimed, pulling him into a hug. "I heard about what happened! Are you okay? She didn't hurt you, did she? Oh, I could strangle that bitch…"

Kit laughed in surprise. "No, Barbie, I'm okay, I promise! Everything's okay."

"Thank god," she sighed, shaking her head. "I never doubted you for a second. Some people thought that it might actually be you that was stealing, but I just couldn't see it. You're a good boy. You wouldn't do something like that. But that Sadie girl…"

Kit couldn't help but be amused at the anger on Barbie's face. He'd never seen her this pissed off before, and knowing that she'd defended him when others hadn't made him even fonder of her. He gave her another quick hug before handing over her decaf drink.

"I need to get back to work, but we're gonna talk later. By the way, you're over twenty-one, right? Me and some other people want to get together and take you out for drinks this weekend!"

"That would be lit," Kit grinned.

"Lit AF, as my kids say. Talk to you in a little bit," she said. She gave a small wave and made her way back to her computer.

Aside from a few other people welcoming him back or congratulating him on figuring out who'd been stealing the money, his day was incredibly ordinary. Nobody made too big an effort to include him or make him feel welcomed, which was much appreciated. Kit wanted things to go back to normal, back before anyone knew about the stealing and the relationship he and Roman had.

With some time to himself, Kit sat down and thought back to the decision he'd made last night. Today wasn't a good day. He needed to talk to Roman and Ari about it before he made any rash choices, but truth be told, he had a feeling they'd agree.

Given everything, it was probably best for him to find another job. Michelle had proven there was a conflict of interest. And not only that, but if for some reason they *did* break up, he didn't want to lose his job again. One time was more than enough for him.

For what he was sure would be one of his last days at Yellow Fall, Kit put his feet up on the sofa and began scrolling through his timeline on Twitter. He needed to find someone who was throwing a party. It wasn't very hard considering most of his New York friends were still looking for jobs and had all the time in the world to throw a get-together on a Tuesday night.

"Aha," he said to himself, smiling.

Niecy, one of the girls he'd met at a party Chad had dragged him to a few months ago, was hosting something. Maybe there was still a spark there, and Chad seeing her would bring it to life once again. He could only hope.

The last thing on Kit's to-do list was to tell his parents off. He'd spoken to Bria briefly, but in the whirlwind of everything, they hadn't had a chance to sit down and really dig deep into this situation. Well, that was going to change soon. He dialed Bria's number.

"Hey, do you know where Mom and Dad are?" he asked.

"Mom's been staying over here, and Dad's still at the hotel. Why?"

Kit took a deep breath. "Because we need to have a family meeting."

34
YOU NEED ME

"Do you think he's going to show up?" Bria's voice was just above a whisper, and though she'd been trying to play it cool ever since Tonya showed up, Kit could tell by the constant stirring of the pot of chicken broth that she was slowly losing her composure. She'd probably been stressing since yesterday, when he called her. He placed a hand on her shoulder.

"Bria, he's gonna show up. And if he doesn't, he knows exactly what he's doing by missing this."

"Okay, but what exactly did you say to him?"

"I told him that the very least he owes me is showing up." Kit had wanted to say more to him than just that. He wanted to yell at Dorian and curse him out, but he knew that if he had any hope of his father showing up at Bria's place, he needed to keep it toned down and hold back until he could actually let it all out.

"I'm sorry for freaking out on you," Bria sighed. "It's just… I thought Trish and I were going to get our own time together when you moved out, but Mom's been staying with us since the whole situation with Dad, and it's unbearable. You know how she gets."

Ever since Tonya had arrived at the musical that night, she'd been buzzing around them like a paranoid, overprotective bee. In a way, Kit had almost gotten used to it. She'd displayed more interest in them during the past few weeks than she ever had when Kit and Bria were growing up.

"You're fine, Bria. We're gonna be fine." Kit knew it was his turn to be the older sibling. Bria had been doing this her whole life, and with Kit finally being in a good place, he could take on the role while she stressed over the situation.

Finally, there was a knock at the door. Bria's hand froze, and Kit looked over his shoulder at their mother. "Mom, can you get that?"

"I don't want to see that bastard," she grumbled, angling herself away from the front door. She propped her head up on her hand and looked out the window. Kit wanted to laugh and roll his eyes at the same time. She was stubborn as all hell, even now.

He crossed the room and opened the door just as

Dorian raised his hand to knock again. Kit stepped aside, allowing his father to enter. For a moment, nobody said anything. The last time Kit and Tonya had seen him, he'd been pandering to his son and proving just how little he cared about mending the past.

"Hi," Bria said quietly.

"Hey, honey. How are you doing?" Dorian crossed the room and gave her a kiss on the cheek.

"I'm fine. I'm making soup for dinner. It's almost ready."

"That sounds perfect." Dorian placed his hat down on the table and took a seat in one of the chairs. "So," he said. "What did you need to see me for?"

Kit shouldn't have been surprised by the casual tone he used, but he was. He couldn't believe that after everything, his father wasn't begging or pleading or apologizing for what he'd done at dinner that night.

"Really?" Kit said. "You really came in here acting like that?"

"I'm not acting like anything," Dorian said.

"Stand up."

"Excuse me?"

"*Stand up*. You don't get to sit down and act like nothing is wrong. Stand the fuck up and look at me like a man." Kit shocked himself with how calm he sounded when inside, he wanted to throttle Dorian. The last time he'd seen his family was when he'd been trying to buy a kidney from his son, and here he was, acting like this was any other day?

"Kit," Bria started.

"No, I want him to stand up and apologize to me. For *everything*. The way Mom did."

Tonya snorted. "That man can't apologize for shit. Never could. He told me we should come to New York to make amends with you and your sister. He wanted to show support for your relationship, Bria. God came to him and told him our behavior was wrong. But none of that was God, was it? It was your doctor, calling you up to tell you that your kidney was as disgusting as your heart."

"That's not why I came—"

"Stand up!" Kit's order bounced around the tiny apartment. Dorian stared him down, finally pushing himself up from the table.

"What do you want, Kenneth? Do you want me to beg for your forgiveness? I spent eighteen years raising you. Taking care of your medical expenses. Feeding you. I kept your ungrateful ass alive, and you want to act all big and bad like you did this shit on your own?"

Kit smiled, but there was no happiness in the expression. No joy, no pleasure, nothing. He took a step closer to the man, getting in his face. "You didn't do shit for me."

"I broke my back for your Black ass."

"You took care of me because the law made you. You took care of me and Bria because you had no other options. Aside from doing what you were legally obligated to do, you didn't do shit. And you don't fucking own me, either. I don't care if you paid every single expense I ever asked. You don't fucking *own* me."

As Kit spoke, he realized he wasn't just talking to his father. He was talking to more than him. He was addressing Dorian, and Jaylen, and the people who'd hurt him before. In a way, he was talking to himself. The side of him that still felt weak. The side that told him to give up when the going got tough.

"You want me to cut myself open for you because you bought me some fruit snacks back in '04? Negro, please." Kit laughed. "I'm gonna be completely honest since this is a family meeting. I've been thinking about it, and I've wondered why it is that I kept hoping you'd come around and realize how insufferable you were. As much as I said I hated you, there was still a little piece of me that wanted the dad everyone on TV had. I wanted the dad that was proud of me. I wanted the dad that talked about me to his friends, that wanted to show me off and encourage me to do whatever it is that I dreamed of. But I didn't get that one.

"I got you. I got the dad that told me all about how I'd suffer for the rest of my life because I let the devil in. You were actually kind of right about that. The moment I let you have an impact on my self-worth, I suffered. And every single day since then, I've hurt. But I'm done now. I'm done holding onto this image of who you're supposed to be, and I'm taking you at face value."

Kit stepped closer again, forcing Dorian to take a step back. "You're spineless. You rely on people being afraid of you, but when they realize that you can't do anything to them, you crumble. We were afraid of you for years, and then when we got out of the house, we found out you were just as weak as everyone else in the world. I thought I needed you, Dad, but it turns out, I'm good on my own.

"I have a job. I have a boyfriend that would move mountains for me. I have a sister that raised me with the love of a mother, a mother that came back to make some changes, and a best friend that would take a bullet for me. You? You have a hotel room with bedbugs and a bum kidney. I don't need you. You need me."

Kit finally stepped back and looked at everyone in the room. "Does anyone have something to add to that?"

Tonya finally turned over on the couch to look at her husband. "Do you have anything to say to him?"

Dorian nodded. "I found out two days ago that I got bumped up higher on the list. So, I don't need you after all, Kit."

Kit expected to feel angry at the sentiment. He was ready for his rage to kick in, or at the very least, his heart to twist at the utter lack of humanity coming from his father. Instead, he felt bulletproof. Dorian's words didn't matter, no matter how cruel he wanted to be.

Bria tapped her wooden spoon clean and wiped her hands. When she was done, she lifted the pot of soup from the stove, stepped up behind Dorian, and raised her arms high, dumping the steaming broth over his head.

"What the hell?" he cried, jumping away in pain. Blindly, he stumbled across the room.

"Get the fuck out of my apartment," she said, raising her voice over his pained shouts. Kit was too stunned to say anything. The only thing he could do was watch as Bria shoved Dorian towards the door. He fumbled to get it open, and when he did, she pushed him again. "Looks like the only thing you need is another trip to the hospital."

And with that, Bria slammed and locked the door. "Who wants Thai food?"

Kitten

———

Kit spent the rest of the night with his mother and sister. As much as he complained and groaned about Tonya being around so often, this was what he'd needed. He'd bared his soul to his father and the only thing he could say was that he didn't need Kit.

He replayed the soup dump over and over again. In his mind, there was no way Bria could ever top telling their parents to "suck her asshole," but somehow she'd done it. He didn't even mind the fact that the three of them had to mop up the soup afterwards. It was a chance to bond with his mother in a way that he'd never done before.

Tonya placed an arm on each of their shoulders. "I'm sorry for your father. I'm sorry I believed him when he said that he wanted to fix this."

"It doesn't matter," Kit shrugged. "You're here. You made the effort. You came back to actually fix us. He didn't, and that's why he's not with us."

"One day your father will look back on this night and realize how badly he screwed up," Tonya murmured softly. "Kit…"

"I'm not going to let him back in. He made it clear that he still wants nothing to do with me. For all I care, he can spend every day of his life suffering. He spit in everyone's faces when we were willing to give him yet another chance."

Bria hugged him tightly. Tonya stood beside them, watching quietly. Without a word, Bria opened her arm for her mother. Tonya stepped inside and hugged the two of them as well.

When Trish returned home with takeout, Kit took a seat at the table while everyone else ate on the sofa. He needed time to himself, at least for a little while. So much had happened in such a short amount of time, and he needed a second to process it. He needed to, for a lack of better words, stew.

For twenty-three years, Kit had wondered what it felt like to be free. He'd wondered what it was like to not have to worry about the nights where he lay in bed, trying to sleep while the demons of his past relationships haunted him. Was this what Roman felt like when Michelle was finally caught?

His phone buzzed. Roman.

"Hey," he said, lowering his voice. Kit stood and stepped out onto the fire escape. It was much quieter out here than it was with the three women inside laughing at the raunchy comedy they'd put on.

"Hey." Roman's voice was like silk. "You left work in a hurry. I wanted to make sure that everything was okay. You are okay, right?"

"I think so. Me and Bria pretty much told my dad to go fuck himself and never talk to us again, sooo."

"What?"

"It's a long story. Just know that I've gotten the last toxic person out of my life."

"Now you can go clubbing with Chad in peace."

"Are you mad that I didn't invite you last night, Romy?"

"Yes."

"Poor baby," Kit teased. He took a seat and brought his knees close to his chest, looking down at the city below. "How about I take you clubbing this weekend and we can get freaky somewhere?"

"Now you're talking my language," he laughed. "Really, though, are you okay? I know your situation with your parents was tough the last time we really talked about it."

"I'm gonna be okay. My mom and Bria are really all that I need. I remember what you said about family. About how important it is to you. And it's that way for me, too. I spent so many years hoping that maybe one day my dad would come around to love me, and because I put so much focus on that, I missed all the people that I actually had. I'm never making that mistake again."

"You're adorable when you're sentimental, you know that?"

"I'm adorable all the time, what you mean? In fact, I'm so adorable that you should come over to my apartment and see. I'll show you."

"Someone's feeling like a frisky kitty tonight."

"I am. So, are you coming, or are you gonna leave me in heat?"

Roman laughed again. "I'm on my way, baby. I'll see you soon."

"I love you, Roman."

"I love you, too."

35
SAFE

Kit stumbled over his own foot, laughing when he just barely managed to keep himself upright. "Roman, just give me a hint where we're going," he whined. He couldn't even walk normally, and here he was, expecting him to walk with hands over his eyes. Roman didn't budge though. He kept his palms flat over Kit's eyes while he steered him in the proper direction.

"If I let you see, it's going to ruin the surprise," he said.

"If I trip and die, that's gonna ruin the surprise too!"

"You'll be fine," Roman said softly. "I have you."

Kit wasn't sure where they were going, but he knew it was somewhere out in the middle of nowhere. The drive out of the city had been long enough for him to fall asleep, and when he woke up, Roman had placed his hands over his eyes and instructed him to carefully climb out of the car.

Using his senses, Kit could hear the sound of water and smell the woods, but that didn't help him pinpoint their location. He was completely at the other man's mercy.

"Okay, now there are some stairs coming up, so be careful," Roman said, helping him take the first one. He guided Kit up the small staircase, praising him. "Ready to see?"

"I've been ready," Kit laughed.

"Ta-da."

Roman pulled his hands away. Kit blinked, adjusting to the bright surroundings. They stood on the porch of an old cabin surrounded by more trees than he'd seen in years. Behind them, a lake stirred softly.

"Where are we?" he asked, turning to face Roman.

"I'll let you figure that out," Roman replied. He placed the key to the door in Kit's hand before heading back to the car to get their bags. Kit unlocked the front door and stepped inside, instantly hit with the smell. It was rustic, like a cabin should've smelled. He wanted to package it into a candle to burn in his house.

As Roman retrieved their bags, Kit wandered

through the cabin, looking at everything. He stopped at the fireplace and smiled to himself. The pictures on the mantel were of a young boy and his parents. Roman. This was their cabin. Kit reached for the picture of Roman in a little bathing suit and large floaties. It looked to be taken right outside, decades before they'd ever met.

Kit ran his finger over the picture tenderly. Behind him, Roman placed the bags down and made his way over. He slipped his arms around Kit's waist and placed his chin on his shoulder. "That's a cute kid if I've ever seen one."

"He's alright," Kit teased. "How old were you in this picture?"

"Three or four, I think. Twenty-six years ago. Damn."

"Tell me about it, old man," Kit smiled. He placed the picture back on the mantel and turned around. "How come you brought me here?"

"I wanted to spend the weekend with you before we had to get back to work. I was considering coming up here for my birthday, but that seemed really personal. Given everything we've been through, though, I've decided it doesn't really matter what I think is personal or not. I want to share it all with you."

"All of it?"

Roman nodded. "All of it. All my baby pictures,

and childhood stories, and the old room I used to sleep in whenever my parents would bring me up here during the summer. We spent three months of the year up here back in the day."

"I was lucky if my parents ever took us to the park," Kit laughed.

"Are you okay? You were vague over the phone about what happened with them," Roman said.

"It was kind of this whole thing," he said bashfully. Kit rehashed the situation with his father. Roman listened intently, raising his eyebrows when it got to the part about Bria and the dragging she'd given their father.

"I don't ever plan on seeing him again. He came here to lie and pay off all his sins from before. But I'm not a kid anymore. I'm done trying to be what he wants. Sorry, I should stop talking about him."

"No," Roman said, brushing a curl of Kit's hair back into place. "Don't apologize. I want to know everything about you and how you're feeling. Even the ugly stuff that no one wants to talk about. I want you to feel safe enough to talk to me about anything, kitten."

Kit didn't know what to say or do other than to hug Roman. It was times like this when Kit had a hard time believing that the person he'd met months ago was the person he was in love with now. Before any of this had started, Kit was sure he'd hate

Roman. He was blunt, determined, and there were times when he'd come off as just plain cruel. But that wasn't the person he was now.

The Roman then would never have taken him to his family's cabin for a private weekend getaway. He'd never ask for complete transparency in their relationship. But underneath that cold, no-nonsense exterior was someone that was looking for affection just as much as Kit was. It was still mind-blowing to Kit that the two of them had ever even gotten to this point.

"I have something for you," Kit said, stepping out of Roman's arms. He hurried over to his luggage to search for the small box.

"What is it?"

"Something I picked up before we left." Kit found the box and returned to Roman's side, handing it over to him. Slowly, Roman pulled the top of the box off and smiled. Inside was a long necklace with a golden cat paw charm. "I made sure that the chain was long enough so that you can tuck it into your shirt."

The smile on Roman's face grew wider. "I love it."

"Here, let me put it on you." Kit slipped it from the box and stepped behind him, pushing up on his toes. He draped it over the front of Roman's chest before he brought the clasps together. "There!"

"It's perfect," Roman said, looking down at the necklace. He grabbed Kit and hefted him into the air, wrapping Kit's legs around his waist for leverage.

"It looks good on you," Kit said.

"It'd look better if it was the only thing on me."

Kit didn't need to ask what that meant. Roman's steps towards the bedroom told him everything he needed to know.

Kit lay in bed with his eyes on the ceiling, lost in his own thoughts. There was a strange feeling of peace that he hadn't experienced much of—if any at all. His entire life had been a constant battle for approval. Approval from his friends, from his family, from his coworkers. He'd gone so long having to prove himself that when the moment came when he *didn't* have to, he wasn't certain how to react.

The pessimistic side of him wanted him to know that this wouldn't last forever. Sooner or later, something bad would come into his life and shake everything up. If something good was happening, it was only a matter of time before it went away. On the other end of the spectrum, these were the times he was supposed to cherish. Things could only get better from this point on. Somewhere in the middle, Kit made a compromise.

This happiness wouldn't last forever, and maybe it was best that way. Without struggle, he would never have understood the concept of happiness. Without the rain, he couldn't appreciate the sunshine. Life wasn't about preparing for the worst, but rather finding a support team that could help him through it. In Kit's mind, he had the best team one could ask for.

His mother was slowly shaping up to be someone he might be able to depend on again. Bria had been there for him since they were babies, and if he had all the time in the world to thank her, it still wouldn't be enough. Chad was in that same category, blood being the only thing separating them from being true brothers. And now he had Roman.

Roman provided him with a different kind of love —one he'd never had before. Roman's love wasn't selfish like Jaylen's had been. It wasn't toxic like so many in the past. It was selfless. It was giving, never taking, and abundant. Kit knew he could never quite fit his real feelings for Roman in a single sentence, but still he tried. He tried every time he told him he loved him.

"I need to talk to you," Kit said, breaking the silence he and Roman had found comfort in. Kit pulled the blanket up to his chest and turned to look at Roman.

"Yes?" Roman's hair was a mess and his smile was lazy.

"I don't know how to tell you this, but… I think it might be time for me to leave Yellow Fall for good. I think this will be my last week with the company."

"What? Why?" The smile fell.

"I know I just got back and everything's good and all, but I'm thinking about the future. I don't want to be a personal assistant for the rest of my life. I want to put my business degree to use. And not only that, but I want to be on equal footing with you."

"You are, Kit."

"No, I mean at work. Even though we're equals here, we're not equals there. You'll always be my boss. You'll always have more power over me. That's not a bad thing, I just don't want to have another situation like when we broke up for like, six days. I don't want to lose you and my job in case something terrible happens again."

Roman was quiet for a while. Kit couldn't read him, but he could tell that he was mulling this over in his head. "That makes sense."

"You're not mad at me, are you?"

Roman propped himself up on one elbow. "Kit, do you really think I'm that selfish that I wouldn't want you to go out and have your own success? I want you to use all of that fire that you have in your heart for something more than just taking our coffee orders and planning out my schedule for the week." He reached forward and brushed his thumb across Kit's bottom lip. "I want you to do whatever makes you happy, even if I am a little sad to see you go."

"I think it would be for the best, for both of us.

Less distraction at work. Less bickering whenever I get in a bratty mood."

"I happen to love your bratty moods, even when they get on my last nerve."

"Thank you for not being mad," Kit murmured. "I was scared you'd think I was insulting you or saying that I didn't believe in us making it through another fight or something."

"No, I know what you mean. I know you're thinking about the future and your goals, and I'd never want to hold you back or keep you tied down to a place you weren't happy with. But I do want you to know that you're the most exciting employee Yellow Fall's ever had."

"No, I'm not," Kit snorted.

"You are. We get a lot of people who've worked in this business for a while, and they don't bring that spark of energy. They don't bring that enthusiasm to the table. But you did. You came in determined to prove me wrong, even in our first interview. That's why you're the most exciting employee. You challenged me, and your coworkers, and even Ari."

Kit rolled his eyes, but he couldn't fight off the blush growing on his face. "You're saying that because you like me."

"Maybe," Roman shrugged. "But it's true. So, even though I'm happy that you're thinking about moving on and finding something bigger and better, I know that so many people are gonna miss having you at work."

"Well, I'm gonna miss them too."

"I have an idea," Roman said. "How about this last week you're here, we make it as fun as possible? We'll send you off the best way we know how. Barbie can throw one of her parties, the whole thing. Would you like that?"

The idea alone was enough to make Kit emotional. He scooted closer to Roman and nuzzled against him. "I would love that."

"Then it's all yours, baby."

36
ONE LAST TIME

THE WEATHER OUTSIDE FELT NICE. THIS WASN'T something Kit could normally say given that New York weather had a vendetta against the people that lived there, but on this particular night, there was nothing more than a cold breeze, enough to justify a comfy sweater. Kit leaned back against the railing on Chad's apartment roof and stared up at the sky. Rarely did he ever see stars, but he could imagine.

Across the terrace, Bria and Trish bickered about the proper way to prepare the barbecue. Trish eventually conceded and let Bria do whatever she wanted. He smirked. That was usually how things worked in their relationship. In a way, that was paralleled in his own relationship. Roman was hardheaded and occasionally challenged him, but once Kit gave him that look or flashed that innocent frown, he got his way.

Part of him wished Roman could be here tonight, but he still had work to do at the office. For the past week, the two of them had been living up their last days together. They spent much of the day talking, unable to stop now that their relationship was out in the open. Not only that, but soon he'd be forced to spend hours away from Roman every single day. He wanted to soak up as much of the man's time as he could before his last day.

Roman also had to look for a new assistant. This was a process Kit was helping with. The only people Roman was allowed to hire were married people, preferably a straight man. Roman laughed when Kit joked about his habit of sleeping with his assistants.

The door beside Kit opened, and Chad stepped out, groceries in his hands. Kit hustled over to take a few of them from him and walked back to the table beside the grill. "Thanks," Chad said.

"What all did you get?" Trish asked, poking through the groceries.

"I got a little of everything. I got them honey barbecue chips that you like," he said. Trish took a step back and pointed at him, smiling.

"You a real one, Chad." She grabbed the bag of chips and popped it open, crunching down on a few of them. Kit cracked open one of the strawberry sodas Chad had picked up. While Bria and Trish returned to the grill, the boys removed all of their loot from the bags, spreading it out on the table. Cookies, chips, soda, beers, and the necessary utensils for eating. He'd even picked up the good kind of potato salad.

"How are you doing, man?" Kit asked, stepping away from the others so they could be alone. In the midst of his final week at Yellow Fall, Kit had given Chad the space he needed to deal with his situation. It had been hell just trying to convince him to have a little party, just the four of them.

"I'm doing alright. It still sucks. I've been reading up on what's going on. Did you see the news?"

Kit nodded. He'd watched the reporter describe the situation at work. Michelle had been described as the car accident victim slash cyberthief. Those first few days after the incident, the media had a heyday with it. They sensationalized her and, just as quickly, tossed her aside when reports of a company's CEO laundering money broke. Like one of the stars Kit couldn't quite see, Michelle shone her brightest right before she burned out.

"I just want to know why she thought it was okay to do this to me, y'know? But that's not something I'll ever understand. Yeah, she wanted to hurt Roman, but she brought us into her game, and that's fucked up." His fist clenched tight, and his eyes cut across to the side of the terrace, avoiding Kit. "It doesn't matter, though. Fuck her."

"Exactly. If you let her continue to hurt you even when she's locked up, you'll never get past the situation. I know it's hard, but you just have to move on."

Chad laughed bitterly. "Thank you for making me do this. I didn't want to, but it's actually kind of nice. No one ever uses the grills up here because they're all WASP-y as fuck."

"Plus, you know they'd just slap the chicken on the grill without even washing or seasoning that shit or anything," Kit laughed.

"Hell yeah they would. Be like, 'A little salt and pepper is all you need, Kenneth. Now, try my homemade green bean and pea casserole!'"

"'Oh, Madeline, these carrots are so spicy, what'd you put on them? What's this black stuff? Pepper?'"

The two of them kept this act going, and just like that, Michelle was gone. Kit couldn't remember the last time he'd laughed hard enough to cry, but here he was, doubling over as they quipped about the bland people that lived in Chad's apartment building.

When it was time to eat, they took their seats at the table and Bria said grace. After her little prayer, she scooped out a handful of potato salad and plopped it down beside her two veggie dogs. Kit cringed at the thought, imagining just how badly those would taste. Then he smiled. Bria would probably get along nicely with the other tenants in this apartment.

After thirty minutes of chattering and talking about the latest political bullshit that they'd seen online, Kit cleared his throat. "I'm gonna be mad corny and say some deep shit, so gimme a second."

"Here we go," Trish teased, rolling her eyes.

"For real! I know we've all been going through it lately, but I want to say that this is all we ever really need. Whether we're going through breakups, bad situations with our parents, or stressful times at work, I know that I'm always safe here with you guys, and I appreciate that. I love the fuck outta y'all."

Chad raised his Styrofoam cup, Dr. Pepper sloshing down one side. "To being there for each other!" The others joined him in the gesture, repeating the phrase.

Kit sat back in his chair and just smiled. He couldn't stop smiling.

———

THIS WAS IT. THE DAY HE'D BEEN DREADING *AND* looking forward to. Kit had come into work a little later than normal, per Roman's request, to find a stranger exiting Roman's office. The man looked straight out of an H&M store, with horn-rimmed glasses and a neatly shaven beard. Best of all, Kit caught sight of a ring on his left hand.

They nodded at each other as he walked to the

elevator. The pep in his walk told Kit everything he needed to know. Whoever this man was, he'd just been given the job.

Kit pushed open the door to Roman's office and smiled at him sadly. Roman frowned and beckoned him inside, pulling him in for a hug.

"Don't be sad, kitten. This is it for Yellow Fall, but it's not over for you. Ira's gonna find you the best place for you sooner than you think."

"I know," Kit sighed. "I'm just sad. Like, I know everyone thought I was a hoodrat scammer bitch, but they're like my second family. I'm even gonna miss Yolanda dragging me for wearing two different socks or having food on my face."

Roman chuckled deeply. "I'm sure she'll miss pointing out all those things too. But remember why you're doing this. You're going to go on to do amazing things. You're going to be huge before you know it."

Kit shrugged, unable to argue. He wanted that to be true. Sure, he had no idea where he was going to go after Yellow Fall, but it was going to be exactly where he belonged. He wanted to be part of a company more than an assistant was, especially one where he didn't have to worry about his boyfriend being his boss. He'd seen too many dramas on ABC to think there wasn't a conflict of interest when it came to dating his boss.

"I hope you didn't eat anything before you came here," Roman said, rubbing Kit's lower back.

"Why?"

"We're sending you off with a feast of sorts. It's corny, but it was Barbie's idea," he said, rolling his eyes. Kit shoved his shoulder lightly.

"Be nice," he warned.

"I'm just teasing. Logan's wife is coming up and she's bringing the baby. He wanted you to meet them before you left."

Kit's smile grew. He couldn't wait to meet them. Most of the time, all Logan talked about was either work or his baby girl. There was something incredibly sweet about the way most men turned to complete mush talking about their kids.

Just like Roman said, Kit was treated like royalty. Barbie finished up with her work for the day as quickly as possible, and by three o'clock, she was free to spend the rest of her time with Kit, lamenting about all the good times they'd had together.

"I promised myself I wasn't gonna cry, but just…" Barbie dabbed her eyes and shook her head, laughing in embarrassment. "You're just like my baby here at work, you know that? And you're growing up and moving on."

"I know," Kit smiled softly, hugging her.

"You really helped me get through my situation

with Kevin. I can't thank you enough, Kit. I don't know what I would've done without you, honey."

Now it was Kit's turn to get emotional. Never in a million years would he have predicted that he'd end up crying over some assistant job with a single mother that had a kid nearly his age. It was so left-field, but it felt so right at the same time.

Behind them, Yolanda cleared her throat. "When you two crybabies are done, Ari wants to talk to Kit," she said. She paused, giving the two of them a small smile before she walked away.

Kit wiped his eyes. "Guess I'd better go talk to him one last time."

"I'll walk with you," she smiled.

Kit straightened up, took a deep breath, and headed over to the meeting room where Ari and his other coworkers sat at the table. Ari rose when he entered the room. At the same time, there was a round of applause. Kit crinkled his face and laughed, confused.

"What's all of this for?" he asked.

"It's for you. For all the help you've been since you started working here," Ari said. "For not holding it against me when I thought you were the one stealing from the company. And for coming back despite it all. Roman can't pick assistants for shit, but he picked a pretty good one this time."

The people at the table laughed, and even Roman cracked a smile. Ari continued.

"Normally, this is how we send off our employees that don't quit or get fired. I say normally because I'm not quite ready to see you go just yet."

Kit made a face. "What do you mean?"

"I haven't had the pleasure of getting to know you as well as I'd have liked, but from what I've heard from someone close to you, you're quite the social guy. You know what's hot, what people are talking about, and what people your age are interested in. At the moment, I'm looking for someone to manage our social media accounts, and I'd like to offer you the position before anyone else."

Barbie gasped, then smiled wide. Kit's coworkers all seemed to be just as shocked as he was.

"Uh—I…" Kit looked to Roman, unsure what to say.

Ari looked his way as well. "Rest assured, Roman won't be your boss anymore. I know that you two are together, and I agree that working in the same department with your significant other can be a recipe for disaster. But if you accept this position, I'll be your boss."

Kit shook his head in disbelief. He'd wanted to leave the company to keep his relationship with Roman safe, but here he was, able to stay with the people he cared about and not have to worry about how he and Roman's closeness would affect their work.

"I... I would love to," he finally said. "Absolutely. I would love to stay here."

There was a second round of applause. Kit couldn't stop his wide grin from spreading, and he didn't want to. He'd been so upset about having to leave, but that was no longer an issue. Their meeting didn't last much longer. On his way out of the door, Ari quietly told him that they'd get the paperwork started next week.

Roman pulled Kit into his arms and held him by the waist, looking down at him. Kit hadn't seen him this happy since they'd played the *Simpsons* arcade game on his birthday. "I thought I was going to lose your presence here at work."

"Is that why you talked to Ari?" Kit asked.

"What do you mean? I didn't say anything to him."

Kit's eyebrows knitted together. If Roman hadn't put in a good word for him, who had? Kit caught Yolanda looking at the two of them, standing still as everyone else returned to their desks. He couldn't explain the feeling, but something in his chest swelled. Yolanda gave a knowing smile, and returned to her work.

"I think I know who it was," Kit said quietly.

Roman lowered his head and pressed his lips to Kit's, stealing away a work-appropriate kiss.

"So, Mr. Social Media Manager," Roman began, steering him towards his office. "I'm going to need you to tell me all about your plans for the future. Will you be weird like Denny's, or savage like Wendy's?"

"I dunno yet. I'm thinking a little of both. Plus, I gotta throw a little sexy in there, for the fans."

Roman's head fell back in laughter. "Of course, for the fans."

Kit didn't know where this new path would take him, or what it would bring. He might go viral with a Facebook status just as easily as he might get into a Twitter war with another brand. If he were being honest, both of them sounded equally fun.

Whichever way his new career went, he knew he'd figure it out. He always figured it out.

EPILOGUE
5 MONTHS LATER

THE SOUND OF OLD SCHOOL JAZZ MUSIC RANG through the house like a trumpet, loud and immediate. Ever since Tonya had become a bigger part of Bria and Kit's lives, he'd grown accustomed to the sound. Whether she was spending the night at his and Roman's place or Bria and Trish's, she brought two things: her white noise machine and her Charles Mingus CD.

Today was no different. He'd invited his family over to the new place because of the space they'd have in the living room to plan the wedding. They needed a large table to spread out pictures of dresses Bria was considering, and Roman was more than happy to have them over. Kit still needed to hear that this was now his home just as much as it was Roman's every now and then. It had only been a month, after all.

Kit followed the sound of horns through the house, stopping when he reached the kitchen. At the table, Trish, Tonya, and Bria sorted through pictures and pages torn from bridal magazines. Trish seemed satisfied with herself, and Bria seemed annoyed by something.

He put on a pot of coffee, and while he waited, he bent down to grab the dog food from underneath the counter. "What'd you do this time, Trish?" he asked, looking at the group of ladies at the table.

Trish gawked. "I didn't do shit!"

"She's lying out her ass right now," Bria said, shaking her head. "She keeps saying we should both just rock tuxes, even though we both already agreed on dresses."

"She does it cause you let it get to you," Tonya said quietly, smiling at the two of them. Trish grinned wider.

"You're such a troll," Kit chuckled. She gave him a playful wink. When he finished dumping a scoop of food into the bowl, he sat it down beside the fridge and called out, "Bosco!" A moment later, a peppy miniature Schnauzer came tottering into the kitchen, sniffing around. When he found the source of the smell, he dug in.

"What's on your schedule today, Kit?" Tonya asked, looking over her shoulder at him.

"Well, I didn't have much planned. Chad's coming home from his trip sometime this week, and I wanna throw a welcome home party, so I should probably start planning that. I also have to do a little work. Oh, and I was gonna have lunch with Roman today."

If he were being honest, taking on the social media manager role was the best choice Kit had ever made. Not only did a lot of the work not require him to be at the office during very specific, rigid hours, but it gave him plenty of flexibility for spending time with Roman without feeling like they were doing anything wrong. Sure, an office romance might not have been ideal to Ari or Kit's coworkers, but it wasn't against the rules. They behaved while they were at work.

Most of the time.

Really, there wasn't much space for the two of them to have private time at work. Roman's new assistant, Dillon, was a married man with two kids, and he was *very* thorough with his job. Kit couldn't get more than ten minutes of time alone with his boyfriend before the man came barging in, informing him that this client wanted to talk to him at this specific time. He was great at his job, and while Roman deserved that, Kit couldn't help but feel annoyed. Some days he just wanted to be thrown down on the desk and ravished.

"Kit, come look at this for a second," Bria said without looking up from her stack of pictures. He did as she said, stepping behind her to see what she wanted. On the table, he found two pictures of dresses.

"What's up?"

"Do you like this shade of white, or *this* shade of white?" She pointed at both of them, then laced her fingers together.

Kit made a face. "Uh... these are the same color."

"No, they're not," Bria said. "This one is a darker white than this one."

He squinted and tried to see the different between the two shades to no avail. "I literally can't tell the difference. They both look cute though. I'd say go with this one, I like the detailing on the front." There were beads that had been placed around the sweetheart neckline.

"That one is pretty cute... Thanks!"

It had been this way for the past couple of months. Ever since Bria proposed to Trish, the girls had been obsessed over the wedding, spending what felt like every waking moment talking or planning the ceremony. Their dedication to detail was as scary as it was impressive.

Kit didn't bother himself with the planning too much, though. Bosco needed to go for a walk, and he wanted to relax and enjoy his coffee. Kit poured some into his thermos, stirred in the sugar and creamer, and hooked the dog onto his leash. A few moments later and they were taking in the fresh air of the neighborhood.

Though he wasn't an expert on the neighborhood, Kit knew his way around the place. His new neighbors were as friendly as could be, constantly talking to him about his relationship with Roman and how exciting it was to have someone younger around. Most of the people that lived here were wealthy older folks. Twenty-somethings that used slang regularly weren't exactly the norm.

It'd been hard to let go of his apartment, but Kit figured giving up his freedom to do whatever he wanted was made up for by the fact that he'd get to see Roman every day and every night. This way, they'd get to spend nights together on the couch, curled up and watching some cheesy thriller movie on the Lifetime channel.

While he walked the dog, Kit dug out his phone from his pocket and checked his personal Twitter account. Last night, Chad had tagged him in a picture on the cruise. In the picture, Chad was posted up in bed between a man and a woman, each of them making silly faces. Kit had never seen him happier.

Since Michelle's dramatic exit from his life, Chad took life by the balls and did whatever made him happy. He wasn't the type to wallow over a girl forever, and he'd made up for that heartbreak two-fold. A month after Michelle was arrested, Chad met Eli and Grace, a couple looking to experiment more in the bedroom. He was the perfect fit for their relationship, and surprisingly, they'd made it work. Kit couldn't imagine taking care of two people's needs at the same time, but Chad had always been good at multitasking.

After sending a quick response littered with emojis, Kit switched over to the Yellow Fall account. Five months ago, he'd made his presence known with a flurry of viral tweets. It seemed that self-deprecating humor was the best route to go for a company well-known for their huge scandal, and the general public had formed an overall positive opinion about Yellow Fall.

The hardest part about the job was making sure he didn't go off on somebody. They received their fair share of trolling tweets and hateful responses, and Kit had never been one to hold his tongue. Any time he wanted to respond to something like that, he double-checked with Ari to make sure he wasn't doing the brand any damage. Every now and then, Ari would give him permission to make some witty quip about the user before getting back to business. Those were the tweets Kit had the most fun sending.

Then of course there was the Facebook page, but nothing really happened there. Most people that were interested in the FB page were business professionals looking for actual information about the company and not snappy one-liners. Whenever he needed a break from the petty users, he switched over there to promote the company.

He'd initially thought this job would be hard, but Kit soon came to realize that as long as he put his mind to it, there was no job he couldn't do. If he could design an entire office with no previous design skills, he could promote Yellow Fall's services and get in contact with potential clients. This new job was much easier than working for Roman had ever been.

Kit spent the rest of his morning back at the house, playing with Bosco in the backyard until the poor pup was exhausted. He collapsed in their bed the moment he jumped on it. Kit laughed.

"Worn out, huh, buddy?"

Bosco didn't respond, but the lazy blink he gave was a good indicator of what he was feeling. Kit scratched behind his ear. He headed to the shower to get cleaned up for lunch with Roman, giddiness rumbling in his belly. Almost a year with the man and those feelings still hadn't gone away. It was almost impressive, the way Roman made him radiate this energy.

He cleaned up and headed out to the company, rapping along to the latest Kendrick song the radio played. Though they censored some of the words, Kit used every explicative. Thirty minutes later, he pulled up outside of Yellow Fall to find Roman waiting for him by the curb.

"Beep beep, it's time to eat," Kit called once he rolled down the window. Roman grinned and climbed inside. He leaned over for a quick kiss.

"Hey, kitten. Thanks for coming to get me."

"No biggie. How's work been today?"

"More of the same," he shrugged. "Yolanda's still terrorizing Dillon, as she's wont to do."

"Ahhh."

Kit had definitely been witness to her berating the poor guy. In a way, he was grateful that he didn't have to endure the smartass comments anymore, but at the same time, he missed them. With his new position and his relationship with Roman being out in the open, she no longer acted like a protective mother, vetting the people who she thought might be interested in him. It was silly, but every now and then, he longed to get into a verbal sparring match with her again.

Barbie was still the same loveable woman, thankfully. Each time Yolanda mouthed off to Dillon, he practically went running to Barbie for reassurance and guidance. It was trippy for Kit. It was like watching his own life from a different perspective.

"What do you want to eat?" Kit asked. He knew the answer, but he still liked asking. Maybe one day he would suggest something else other than the little Greek place down the street.

"Actually, I'm in the mood for something else," Roman said, directing Kit to park around the back of the building.

"This is bad," Kit laughed. "Someone could walk out here and see us!"

"What, like you mind?"

"I don't want to get in trouble—"

Before he could finish his sentence, Roman's lips were on his, hungry and passionate. Only when they parted did he take a breath, staring into the other man's eyes. Before Roman, Kit would have never believed he could be so interested in someone. With all this wedding talk, he wondered what it would be like to marry Roman. Would they have a perfect marriage, or would they end up bickering for the rest of their lives, showing their love through sarcastic retorts?

Kit didn't worry himself too much about the future. He was far too young to get married or even think about marriage. Right now, all he wanted was to get money, eat good food, and fool around with his boyfriend every single chance he got.

Roman stole another kiss and said, "Get in the backseat, kitten. I want to eat."

A deep blush made its way up Kit's neck, and he did exactly as he was told, stripping down to his boxer briefs. In the darkness of the car, no one would be able to see what they were doing, but it still felt thrilling. Roman climbed into the back a moment later, his hands on Kit's hips.

"You can only eat if you promise me one thing," Kit said, stopping him.

"What's that?"

"That you're gonna lick the plate clean."

Roman simply laughed. Then he got down to work.

About the Author

Jack Harbon is your typical, eccentric twenty-something writing stories much more interesting than his real life. If he's not writing, he's either reading domestic thrillers about women in peril, watching trashy reality TV shows, or playing *The Sims*.

Also by Jack Harbon

Sweet Rose
Meet Cute Club (#1)

Encounters
The Babysitter (#1)
The Brother (#2)
The Intern (#3)

Endearments
Daddy (#1)

Standalones
Unwrap Me

Printed in the USA
CPSIA information can be obtained
at www.ICGtesting.com
CBHW051710191124
17646CB00034B/525